The Hidden

Alison Knight

In the same series:

MINE - mybook.to/minedarkstroke
THE LEGACY - mybook.to/thelegacydarkstroke

www.darkstroke.com

Copyright © 2021 by Alison Knight
Artwork: Adobe Stock, © TrapezaStudio
Design: Services for Authors
All rights reserved.

No part of this book may be used or reproduced in any manner whatsoever without written permission of the author or Crooked Cat/ darkstroke except for brief quotations used for promotion or in reviews. This is a work of fiction. Names, characters, and incidents are used fictitiously.

First Dark Edition, darkstroke, Crooked Cat Books 2021

Discover us online:
www.darkstroke.com

Join us on instagram:
www.instagram.com/darkstrokebooks/

Include **#darkstroke** in a photo of yourself holding this book on Instagram and **something nice will happen.**

This book is dedicated to the people who will fight to protect their family and friends; to the people who have the courage to speak out against wrong-doing; and for faithful dogs everywhere (but especially Arnie, a British Bulldog, and Milo, a Golden Labrador, both much-loved companions in our family).

Acknowledgements

I seem to be making a habit of being inspired by a previous book and The Hidden is no exception. This story was inspired by a character in The Legacy – I won't say which one as they have changed their name and started to build a new life. I hope it will soon become clear to you.

Have you ever met someone you felt was a really horrible person? Did you ever wonder why they were like that? Well, in The Hidden, we meet a selfish, uncaring woman who seems to have a knack for being unpleasant and standoffish. But no one is born like that, so what has made her into the person that we meet here? I hope that, as the story unfolds, you will begin to understand what makes her tick and how a damaged hero and his family and friends are able to help her to release the scared but caring woman hiding inside her.

Once again, my thanks to Laurence and Stephanie Patterson at Darkstroke, and my wonderful editor, Sue Barnard. The Darkstroke community of authors are a worldwide family of Cats and Darklings who support and encourage each other. I'm so grateful to be part of it.

My thanks also go to everyone who has read my books. I hope that you'll enjoy the connections in The Hidden to my last book, The Legacy.

About the Author

Alison has been a legal executive, a registered childminder, a professional fund-raiser and a teacher. She has travelled the world – from spending a year as an exchange student in the US in the 1970s and trekking the Great Wall of China to celebrate her fortieth year and lots of other interesting places in between.

In her mid-forties Alison went to university part-time and

gained a first-class degree in Creative Writing at Bath Spa University and an MA in the same subject from Oxford Brookes University, both while still working full-time. Her first book was published a year after she completed her master's degree.

Alison currently has a trio of novels published by Darkstroke. The first, Mine, is a domestic drama set in 1960s London based on real events in her family. She is the only person who can tell this particular story. Exploring themes of class, ambition and sexual politics, Mine shows how ordinary people can make choices that lead them into extraordinary situations.

The Legacy, a drama set in London in 1969, was inspired by a scene in Mine, and explores how an unexpected legacy can be both a blessing and a curse. The Legacy looks at themes of greed and expectations, and the lengths people will go to when they are desperate.

The Hidden, available from September 2021, is a romantic suspense that picks up the story of one of the characters in The Legacy. Set in Montana in 1973, two wounded, damaged people are forced together, each guarding their secrets. Can they learn to trust each other? And will their nightmares ever end?

Alison teaches creative and life-writing, runs workshops and retreats with Imagine Creative Writing Workshops (www.imaginecreativewriting.co.uk) as well as working as a freelance editor. She is a member of the Society of Authors and the Romantic Novelists' Association.

She lives in Somerset, within sight of Glastonbury Tor.

The Hidden

Chapter One

As she left the witness box there was a flash of blinding light and the courtroom filled with smoke. She froze, terror holding her trapped, unable to escape. Around her, court officials called for order, women screamed and there were thuds and crashes as furniture was overturned.

"Get out!" she heard her brother shout.

She looked around in a daze. "Percy?" It couldn't be him. He was dead. That's why she was here, why she'd spilled their secrets.

For a moment the smoke cleared, and she saw a figure in a balaclava running towards her. He was clad all in black. His eyes were filled with hatred. She knew why he was there. It was her time to die. He raised his arm and she saw the glint of steel in his hand. She closed her eyes as the knife descended and slashed the side of her face.

At last her survival instinct freed her from her terrified paralysis. She turned, desperate to get away, but she felt the blade pierce her body. She wanted to crawl away from the stinging slashes, but she was trapped, unable to move. She felt moisture on her skin – her blood or her tears?

"It's all right," she heard Percy whisper. "It's not your time yet. You've won, Sis. Don't give up now."

"Percy!" she screamed, reaching out for him ...

Montana, USA, 1973

Her hand touched fur. *Fur?* She opened her eyes, blinking as she registered the soft whining of the dog on the bed next to her. The vivid images of the London courtroom faded away as she took in her surroundings – the moonlight flooding through the window where she'd forgotten to close the curtains again; the patchwork quilt on the big wooden bed; the large pine chest and smaller matching bedside cabinet.

She sat up, bringing up her knees and leaning her elbows on them as she rubbed her face. The dog nuzzled her cheek, trying to lick up her salty tears. She pushed him away.

"It's all right, Bear," she said, scratching behind his ear. "It was just a dream."

The same dream. Every. Bloody. Night. It's been three years now. Will it ever go away?

Knowing she wouldn't get back to sleep, no matter how tired she felt, she got up and padded barefoot to the window. It was a clear night. She could see the dark silhouette of the mountains that stood guard above the fertile valley. Above them were millions of stars. It never ceased to soothe her, looking out at the moon and the endless sky above her. It reminded her of how huge the universe was, and how small and insignificant she was in comparison.

There had been a time when she hadn't bothered to look around and to enjoy the beauty and majesty of her surroundings. Instead, she'd focused only on herself – her wants, her opinions, her pleasures. No one else had mattered. *And look where that got me,* she reminded herself. Today, she hid herself away in this valley, thousands of miles away from her old life. It was her penance, her punishment. She wasn't the same person any more. The trouble was, she had no idea who she had become.

She hadn't had the nerve to test it. Instead she kept herself to herself, with Bear, some chickens and a horse for company. She should be at peace, but every night the dream reminded her of why she couldn't relax.

They wouldn't find her here. Or could they? She was half a world away, and didn't even look the same. She ran her hands through her long, dark hair, draping it across her left cheek and shoulder, hiding her scars. It was an automatic reaction, even when she was alone and knew that, logically, she was perfectly safe. The surgeon had done his best, and three years had served to reduce the vivid red marks to thin white lines. Her attacker had been jailed and wasn't likely to be released any time soon. But he was only one man. There were others out there, and they had long memories.

Maybe that's why I keep having the dream – to remind myself I can't let my guard down.

As if to reinforce her thoughts, Bear got up and padded over to her side. At the same moment, a movement in the distance caught her eye. She frowned as the headlights of a vehicle turned off the road a few hundred yards from the house onto her drive.

She didn't wait to see who it was. Instead she turned and grabbed the pile of clothes she always left ready, and dressed quickly, throwing her nightdress on the bed and not bothering to put on a bra. She had maybe a couple of minutes – the drive was potholed and treacherous, and she left it like that deliberately to hold up all but the most stupid driver. A quick glance out of the window confirmed that the vehicle had slowed to a crawl and was negotiating the worst of the holes.

The dog whined again, and she shushed him as she reached under the bed and brought out a small rucksack and her shotgun. She broke the barrel to check it was loaded, then closed it and headed for the bedroom door.

"Come on, Bear," she whispered. "Time to go."

With a final glance behind her, she closed the bedroom door and headed across the dark living room to the kitchen at the back of the cabin. She wouldn't let herself acknowledge the despair she felt. This place had been a haven for her. But her sanctuary had been breached. It was time to start over again. She grabbed Bear's leash and slipped it on him, unlocked the back door, crept outside and began to run. A few seconds later, she was concealed in the shadows inside the interior of the barn.

Behind her, a car door slammed. She flinched at the noise, and again Bear whined. She opened the door of her pick-up truck as quietly as she could and urged the dog inside, but he resisted.

"Come on, Bear," she whispered, pulling on his leash. "I don't have time for this. Get in!"

The dog sat back on his haunches, resisting her efforts to get him into the truck. Her heart sank. She couldn't afford to waste time, and he was so big there was no way she could lift him into the cab. But she still hesitated. Bear and Ebony, the elderly horse standing quietly in his stall behind her, were her only friends these days. The thought of leaving them both behind broke her heart. But her survival instincts were stronger. If she was dead, she'd be no good to them anyway. As if understanding he was about to be abandoned, Ebony gave a soft whicker, making her flinch at the sound.

She gave one final, desperate tug, but she was no match for the dog who got his name because he was as big and furry as a damned bear. Admitting defeat, she dropped the leash and whispered, "Stay!" But Bear had other ideas. He leapt up and headed out of the barn, barking like a mad thing.

"No!" she cried, torn between chasing after him and making her escape before whoever was out there realised where she was hiding.

Chapter Two

He was dead on his feet. It felt like he'd been travelling for days. The adrenaline that had kept him going was slowly seeping out of his system, leaving him barely able to keep his eyes open. He supposed he should have called the family when he got into town, but it was the middle of the night and he needed sleep. He'd report in tomorrow.

He grabbed his stuff from the passenger seat and shut the car door. He didn't bother locking it; there was no one around for miles. He paused, looking around at the moonlit landscape. The paddock at the side of the house looked good, the fences stood firm and the grass looked well-cropped. The barn was looking tired in the pale light, the doors hung open, and from the interior he heard the soft whicker of a horse.

He frowned and dropped his bag. He cast a look at the house – a single-storey log cabin with a wrap-around porch. It was in darkness, as was the barn. But his instincts led his footsteps towards the open barn doors.

As he approached them, he heard a sound and then a dark figure exploded into the yard. He didn't have time to react before a huge beast leapt at him, sending him sprawling on his back with it on his chest. His head snapped, making contact with the hard earth, and he saw stars.

"What the hell?" He shook his head, trying to focus as a hot, wet tongue scoured his face and barked loudly in his ear. "Get off me, you damned mutt!"

He tried to push it off him, but his strength was just about done. He'd used it up in his desperate race to get here. With a sigh he gave up and lay back down. The dog continued to assault him with its tongue as he stared up at the stars and waited, hoping the beast would grow tired of playing with him before it decided to take a bite out of his sorry hide.

It was a click and a soft voice that finally stilled the dog and got his attention as well.

"Don't move, or I'll shoot."

He felt the adrenaline that had deserted him a few minutes ago rush back into his system. He turned his head in the direction of the barn. A woman stood, half-concealed in the shadows just outside the doors. The moonlight glinted on the barrel of a shotgun. The dog lay over him, panting.

"You might want to put that down, lady. We wouldn't want to have an accident with that thing," he said, trying to keep his voice calm.

"There'll be no accident," she said. "I know how to use this and I'm not afraid to shoot you if you move so much as a muscle." She stepped into the light and raised the gun to her shoulder. "Good dog, Bear. Come here, boy."

He frowned. "Bear? What the hell is Bear doing here?" He peered up at the beast. "Goddamn, it *is* you! How you doin', buddy?"

"How do you know his name?" she asked.

"Because he's my dog," He lifted his hand to touch the dog's nose.

"I said don't move!" she shouted.

He froze but Bear didn't. The dog barked and resumed licking him. The woman tried to call him again but she was ignored.

"Look, I don't know who you are, lady. But I'm not the enemy here. If you don't believe me, ask Bear here. You know me, don't you, buddy?"

"That doesn't mean a thing. He's a friendly dog," she said, her voice as cool as the ice that covered the lake out back in the winter. "You're trespassing in the middle of the night. In the circumstances, I think I'd be justified letting you have it with both barrels, don't you?"

"Wait," he frowned, wondering if his sleepless state was playing tricks on him. "Are you English? What the heck are you doing in Montana?"

"It doesn't matter where I come from. You shouldn't be here. I've called the Sheriff and he'll be here soon. So I suggest you get in your car and go back to where you came from."

He sighed. This was getting him nowhere. There wasn't a phone in the house, so he knew she was lying about the call. He didn't know where this damned woman had come from – but he wasn't about to argue with a shotgun aimed at his head.

"Okay, lady. You win. I'll go quietly. Just call the dog off."

"Bear. Heel," she said.

This time the mutt obeyed, and a moment later he was free.

"No fast moves," she warned.

He rolled onto his side and tried to get up, but pain shot up his thigh and he lay back and groaned.

"Get up," she ordered.

"Trust me, lady, I would love to. But I might need some help."

"Don't be ridiculous. Just get up."

He tried again, feeling sweat break out on his forehead as he gritted his teeth and forced himself to stand. He leaned his weight on his good leg, until he stood crookedly, staring down the barrel of the gun.

"Now turn around," she said.

He took a deep breath. "I can't."

"If you don't want to get shot, you'd better do as you're told," she said.

"I would love to do as I'm told, I really would," he said, trying to keep the anger out of his voice. This was not what he expected. "But unless you hand me my walking cane, I'm likely to end up eating dirt again." He pointed at the stick on the ground between them.

She glanced down, her shock registering on her face. He knew now was the time to jump her and wrestle the gun from her while she was distracted. But he could feel blood seeping down his leg, and the pain from his wound was making him feel woozy. He needed his pain meds and a damned good sleep before he could muster the energy to fight this crazy woman.

"You're bleeding," she said.

"Yeah, I know. I guess Bear's welcome ripped my stitches."

"What happened to your leg?"

"I met someone with a gun who didn't want to talk before he shot me." He shrugged, beyond caring. "Wouldn't have understood a damned word he said anyway. Vietcong spook."

"You've been in Vietnam?"

"Yeah. Just got back. Wanna see my purple heart?"

She shook her head. "No. I want to know who sent you."

He put a hand to his head and rubbed his eyes. "Lady, I don't know what the hell you're talking about. I've been in 'Nam for the past three years, got shot and sent Stateside. I just got out of the vet's hospital in Virginia and headed home." He pointed at the cabin. "And there it is. My home. Now, are you gonna give me my stick, or shoot me? 'Cause right now, I don't give a shit either way."

She stared at him, her grip on the gun firm. She had nerve, he'd give her that, considering he was a good foot taller than her, even all hunched up and trying to keep his weight off his gammy leg.

"Who are you?" she asked.

"Jefferson Mackay." He pulled at the chain around his neck and showed her his army tag. She stayed where she was. He didn't blame her. He was getting pissed off now. If she got close enough he'd probably take his chances and grab her.

"Now I know you're lying," she said. "I know Jefferson Mackay. Or rather, I knew him. I went to his funeral two weeks ago."

He closed his eyes. "That was my dad," he said, his voice tight. "They wouldn't let me out of the hospital to get here for it." He still hadn't come to terms with the fact that his father was dead. No doubt it would hit him now he was home. But he didn't want to think about that right now. If this crazy woman had her way, he might just be joining dear old Dad in the town cemetery.

Bear whined and moved to his side and licked his hand. The woman remained silent. He could almost see her furious thinking.

"Look, babe. I'm dead on my feet here," he said. "I don't know who you are or why you're here. But this is my damned house. I've been travelling for days, I need my pain meds and a fresh dressing on my leg. Then I intend to sleep for as long as it takes to make me feel human again. So can you give me my cane, or do I have to hang on to Bear here and hop to my bed?"

The woman's shoulders slumped and she lowered the gun. He let out a breath he hadn't realised he'd been holding.

Chapter Three

"I'm not your babe," she said, bending to pick up his stick. She shoved the cane into his hand and stepped back, still not sure he wouldn't do her harm.

He shrugged. "Sorry, Princess."

She scowled at him.

"I'll call you by your name if you tell me what it is," he said, straightening up as he shifted his weight and anchored himself with the cane.

She still didn't know whether to trust him, even with the dark patch of blood staining the leg of his khaki trousers. She was still in fight-or-flight mode, even though logic told her that the son of her landlord wouldn't have been sent to kill her. And now she studied him, she could see the likeness to the older Jefferson MacKay.

He took a step and grimaced in pain.

"Do you need a doctor?" she asked.

"Nah. I've had it with medics for a while. Even nurses lose their appeal when every time they look at you they stick a needle in your ass."

She could relate to that, but she couldn't bring herself to smile. She saw nothing amusing about this situation. If she could have persuaded him, she'd have driven him to the nearest clinic and left him there. But she knew what it felt like to be stuck in a ward and helpless.

"But I would appreciate some help," he went on.

"I'm not very good with sick people," she said, still unwilling to get close to him.

Memories of a man ... A hotel room somewhere in France ... Him retching and clutching his stomach and begging her for help ... She shivered. *He'd been faking it and she had fallen for it, letting him send her on her way, knowing he'd betrayed her and was sending her into danger.* Why the hell should she trust this stranger?

He raised his eyebrows and ran his free hand through his hair. It was cut short, military style. Nothing like the longer-haired shop boys and mechanics she encountered on her rare visits to town.

"I don't need nursing, Princess. I just don't think I can get these pants off without some help. If I don't get the dressing off before the blood dries, it'll be a bitch to change later."

She sincerely hoped he meant his trousers, and not his actual underpants.

"Faye. My name's Faye. Stop calling me Princess."

He nodded. "Faye. Okay. I'd say it's a pleasure, but right now it would be a lie and we'd both know it. So, Faye, you gonna help me get inside or not?"

"But …"

He rolled his eyes. "What?"

"I don't think you understand. This is my home. I paid rent in advance to Jefferson Mackay – the older one."

He closed his eyes and groaned. "I don't believe this." He took a deep breath and turned, leaning heavily on the walking cane as he made his way towards the house.

"Where are you going?" she asked, following him.

"Inside."

"You can't. I told you—"

"And I'm telling you, Faye whoever-you-are. This. Is. My. House. My dad had no right to sign anything with you. I'll get the estate to refund your money, but it ends now. I'm home and I'm not going anywhere."

She glared at him, her mind in turmoil. "I should've bloody shot you when I had the chance," she muttered.

He ignored her and made his painful way up the steps to the porch. If he noticed that she'd painted the posts and railings and added cushions to the rocking chairs, or that she'd added some tubs bursting with scarlet geraniums, he didn't comment.

Of course he won't notice them in the dark, she reasoned as she left him there and ran round to the back door, let herself in and locked the door behind her. She crossed the kitchen as he banged on the front door.

"Where'd you go? Dammit, who the hell locks their doors around here?" he yelled.

"I do!" she shouted back. "And I've just locked the back door too. And is it any wonder? You turn up here in the middle of the night, frighten the life out of me, and then tell me you're going to evict me."

She was shaking. She wished he would just get in his car and drive away. Or that there was a phone in the cabin so that she could actually call the Sheriff to come and send this man away. Despite being prepared to run when she thought her life was threatened, she didn't want to leave this house. She'd been running for years now, and over the last six months here she had found some measure of peace. If he really did own the place, she knew it was inevitable that she would have to go, but right now she wasn't going to make it easy for him.

She heard him swearing and moving around the porch. If he was looking for the key that used to be left over the door frame, he'd be out of luck. The first thing she'd done was to take that down and have bolts fitted. Even if he could pick a lock, both doors were firmly bolted as well. Ramming them with anything less than a wrecking ball wouldn't damage the solid wood. As he was handicapped by his injured leg at the moment, he was unlikely to be able to climb in through any of the windows.

It went quiet. She frowned. She crept into the living room and peeked out of the window. He was nowhere to be seen, but his car was still there. *Where the bloody hell was he?*

Bear started barking at the side of the house. There were no windows there, so she couldn't look out from her position of safety. She rushed into the kitchen to see if he'd moved round the back, but the moonlit garden was undisturbed. There were no shadows moving in the trees beyond. She went and checked the bedroom window. Still nothing.

Bear continued to bark. She started to wonder whether the man had fallen, or passed out. Her conscience started to niggle at her. To any normal person, it would have been obvious he was in pain and it would be hard to fake the blood seeping through the leg of his trousers. But she'd been fooled before and it had nearly killed her. He might just be waiting for her to panic and rush out to find out why Bear was barking so frantically.

But then the barking stopped.

She waited, her heart hammering in her chest, her senses on full alert. The rapid thud of her pulse and the raspy sound of her breath made it hard for her to listen. She'd put the shotgun down by the kitchen door when she'd bolted it. She left the bedroom, intending to retrieve it. If he was still out there, she'd feel better with the gun in her hand.

As she entered the kitchen she was blinded as the light came on. She gasped as her vision cleared and she came face to face with Jefferson Mackay Junior, her shotgun in his hand.

"How did—?"

He smiled, but his eyes remained cool. "I helped rebuild this place. I'm guessing you haven't been using the root store." He inclined his head. The door to the small pantry was open. "There's a trapdoor in there."

She closed her eyes. *How could she be so stupid?* She had known about the root store under the house, but thought it was only accessible from outside. She hadn't even been down there. If she had, she'd have realised this was a vulnerable spot and would have taken steps to make it secure.

With a sigh, she raised her hands in surrender.

"More fool me," she said, concentrating in keeping her hands and voice steady. "Now what?"

He shook his head. "Damn, you're a cold bitch."

She felt her heart stutter but refused to let him see he'd got to her. "So I've been told," she said. Although if she was as bad as he and others thought, she'd have shot him the moment she had a clear target. But, like a fool, she hadn't.

The sound of him cracking open the gun made her jump. He looked at her, one eyebrow raised. "Sorry if I make you nervous, Princess," he said as he emptied the chambers and slipped the cartridges in his pocket. He closed the gun with a snap and propped it by the back door where she'd left it. She realised she'd left her emergency rucksack on the seat of the truck. She had backup weapons in there – a handgun and a couple of knives. If she was quick, she might reach the cutlery drawer and grab a kitchen knife before he reached her, but then what? He was bigger than her, and a trained soldier. No, fighting her way out of here wasn't an option. He had the control. She was at his mercy.

Chapter Four

Jeff watched her. He noted the slight tremor in her hands, and the way she blinked rapidly against the harsh electric light. She was a tough one. Even when he had the gun in his hand she'd kept her blue eyes on his face, daring him to shoot her.

Why the hell didn't Dad tell me about her? And why did he let her live in my house? I asked him to keep an eye on the place, not find a damned tenant.

A memory hovered at the edge of his consciousness. An English voice. A man. Someone his dad had known in his military days … He shook his head, trying to make sense of why this memory came to him now when he should be focusing on dealing with this damned woman. But the pain in his leg, made worse by having to climb in through the root store and up the rickety steps to the trap door into the pantry without making any noise, was starting to make him feel queasy. He needed his pain meds and a fresh dressing.

"Open the front door," he told her. "My bag is out there, by the car. Go get it for me."

"How do I know you're not just going to slam the door behind me and leave me out there?" she asked.

He sighed and leaned against the countertop, taking the weight off his leg. "Because I need what's in my bag, and my cane which is out by the root store, and we need to let Bear back in, don't you think?"

As if he'd heard his name mentioned, the dog scratched at the kitchen door and whined.

"All right," she said. "I'll bring your bag and walking stick. You let the dog in." She turned towards the living room but paused as she looked over her shoulder at him. "But I'd better warn you, if you try to lock me out of here you will regret it."

Jeff raised his head and glared at the ceiling as he blew out a long breath. "For fuck's sake, woman. I'm in no fit state to throw you out, much as I want to. But that doesn't mean I'm leaving either. Just get me my meds, will ya?"

With a huff she did as he asked. He unbolted and unlocked the back door and let Bear in.

"Hey, boy. You okay?" He ruffled the dog's fur. "It's so good to see you, buddy."

For a moment he felt emotions welling up through his chest as memories of times spent with Bear came rushing into his mind. But the slam of the front door brought him back to the present and he straightened up. If she had another gun, things could get rough. He glanced at the shotgun and reached into his pocket for the cartridges.

Faye stepped into the room, dragging his bag with one hand and carrying his cane in the other.

That don't mean she hasn't got a pistol stuffed into her waistband, he thought.

But as she heaved the bag onto the kitchen table, he noticed her t-shirt rode up, exposing the pale skin above the waistband of her jeans. No gun. No suspicious bulges. Just smooth, creamy skin.

She turned and scowled when she saw him checking her out. She picked up the cane she had rested against a chair and offered it to him, keeping the length of her arm and the cane between them.

"What now?" she asked.

He took the cane and leaned on it with relief. "Side pocket of the bag. Pills and dressings," he said as he pulled out the chair at the end of the table and sat down, straightening his leg with a groan.

She found what he wanted and put them on the table in front of him. Without a word she turned to the sink, pulled a glass from the cupboard next to it and filled it with water.

"Thanks," he said as he took it from her and tipped a couple of pills into his hand. He took the medication and washed it down. He kept drinking until the glass was empty.

"Damn, I forgot how good the water is here," he said with a crooked smile.

"More?" she asked.

He shook his head. "No, thanks. But I'll need some warm water in a bowl."

For a moment she looked like she was going to refuse. She opened her mouth then shut it again, then turned her back on him as she filled a kettle and put it on the stove, then searched the cupboards for a bowl and some clean cloths.

Jeff watched her, waiting for the meds to kick in. He didn't expect an instant result. If he could get his dressing changed and get to his bed, he expected they'd be working by then and he'd be able to sleep. In the meantime, he tried to ignore the problem of what this woman's presence meant to his plans for a peaceful rehabilitation.

When the water was warm, she poured it into the bowl and brought it and the cloths to the table.

"Now what?" she asked again.

He looked down at his blood-stained thigh. "Now, I need to get these pants off."

"I'd better leave you to it, then," she said, turning away.

He reached out and grabbed her hand. "No."

She froze and looked at him.

"I need some help," he admitted. When she didn't re he went on. "Look, I know you said you don't like sick but—"

"I didn't say I didn't like them," she said. "I said I' good with them."

He shrugged, not letting go of her hand. Instead thumb over the back of her hand. He noted her sl her gaze was clear and fearless. "I don't care," help and you're all I've got. Can we call a tru with this?"

She pulled her hand away from his. "W to the clinic in town?"

He shook his head. He wouldn't leav sure she couldn't lock him out again. " I just need to get my damn pants dressing."

"What if you need stitches?"

He sighed. "We won't know until we get a look at it."

She looked at him. He stared back, waiting. Eventually she took a deep breath and huffed it out. "All right. Let's get this over with." She reached for his pants and undid the button before unzipping the fly. "You'll need to stand up again."

The meds had started to work. He welcomed the woozy, warm feeling that was slowly taking over his senses, banishing the ache in his bones.

"Jefferson, concentrate!" she snapped. "You need to stand up."

He blinked. "Yes, ma'am." He braced himself on the solid pine table and attempted to stand. A bolt of pain shot through his body, over-riding his narcotic haze. With a curse he dropped back into the seat. Sweat broke out on his forehead as he closed his eyes and panted through the pain.

"Are you all right?" she asked. "You're not going to pass out on me, are you?"

He shook his head. "I just can't get up. Sorry."

After a few moments he opened his eyes and peered up at her. She stood beside him, her arms crossed over her chest and frowning. When she saw him looking at her, she seemed to come to a decision.

"I hope you've got some more trousers in that bag, because I think the only way we're going to be able to sort this out is to cut those off." She pointed at his khakis. "Are they army issue? Will you get in trouble if we destroy them?"

"Not a problem," he said.

"Do you need more pain-killers?"

"No. The ones I took should be enough. I just shouldn't have to move so soon." He leaned his elbows on the table and his head in his hands. "Can we just get on with this?"

He heard her move behind him and pull open the cutlery drawer. He hoped like hell she wasn't picking out a knife to stab him with. She shut the drawer and he raised his head to look at her. She waved a pair of scissors. "Do you want to do it?" she

He shook his head. "I trust you," he said, knowing he was probably too far gone with the combination of pain, exhaustion and narcotic haze to be able to help himself. He just needed to get through this.

"Okay. Hold still," she said, kneeling at his side.

She took hold of the hem of his trousers and began to snip, opening the material to expose his leg. She kept cutting until she reached the blood-soaked patch above his knee. As she hesitated, he waved her hands away. He reached down and grabbed the material and ripped it apart, exposing the soiled dressing underneath.

She sat back, scissors in her hand, and surveyed it as he leaned against the table and rested his head in his hands again.

"I think the bleeding must have stopped," she said. "It looks like it's drying."

"Just rip it off," he said.

"No. It could start bleeding again. Let me think … Ah, I know."

He turned his head and opened one eye to watch as she soaked a cloth in the warm water and brought it to his thigh. With gentle hands she rinsed the drying blood away from the edges of the dressing until she could slip the blade of the scissors under it and cut it away from his wound. She kept stopping and dabbing more warm water on it to ease the bandages and lint away from his skin until she finally got it all off, exposing the jagged scar on his thigh.

"That doesn't look like a bullet wound," she said.

"They had to dig it out. Took a while. They had to sew up some muscle and the artery."

She sucked in some air with a sharp hiss. "You could have died."

"Yeah. But I guess it wasn't my time. I was lucky I was with a guy who knew what to do. He saved me from bleeding out."

She nodded, her eyes never leaving his wound. Her brown hair fell around her face. Without thinking, he leaned over to brush it behind her ear. He had a brief glimpse of a thin white line running down her cheek just in front of the hairline before she flinched back and glared at him.

"Keep your hands off me!" she snapped, sweeping her hair over the scar.

Chapter Five

Faye glared at him, fighting the urge to get up and run. She hadn't been touched by another human being for so long that his soft caress had taken her by surprise. She felt exposed and vulnerable, and she hated it.

"Keep your hands off me," she snapped.

He stared at her, looking bewildered. He was still leaning on the table, his head resting on his other hand. "Your hair was getting in your eyes."

"I don't care. Don't touch me, all right?"

"Princess, do I look like I'm about to ravish you?" he asked, his voice slurring.

"You look like you've invaded my home," she said. "And you look like you need my help. So keep your bloody hands to yourself or I'll leave you to sort yourself out."

He actually rolled his eyes at that. "Can we fight about the home invasion issue later? I really need you to help me with this." He waved his free hand – the offending one – in the direction of his thigh. "Please?"

He really did look dead on his feet. She took a deep, calming breath and turned back to her task.

"All right. But keep your hands to yourself," she muttered as she grabbed a fresh cloth, soaked it in the water and began to clean the wound.

A couple of stitches looked like they'd come loose, but the rest seemed to be holding the sides of the wound together. She didn't know whether there was any damage under the skin, but if the stubborn man didn't want to get a doctor to look at it, there wasn't much she could do about it.

He was silent as she finished cleaning the blood away and dried the area. She picked up the dressing pack, tore it open and applied it to his wound. Aware of his stare, she refused to look at his face, letting her hair fall forward, hiding her expression from him.

"Right. All done," she said, sitting back on her heels. "What now?"

"Bed."

"I beg your pardon?"

"I need to get to bed. Meds are kickin' in. Unless you can carry me, I need to get my head down before I pass out."

His words were slurring, his eyelids drooping. She couldn't leave him there. Nor could she dump him on the couch in the living room because he was far too big for it. With a sigh she got up. It would have to be the bed in the main bedroom – her bed. He wouldn't fit anywhere else. At least with him sleeping off his medication she wouldn't have to worry about fighting with him or of him attacking her.

"All right, big boy. Let's get you to bed," she said as she stood and grabbed his walking stick.

He sat up straight, rubbing his face.

"Here," she said, putting the cane in his hand. "You're going to have to do some of the work. You're too heavy for me to move."

He nodded but didn't move. His eyes closed. She shook his shoulder.

"Jefferson! Wake up! Come on, spit spot." She groaned. "Bloody hell, now you're turning me into Mary Poppins," she muttered.

He smiled and squinted at her. "Are you going to sing to me, Princess Faye?"

"Not in this lifetime," she said. "Move yourself or I'll leave you here."

He huffed out a breath. "Gotta work on that bedside manner, nurse. Okay, okay. I got this." He squared his shoulders and stood, grimacing and leaning on the cane.

Faye stepped closer and he put his free arm around her shoulders. He leaned on her and she staggered, fighting to keep them both upright.

"Whoa, you're a little bitty thing, ain't ya?" he said, looking down at her from his great height.

"I'm all you've got, big boy, so let's get this done." She pointed towards the living room. "Move."

It took a few tries until they got into a rhythm and moved slowly through the cabin to the bedroom door. Faye opened it and they moved towards the ruffled bed.

"Who's been sleeping in my bed?" he said, a sly grin on his face as he looked at the silky nightdress she'd abandoned on it. "Was it you, Bear?"

The dog had been sitting quietly, watching the two of them in the kitchen, but now he was at their heels. At the sound of his name, he let out a short woof that could have been a laugh or a confirmation. Faye shook her head.

"Just get on the bed before we both fall over," she said, pushing him in the direction of the mattress.

"Wait," he said. She halted.

"Now what?"

"Can you get these off me?" He nodded towards the shredded trousers.

"All right. Lean on your stick a minute." She pulled the remnants down to his ankles, leaving him in a dark t-shirt and boxer shorts. Then she pulled back the bedding. "Right, sit down."

He sat on the edge of the mattress then lay back with a sigh. Faye dispensed with his boots and socks, then pulled the remnants of his trousers off. She stood up. He was almost out. She plumped up the pillows and shook his shoulder again.

"Jefferson."

"What?" He didn't open his eyes.

"You can't sleep like that. You need to move."

Muttering under his breath, he let her help him move onto the pillows and lift his legs onto the mattress. He hissed as she moved his injured leg, but she didn't stop. It had to be done. Once he was properly in bed he could relax. She wasn't about to waste any more time on this. She was exhausted.

At last he was settled in the centre of the bed. Faye pulled the covers over him and realised he was already out of it. She listened for a moment, wondering whether he'd lost consciousness, but his breathing was deep and even, so she thought it was safe to assume he was finally sleeping.

As she straightened up, Bear moved to the other side of the bed and jumped up. Faye held her breath in case the movement had jarred the man, but he slept on. Bear settled himself against the stranger's side and the dog settled with a sigh, head on his paws, his gaze fixed on the man's face.

"Traitor," she whispered. "I thought you were my friend."

The dog ignored her.

She turned away, disgusted by how much it bothered her that she had been so easily replaced in the dog's affections. So what if Bear had apparently known Jefferson for far longer than he'd been with Faye? He'd been her dearest friend, and now she was being ignored in favour of this ... this beast of a man who had invaded her sanctuary. They still hadn't resolved that issue, either. She didn't want to leave and he clearly intended to stay. An impossible situation.

"What the hell am I going to do?" she muttered as she closed the door behind her.

She surveyed the living room, its only illumination the light spilling in from the kitchen and the moonlight pouring in through the window. The couch was fine for sitting on, but not for sleeping. She ran a hand through her hair. She didn't know if she'd sleep now anyway, even though she felt exhausted. The fear and anger that had driven her for the past hour was draining away, leaving her feeling weak and fed up. She just wanted to curl up, close her eyes and ignore the world for a few hours.

There was only one other place where she could sleep – there was a day bed in the studio up in the attic. That would have to do for now. The decision made, she went into the kitchen and checked that the trap door to the root store was closed and that all the doors were locked and bolted. She would have to work out what she was going to do about the root store later ... if she was allowed to stay.

Turning out the kitchen light, she climbed the ladder to the attic. Moonlight flooded in through the skylights so she didn't need to put the light on. Instead she kicked off her boots and collapsed onto the day bed. She lay there, staring up at the stars, wondering what would happen tomorrow.

Chapter Six

"Where the hell is my stuff?" Jeff roared in frustration as he rifled through the dresser and came up with silk underwear and women's clothes. "Jesus Christ, what the fuck is going on around here?"

When no one answered, he slammed out of the bedroom and limped through the cabin in just his underwear. He'd thought he'd dreamed about some woman trying to run him off his own property, but maybe he hadn't imagined it. There was no one there now. But she couldn't have gone far because there was a pot of something simmering on the stove. He sniffed, his mouth watering. He had no idea what was cooking, but it smelt damned good to a man who couldn't remember the last time he'd had a decent home-cooked meal.

The sound of quick footsteps on the back porch steps drew him to the door. He opened it just as Faye arrived. She stopped, taking a step back.

"Is there any chance of you putting some clothes on?" she asked, sounding like the English Queen.

"I would, but some asshole has stolen my stuff and replaced it with women's underwear," he said, resting his hands on his hips. "Know anything about that?"

If he expected her to be intimidated by an almost-naked man blocking the doorway, he was disappointed. She ran her gaze down his body and up again before she raised an eyebrow and mimicked his stance, hands on hips. If he wasn't so pissed off, he'd have laughed at her sass.

"I asked if you had any spare trousers in your bag before I cut the other ones off you," she pointed out. "I believe the rest of your clothes must be at your father's ranch. He took some boxes away when I moved in here."

"I'll bet you used all the hot water for the shower as well," he muttered, turning away from the door.

She followed him in and moved to the stove to check whatever was cooking. She gave it a stir and put the lid back on before turning the heat down a little. "I had my shower hours ago, so it should be okay. Just don't get your stitches wet," she said.

He rolled his eyes. He didn't need another damned nurse ordering him around. "What time is it?"

She shrugged. "About twelve-thirty, I think."

"I slept for twelve hours?"

"Actually, you slept the clock round. You arrived in the early hours of Tuesday and it's Wednesday afternoon now."

He frowned. He knew he'd been exhausted, but to have slept – what? – thirty-six hours?

"You were a bit restless yesterday morning," she went on. "So I offered you some more pain-killers. You took them and went out again."

That would explain why he wasn't in more pain. His leg ached, but it wasn't nearly as bad as it had been after the long drive here and his tumble in the dirt with Bear. When he didn't say anything, she gave him a cool look.

"You're welcome," she said.

"Is that English sarcasm, or good old American snark?" he asked.

She rolled her eyes. "Just go and get washed and dressed. I assume you're hungry now, so I'll put your terrible manners down to that. I'm dishing up in twenty minutes, and if you're not at the table suitably attired, you can go without."

"Any chance of a coffee?"

"Sorry. Haven't got any. I only drink tea."

With a grunt of disgust he went into the bathroom.

He had to make do with a strip-wash so that he didn't get his dressing wet. He would have to get some new supplies – he only had enough to see him though a couple of days. At least the bleeding had stopped. He thought about shaving, but decided against it. He didn't want to stand for too long. And anyway, he didn't have any officers hanging around ready to put him on a charge for looking like a slob. Instead he dunked his head into the water and shampooed his hair. It wasn't until he rinsed that he realised he'd used something that smelled of damned strawberries. He rinsed again, hoping to get rid of the smell, but it clung to him.

He dried off and ran his fingers through his hair, wondering where his comb was. He didn't want to use the fancy hairbrush on the shelf. It was obviously hers as some of her long brown hairs clung to it. Today she had it in a loose braid over her left shoulder. No doubt she smelled of strawberries too.

He wrapped a towel around his hips and wandered back into the bedroom. He located his comb in his bag, together with a fresh shirt, underwear, socks and pants. He sighed as he pulled on the khakis. He'd not expected to have to wear them ever again. For the first time in years, he was a civilian. He couldn't wait to slide into some Wranglers and a plaid shirt. But he guessed that could wait another couple of hours. First, he needed to eat. He struggled into his socks, grimacing against the pull on his thigh. Once they were on, he donned a clean khaki t-shirt and a black sweatshirt and rested his hands on his knees for a minute to catch his breath.

A clatter of plates from the kitchen got him moving again. He wouldn't put it past her to feed his lunch to Bear if he didn't show up on time.

There was something about this woman – something brittle, even cold. Yet she'd been gentle when she'd cleaned his wound, and she'd been humane enough to check on him and give him more pain meds when he needed them. He still had no idea why the hell she'd taken up residence in his house. Something about his dad letting her rent it didn't make sense. But with the old man gone, Jeff reckoned he should be able to handle this. A quick call to the family lawyer and an eviction order should restore his home to him in no time.

Who knows? he thought. *Maybe now she's had time to think about it, she could be planning on moving on anyway.*

But evidently not before eating whatever she'd been cooking when he woke up. He found her standing at the kitchen table, ladling a rich beef stew into bowls. Bear sat beside her, his nose twitching and his eyes pleading, but the woman ignored him.

On the radio, *Mr Tambourine Man* was playing and she moved her head and hips in time to the music. For the first time in months he felt the stirrings of desire, but he banked it down. She wasn't just some chick he met in a bar. She was in residence in his home and refusing to leave. Taking her to bed might scratch an itch, but it sure as hell wouldn't make getting rid of her easy.

She looked up and saw him standing in the doorway. If she realised he'd been watching her dance, she didn't show it. Instead she slid a full bowl of food across the table, where she'd already laid out cutlery and a glass of water.

He sank into the chair while she turned off the radio before sitting opposite him with her own meal. He tried to keep his gammy leg as straight as possible. Bear came round to greet him, resting his head in Jeff's lap. He smiled down at the dog and scratched between his ears.

"Bear, in your bed." Her sharp command had the dog slinking onto the doggy bed in the corner of the kitchen. "If you let him sit near the table while you're eating, he'll steal the food off your plate."

"I know," he said. "He's always been like that."

"Well, he gets plenty of grub, so I won't put up with sharing my meals with him."

He glanced over at the dog, who gazed back at him longingly.

"How'd you get him to do what you say? Dad reckoned he was untrainable."

She shrugged. "My father said there are no bad dogs, just bad owners. You have to let them know who's boss. Bear wasn't hard to train."

"Until I showed up," he said. "He ran out of that barn where you were hiding and nearly loved me to death."

She glared at him. "I was hoping he was going to savage you. It's no more than you deserved, sneaking in here in the middle of the night." She huffed out a breath. "Anyway, are we going to eat or what?"

He looked at the rich stew in front of him and sniffed. It smelt delicious.

"I'd love to eat. But how do I know you haven't laced this with arsenic?"

She rolled her eyes and tutted. "For God's sake. If I was going to kill you, I could have slit your throat while you slept. But if you really don't trust me …" She reached for his bowl and switched it with hers. "There. Now eat."

He waited until she started eating, then took his first mouthful. Rich flavours of beef and herbs and something else burst on his tongue.

"Oh man, that's good," he groaned after he swallowed it down. "What is this? It's not plain stew."

"It's beef bourguignon," she said. "Just stew with some herbs and wine."

"You know French cooking?"

She nodded. He waited to see if she'd say more, but she ignored him and carried on eating.

"Where'd you get herbs and wine around here?" he asked. "This is plain meat and potatoes country."

"I grow some herbs and I got some wine shipped in. Just because this is the middle of nowhere, it doesn't mean I have to live like a peasant."

He sat back, chewing, trying to figure her out. "Sorry, Princess. I guess us peasants don't know any better."

"Well, I do. So I do what I can to make life bearable."

"Wouldn't you be better off in a city, where you can get all these fancy ingredients any time?"

"Been there, done that. I don't like people very much, so at least here I can enjoy my splendid isolation." She gave him a cool glance before turning her gaze back to her food. "At least I could, until you showed up."

"How old are you?" he asked.

She dropped her spoon and stared at him. "What's that got to do with anything?"

"Just curious."

"You're also very rude. Don't you know you should never

ask a lady her age?"

"You're a lady?" he smirked.

He knew he was being mean. She was all woman and he was finding it hard to not want to touch her. But she had that antsy attitude that got him right in the gut. He needed to keep on pushing, to find her weak spots.

She laughed and picked up her spoon again, shaking her head. "Eat your lunch," she said.

He wanted answers, but the food was too good to ignore. He went back to eating, enjoying the rich flavours and textures of the meal. It was a far cry from army rations and hospital food. Hell, he'd consider keeping her around if she fed him meals like this every day. That thought brought him up sharp. He frowned at his now empty bowl.

"Do you want some more?" she asked. "I make up big batches and freeze what's left for another day. There's plenty."

He shook his head. He probably could put away another couple of bowls full but then he'd get sleepy again. He needed to stay alert.

"No thanks. It was good, though."

She inclined her head like she was the Queen of England. She didn't look like the Queen, even though she sounded like he imagined the monarch would talk. But she had a look that he never saw around these parts. She wasn't from some small-town, ranching stock. She had a delicacy about her features, and an elegance in her posture that spoke of high-class breeding. Where the women around here were like working ponies, this woman was a thoroughbred. And she knew it.

"So, you won't tell me your age. How about you tell me how you ended up here?"

"A friend recommended it. I saw it, I liked it. End of story."

She got up, collecting theirs bowls and took them to the sink. She ran some hot water into the basin and began to wash up. She'd obviously cleaned up as she cooked, as there was nothing else to scrub. He thought about grabbing a towel and joining her to share the chore, but that might be a bit too cosy in the circumstances. She was still a squatter in his house. He had to remember that.

"So," he leaned back in his chair and watched her. "You're a city girl in your, let's say, mid-twenties. You don't like people but you like life's luxuries."

She snorted. "A few herbs and a decent bottle of wine are hardly luxuries."

"They are round here, Princess."

She glared at him over her shoulder. "I told you …"

He waved a hand. "Yeah, yeah, yeah. 'Don't call me Princess,'" he mimicked in a falsetto voice and a terrible English accent. "But the thing is, you act like one. I just can't help it. In fact, if I didn't have a gammy leg, I'd probably be curtseying every time you open your mouth."

She turned away, but not before he saw her reluctant smile. "You're ridiculous," she huffed, pulling the plug and letting the water drain out of the sink.

He watched her in silence as she dried the bowls and cutlery and put them away. He caught a glimpse of the inside of the cabinet as she stacked the bowls inside. It wasn't the messy clutter he'd left there when he'd left for his last tour. Someone – probably Faye – had reorganized it so that everything stacked neatly. Nothing was likely to fall off the shelf onto your head when you opened the door. The soldier who appreciated discipline and order appreciated that. The guy who had rebuilt this cabin, and hadn't had the chance to do more than throw everything into the cupboards before his army leave was over, resented that she'd got there first.

She hung the towel on a hook that he didn't remember being there the last time he was home.

"Who put that up?"

"What?" she asked. He pointed at the hook. "Oh, one of the ranch hands, I think."

"What else have you done to my place?" he asked, trying to keep a scowl from his face.

She opened her arms. "See for yourself. It's a lot cleaner than you left it."

"I left it clean enough," he growled.

"I'm sure you did. But it was empty for a couple of years, wasn't it? I had to battle through cobwebs and dust to make it habitable."

So much for Dad looking after the place for me, he thought.

He opened his mouth to respond, but she was turning away. "I have work to do," she said and walked out of the back door.

He debated going after her, but decided to get a better look around the house first. The kitchen didn't look so different – apart from some herb plants on the window ledge above the sink. He peeked into the pantry. He had a vague memory of coming in through the trap door from the root store after she'd locked him out, but now he took in the shelves filled with cans and jars. He picked up a round, brown jar. Yeast extract? What the hell was that? He opened it an examined the dark goo inside. He dipped a finger in and tasted it. It was salty. He didn't know whether it was good or not. He had no idea what anyone would do with it. Next to it was a jar of marmalade. He knew people had that on their breakfast toast – his dad's English friend had introduced him to it and shipped it to Dad on a regular basis.

There were cans of vegetables, boxes of flour, rice and spaghetti. A couple of bottles of wine. He opened the chest freezer and saw that it was well-stocked with packs of meat and containers marked as holding cooked dishes, just like she'd said. She had enough supplies to survive here for months.

In the living room, his old brown sofa had been covered by a scarlet blanket and a few cushions – a sure sign that a woman had taken over the space. There was a bookcase that hadn't been there before but looked familiar – had it come from the ranch? The shelves were packed with books – novels, gardening manuals, history books and a couple on livestock management. He recognized a couple of the titles. He was sure they'd belonged to his dad.

He didn't need to look in the bedroom. He already knew she'd taken his plain, neutral bedding and switched it to make it a woman's boudoir. He frowned as he wondered where she'd slept since he'd reclaimed his bed. He'd have to ask her.

It occurred to him that there were no photographs, not one single image of family or friends, no reminders of places she'd been or things she'd done. Instead, she'd put up a few paintings, mainly local scenes of the mountains and forests. That was about the only change to the place he approved of.

The bathroom was as he remembered it, but with fluffier towels, and shampoo and soaps that smelt like flowers and fruits.

Outside, the wraparound porch looked smarter, with tubs of scarlet flowers on either side of the door. She'd painted the posts and railings around it – or got someone to do it for her. Even the old rocking chairs he'd rescued from a yard sale had been rubbed down and varnished. She had put seat pads on them, and there was a dark blue blanket hanging over the back of one, as though she sometimes sat out there snuggled into it. He sank into a chair and stared out over the front lot. He'd noticed the paddock fence had been repaired and the grass was neatly cropped. A movement in the far corner caught his eye. There was a horse, his head down, grazing. He frowned. It looked familiar. Had Dad given her one of the ranch horses as well as Bear?

Damn! I need to find out what the hell has been happening.

He got up and stalked around to the back of the house. As he rounded the corner, he stopped and blinked. What had been a rough plot between the cabin and the barn and the woods beyond was now neatly divided into a vegetable patch and a flower garden. In between rows of beans and potatoes and tomatoes, Faye was picking pea pods and dropping them into a basket. Bear lay on the dirt, chewing on a bone. The dog didn't even acknowledge him.

He moved forwards and Faye noticed him. She straightened up and watched him, her expression guarded.

"Did you do all this?" he asked.

She nodded. "Your father gave me some advice and loaned me some books. I've been quite pleased with how it's gone. I never thought I had green fingers."

"You English need all your fingers to be green, huh? American gardeners only need green thumbs."

She didn't respond. She simply looked down at her hands, protected by gardening gloves.

He smiled, although it didn't reach his eyes. He should have guessed Princess Faye wouldn't want her hands getting rough with all this manual work.

"Do you want to go to the ranch?" she asked. "I expect your sister will want to see you."

He frowned. "Trying to get rid of me?"

"That would be nice," she said, her expression cool. "But I doubt you'd make it that easy for me. I just thought you might want to locate your personal belongings and catch up with your family. It's been hard on your sister, not having you around when your father died."

He felt himself tense. "I was in the hospital."

"Yes, but you're not now, are you? I think she could do with some moral support."

"If my dad had done as I'd asked and put in a phone line to here, I could have called her."

"Well you can blame me for that. I didn't want a phone."

"Why not?"

"There's no one I want to call." She shrugged. "So I didn't see the point."

She seemed okay with that, which didn't seem right. In fact, the more he thought about it, the more he felt something was off about this whole set-up. She was a virtual recluse, living like some mad old spinster who had scared all the eligible bachelors away in her youth, only to end up bitter and alone in her old age. Yet this woman was young – in her twenties, maybe? Certainly no older than thirty. What the hell had happened to send her running from England to the wilds of Montana to hide from the world?

"So your claim to have called the Sheriff was a lie."

"Maybe I used the CB radio in my truck," she said.

He smirked. "Oh yeah? What's your handle, Princess?"

"Lavender Lady," she shot back, cool as a cucumber. "I seem to have some novelty value on the airwaves."

"I'll bet you do."

"Anyway, I've got to go over to the ranch myself, so I could give you a lift," she said, picking up the basket of peapods. "I share my produce with them – I couldn't eat all these myself."

She looked up at him. "Or even with a guest."

"I'm not a guest. This is my place," he growled. "You're squatting in my home."

"Check the accounts with your sister. I pay rent. I'm a legal tenant."

He sighed and ran a hand through his hair. It was still short but growing fast. He couldn't remember the last time he'd had hair long enough to tangle his fingers in it.

"Maybe going together is a good idea. I don't trust you not to barricade yourself in the house while I'm gone."

She smiled. "I've already fitted bolts to the root store and trap door while you were sleeping. But going together is a good idea. I trust you about as far as I can throw you," she said, looking him up and down. "Which isn't far, given the size of you."

"Good call. You never know when you'll find your silky lingerie and frou-frou cushions tossed out onto the porch."

She reached the back porch steps and rolled her eyes. "So we agree that neither of us trusts the other. Fine. If we leave, we leave together. Just don't start criticizing my driving."

"I can drive."

"Much as I'd like to see you get in the car you arrived in and drive out of my life, I'm afraid you didn't shut the door properly. It left the interior light on and drained the battery. It's going nowhere. I, on the other hand, have a vehicle in the barn and am prepared to drive you to see your sister and her family in the hope that she can talk some sense into you." She held up a hand when he opened his mouth to speak. "And no, you can't drive it because it's what you people call a 'stick shift' and I doubt you could use the clutch pedal with that leg of yours."

"Are you finished?" he scowled.

"Yes."

"Good. Let's go."

Chapter Seven

Faye drove the truck along the dirt roads between the cabin and Jeff's father's ranch. It was a couple of miles, and all of the land they crossed belonged to the Mackay family. The parcel that the cabin was situated on was on the Western boundary of the Mackay estate.

At her side, Bear sat at attention while Jeff held onto the dog with one hand and clung with the other to the handle above the passenger door. No doubt he was trying to keep his leg from being jolted as they barreled over the ruts and potholes of the track.

He was sulking, she knew. Apparently he'd learned to drive in this old truck, and couldn't accept that his father had parted with it.

"I paid good money for it," she told him. "And then spent more on getting the damned thing roadworthy. I don't think it had ever been properly serviced. It drives like a dream now," she crowed, stroking the steering wheel.

"Where the f– er, heck did you learn to drive, lady?" he demanded as she sped along, not bothering to brake before any of the turns.

She grinned. "On a farm, of course. I can drive a tractor, too. I'd prefer a nice little convertible, but it wouldn't last five minutes around here."

Men were always surprised by her confident driving style. The memory of driving in France, with her companion complaining and whining all the time, wiped the smile from her face. She sped up momentarily, before she realised that she couldn't outrun the memory. All she could do was to refuse to let it drag her back to the life she'd left behind. She took a deep breath and slowed the truck, keeping her gaze on the track ahead. She could sense him staring at her.

"You're no farm girl," he said.

"Only in the holidays. My grandparents lived on the farm."

"Is that where you learned to handle a gun?"

"No. That was with my other grandparents. Grouse shooting in Scotland."

He whistled. "You may deny the princess tag, but you're not far off it, are you?"

She was silent for a moment. "I could be a servant's daughter," she said, still not looking at him.

"Not with your taste in lingerie, Princess."

"You sound so disapproving," she sneered. "I'll bet you got off just rifling through my drawers."

She pulled into the yard of the ranch house before he could respond.

"Ready to greet the family?" she asked, finally looking at him.

He was pale. She wasn't sure if it was hospital pallor, or fear generated by her driving style, or nerves at the thought of seeing his family again – now reduced following his father's sudden death – after years away. She wouldn't pity him. He had the power to evict her from the first place she'd felt safe in a long time. Instead she leaned on the horn to announce their presence and then got out of the truck, followed by an enthusiastic Bear.

The front door of the main house opened and a boy of about ten rushed out. He was halfway across the yard, heading for Bear, when Jeff slammed the passenger door of the truck. The boy slid to a halt, staring at him.

"Uncle Jeff?"

"Hey, Pete. Good to see you, bud," he smiled.

With a whoop the boy rushed towards his uncle. Faye dashed over and grabbed him under the arms just before he slammed into Jeff.

"Whoa there, little man! Mind his leg. You wouldn't want to see a grown man cry, would you?"

"Huh?" Pete looked at Faye. "What's the matter with his leg?" He turned to his uncle. "Why you got that stick, Uncle

Jeff?"

Jeff looked embarrassed, shooting an annoyed look at Faye. She shrugged. If he'd rather end up on his backside and rip his stitches again, she'd let him get on with it next time.

"It's only temporary, bud. Got shot." He tapped his thigh.

"If you ask him nicely, he'll show you his medal," she said. "Is your mummy around?"

"Right here."

They all turned towards the porch. Sally Mackay-Henderson stood there, wiping her hands on a towel. A little girl with blonde braids peeked out from behind her mother.

"Hey, Sal," said Jeff. "And is that little Amy? Man, you're all growed up!"

"'Bout time you showed up," said Sal. "Where the heck have you been? I called the hospital and they said you left five days ago."

"Yeah, well, took me three to drive home."

"And?" She stood with her hands on her hips, glaring at him.

Faye stepped forward. "And then Bear was so pleased to see him he knocked him off his feet and opened his wound. I had to administer first aid and painkillers, which knocked him out. He's been sleeping it off until a couple of hours ago."

Bear woofed at the sound of his name and leapt up the porch stairs towards Jeff's sister. Sally put out her hand and the dog stopped in his tracks and sat, staring up at her with adoration.

"Damn! He does that for you as well? I could never get that dog to do anything." Jeff shook his head.

Sally shook her head, laughing and crying at the same time. "Get in here, you idiot!"

Faye held back as he limped towards the stairs. No one else moved as he hauled himself up the steps and finally dropped his stick and opened his arms to pull his sister into a hug. Amy joined in, hugging his leg – thankfully his good one. Pete joined them, leaving Faye and Bear looking on as the family welcomed their lost boy home.

Faye felt her habitual sneer forming, but tightened her jaw

to fight it. She was glad the family were reunited. Really. Just because she'd always looked down her nose at lovely-dovey people, never understanding why they would get themselves so worked up about family ties, it didn't mean she should spoil this moment for them. Their lives were different from hers. In her experience, family gatherings were cold, dutiful events to be endured until you could make your excuses and leave. There was no laughter unless it was a means of putting someone down; none of her family would ever allow anyone to see them doing something as weak and pathetic as crying, for God's sake! Instead, she turned away, retrieving her baskets from the back of the truck. By the time she turned back the huddle had split apart, the kiddies were fussing over Bear, and Sally and Jeff were talking quietly.

Faye hefted the baskets up the steps to the porch.

"Shall I put these in the kitchen?" she asked.

"Oh, yeah," said Sally. "Thanks. What have you got?"

"Peas, spinach, lettuce and spring onions. Oh, and some eggs."

"Great."

Faye smiled and walked round them to enter the house. She knew the way to the kitchen and was glad to be able to leave the siblings on the porch getting reacquainted. So what if she had an ache in her heart as she thought about her own brother? She couldn't ever remember getting a hug from Percy. If she had showed him any affection he'd have immediately have been suspicious of her motives. She still missed him, though, she realised.

Which is bloody stupid, she thought. *He'd laugh his head off at the idea.*

The others followed her into the room.

"Have you eaten?" Sal asked her brother.

"Yeah, thanks. But I'd kill for a coffee," he said, inclining his head towards Faye. "She drinks tea."

Sal laughed. "I know. Weird, huh? Sit down. I'll put a fresh pot on." She turned to Faye. "D'you want some tea? I've still got some of those bags you brought over."

She shook her head. "No, I'm fine, thank you. But I need to

make a call. Long distance."

Sal sighed. "You'd better use the office phone."

"Thanks. I'll keep it short. Just let me know how much when your bill comes in and I'll settle up with you."

"Yeah, I know."

Faye turned and left the kitchen, but not before she caught the frown on Jeff's face. *He still doesn't trust me,* she thought. *Good.*

The late Jeff Mackay Senior had run his empire from a huge old pine desk in a wood-panelled study. There were guns and cattle horns as well as family photos on the walls, and a large picture window looking out over the pastures. Even though it had a Western feel, the room always reminded her of her father's study in London. Except this room was one where she'd always been made welcome. She'd never enjoyed visiting her father's study – she was usually only summoned there when he was displeased with her.

Faye closed the door behind her and felt a pang of regret that the gruff old American was no longer there to greet her. They'd been complete opposites – him a rough cowboy, her a self-confessed spoilt brat – but they had developed a mutual respect and friendship that had surprised everyone. But now he was gone and his son had returned.

With a sigh, she sat in Jeff Senior's chair and reached for the phone. She didn't need to look up the number, she knew it by heart. She dialled and heard the distinctive sound of a British ring tone. She just hoped he'd be home.

"Grainger," the clipped voice answered.

"It's Faye," she said.

"Hello there. What can I do for you?"

She smiled. No 'How are you?' or 'Faye who?' He never wasted time or made her feel she shouldn't have called – not that she did very often anyway.

"Jefferson Mackay has died."

"Yes, I heard. Shame. He was a good man."

"Yes," she replied. "I'm going to miss him."

"Is that why you called?"

"No. His son, Jefferson Junior, has come back from

Vietnam and wants me out of the cabin. He says it's his."

"I thought he was a career soldier. Old Jeff didn't expect him back any time soon."

"Yes, well. Rather inconveniently he got shot by an enemy sniper and has been sent home with a purple heart and a desire to take up residence in his own house. He's bloody lucky he didn't get shot again when he turned up on my doorstep in the middle of the night. I had him in my sights but I didn't want to shoot the dog who leapt all over him."

Grainger chuckled. "Lucky man."

"Yes, but that means I'm in a bind. I'm refusing to leave, but I doubt I can hold out for too long. I can't get involved in a legal tussle. But I've got a dog, a horse and some chickens now, and I don't want to leave them behind."

"Goodness, you really have changed your life, haven't you?"

"Don't patronize me, Mr Grainger," she snapped. "It's not like I had much choice, is it?"

"My apologies," he soothed. "I'd heard from Jefferson that you were doing well."

Faye wasn't sure she liked the idea of the old cowboy reporting back to Grainger about her.

"Well, now I'm about to be homeless again, and without Jefferson I don't have anyone else to turn to for help."

"Does the son know your situation?"

"Of course not," she scoffed. "I'm not likely to spill my secrets to the man who's trying to evict me, am I?"

"I suppose not. What does his sister say about it?"

"I don't know. We've just arrived at the ranch. I left them having their grand reunion while I called you."

"I doubt if she's aware of what we arranged with her father."

"She isn't."

"Mmm."

Faye sighed. "But now he's dead, I don't suppose it matters what was agreed. I'm going to have to move."

"Can you stall them? It could take me a while to make new arrangements for you."

"Stall them how? I may have made changes in my life, but I'm still the same person, you know. I don't do nice. I don't know how. No doubt he'll be ready to throw me out sooner rather than later."

He was silent for a moment. "I think you underestimate yourself, my dear."

She closed her eyes. Grainger had always been like this, even when she was in her deepest, darkest place. "He's an arse," she declared. "I already regret not shooting him."

"Try to restrain yourself, just for a week or two. I'll get my people on the case as soon as possible."

"I'll do my best," she said. "Just be quick, please."

"Trust me, Faye. It will work out. I'll get back to you as soon as I can. Should I leave a message through Jefferson's daughter? Or shall I speak to the lawyer?"

"Whatever you like," she said. "The sooner the better."

She ended the call and sat for a moment, staring out at the pastures. She felt drained. Calling her handler always made her edgy. He was her only link with her former home and the life she used to live, and she wished with all her heart she could cut that final chain holding her. But she wasn't stupid. She needed Grainger. Without him she was a sitting duck. His organisation kept her safe. Even though she really didn't deserve it.

Chapter Eight

Even though Jeff told Sally he'd eaten not long ago, his sister insisted he stayed for dinner.

"I need to go back with Faye."

"We can give you a ride back."

He was about to argue when Faye walked back into the room.

"He doesn't trust me, Sally," she smirked. "He thinks if I leave him here I'll barricade the house and leave him outside."

Sally frowned, looking from him to the Englishwoman.

He shrugged. "Hey, I'm not the one who bolted the doors against a bleeding man."

Faye rolled her eyes and Sally gasped. "Say what?" she asked.

"Yeah, she met me in the yard with a loaded shotgun and set Bear on me," he told her. "Then she ducked into the cabin and bolted the doors." His eyes were steely as he smiled. "But she forgot about the root store, so I got in anyway."

Faye sat down at the table. "You know, you two look much more alike when you're both scowling," she said in a light conversational tone.

"Why did you attack my brother?" asked Sally.

Faye looked at the children who were also sitting at the table. Their wide eyes and open mouths were almost comical. She smiled.

"I did not attack him, and neither did Bear."

Young Pete looked relieved. Amy looked confused. Sally still looked pissed off.

"He arrived unexpectedly in the middle of the night," Faye explained. "What was I supposed to do? I was actually hiding in the barn, trying to get Bear into the truck so we could escape, but the stupid hound rushed out and knocked Jeff over.

I thought he was going to lick him to death."

Amy giggled. No one else smiled.

"Look, if you were at home alone and some stranger arrived in the middle of the night, wouldn't you grab a gun and try to defend yourself?" Faye asked Sally. "He might be your brother, but I had no idea who he was or what he was doing there. I mean, it's hardly polite to roll up somewhere at three in the morning, is it?"

Sally relaxed a little and looked sideways at her brother. He glared at her and then at Faye.

"That does not excuse locking me out of my own house – dammit, I told you who I was!"

Sally slapped his shoulder. "Watch your language in front of the kids," she said.

He wanted to roll his eyes, but knew his sister would get even more pissed off if he did. Instead he closed his eyes and counted to ten in his head.

"I'm not the bad guy here," he growled. "And I'm not letting her go back there without me."

"Then you'll both have to stay for dinner," his sister declared. "Maybe we can talk about this when the kids have gone to bed, and see what we can do about it."

Faye shrugged. "Fair enough. Maybe you can talk some sense into him."

Sally raised her hands. "Woah, don't drag me into this. If you guys can't work it out, we'd better call Tom Hastings. He wanted to know when you were home anyway, Jeff. We need to read Dad's will."

Tom was an old friend of his dad's, and the family's lawyer.

"Why didn't you do it after the internment?" he asked, confused.

"Tom said you needed to be there. He knew you were Stateside because I told him. He said we should call him when you got here. I'll do it now."

She went to the phone on the wall and dialled. The kids asked if they could go and play, and she nodded. They ran out and he heard them clattering up the stairs like he and Sally used to do way back when. He half-expected to hear his dad's voice yelling at them to slow down and stop that godawful racket.

For a moment he felt a pain in his chest at the realisation that he was never going to see his old man again.

"Are you all right?" asked Faye. "Only you've gone all pale again. Do you need your medication?"

He shook his head. "I'm okay. It just hit me that my dad isn't here any more."

"But you've been away for, what? Two, three years?"

"You think that makes a difference?" he snapped. "Until now I could call home and talk to him anytime I wanted to. Now he's gone. I don't suppose you'd understand how that makes me feel, Princess."

She stared at him, looking confused. "Why do you say that?"

"I guess from our brief acquaintance that you don't much care for anyone but yourself. You're not likely to suffer much if anyone dies."

For a moment he saw a brief flash of pain on her face, before she took a breath and wiped the emotion from her expression.

"You know nothing about me. Nothing at all. Don't presume to judge me. I've known loss. I just don't whine about it."

"Whining – you think I'm whining? Jesus Christ, you're a damned annoying woman. Why my dad didn't kick you off our land, I'll never know."

They had been speaking in low tones while Sally had been talking to the lawyer. She now ended the call and turned to face them. They glared at each other.

"Well, that's odd," said Sally, joining them at the table. "Tom wants to come over right away."

"Tell him we can go to him tomorrow," said Jeff.

"I did, but he said it would be better to do it now." She looked at her watch. "I'd better get the kids ready for bed. Nick will be back soon – he's been working out in the Eastern pastures today. If Tom's coming straight over, we might have to hold back our dinner for an hour."

"I'd better leave you to it, then," said Faye, standing up.

"No," said Sally, putting a hand on Faye's arm. "Tom said you need to be here too."

Faye frowned. "Why?"

"I don't know. Maybe Dad left you something," she replied.

Jeff frowned. Faye shook her head.

"No, he wouldn't. And even if he did, I don't want it. It should all come to you two."

"Well, you'll have to stay and tell Tom. He said you have to be here."

With an exaggerated sigh, Faye sat down again. "This is ridiculous. I've got to get my horse settled for the night."

"That old horse can wait an hour. He's not going anywhere and it's a warm night. Tom was adamant. He won't read the will without the three of us being there."

Jeff felt his anger rising. *Who the fuck is this woman, and what the hell did she do to Dad?* He never in a million years would have imagined his dad having his head turned by a pretty face. Yet this Faye – this British stranger who acted like she was some damned entitled princess – seemed to have cast a spell on the old man. He'd given her Jeff's cabin to rent; and handed her his dog, and even his battered old truck...

"What horse?" he asked.

"Say what?" said Sal.

"I beg your pardon?" replied the princess, looking down her straight, perfect nose at him.

"What horse do you have?"

She frowned. "His name is Ebony."

He shook his head, putting a hand to his forehead. "Ebony is a working ranch horse. A valuable animal. What the hell was Dad thinking, giving him to you?"

"Jeff–" Sally reached a hand out to him.

"He was a working horse, until he stumbled into a rabbit hole and broke his leg," said Faye. "I helped look after him. And when it was clear he wasn't ever going to be able to work again, your father gave him to me. He's living a very nice life in retirement, and I get the occasional ride, which we both enjoy. Would you rather he'd been put down?"

"No, of course not. I'm just getting a bit pissed off that every time we talk I discover something else that you've appropriated from my family, that's all."

"Appropriated?" Faye snapped. "Goodness! That's a big word for a cowboy soldier, isn't it?"

"Seems like the right word in the circumstances," he said.

A shrill whistle cut through their anger. Sally stood, hands on hips and glared at them both. "Will you two quit it? Now, I have to go see to my kids, and Nick will be home from work any time. Is there any chance I can leave you two alone? I don't want to come back to find blood on my floor." She paused, but neither of them spoke. "Look, Tom will be here in about twenty minutes. Let's get the will read, and then maybe we'll all get some answers. Okay?"

Jeff wanted to argue. He wanted to snap and snarl and throw this damned woman off Mackay land and wash his hands of her. But he could see the tension in his sister and didn't want to make her feel any worse. She'd been through enough lately, having to deal with Dad's sudden death as well as taking over the management of the ranch with her husband Nick.

"Okay," he growled.

"Fine by me," said Faye, irritating him with her calm manner. "Is there anything I can do to help?"

"Yeah, there's a chicken in the fridge ready to go in the oven. And potatoes to peel."

Jeff thought Faye was going to refuse. She probably expected to be waited on. But even as he thought it, he realised he was wrong. She'd cooked him a damned fine meal today. She knew her way around a kitchen.

Faye nodded and rose to start the dinner as Sally ran upstairs calling the children.

Jeff wondered whether he should offer to help, or maybe he could go upstairs and see the kids. He thought about how much his niece and nephew had grown. He looked forward to having some fun times with them soon. But the ache in his leg stopped him from attempting the stairs, and the image of other children – malnourished, frightened, bedraggled – filled his mind.

The clatter of the cutlery drawer opening dragged him back to the present. He opened his eyes to see Faye holding her hands out.

"Here," she said, passing him forks, knives and spoons. "Make yourself useful and lay the table."

He took them without a word and did as she ordered. In the meantime, she got busy, stuffing onions into the chicken carcass and putting it into the oven to roast. He pulled plates and water glasses out of the cupboards, while she hauled some potatoes from the pantry and began peeling them. He got napkins out of the dresser drawer. She got out some of the spinach she'd brought with her and left it in a colander, ready to wash and cook. Neither of them spoke. They just worked alongside each other in silence.

His brother-in-law arrived just a couple of minutes before the lawyer. Jeff found himself engulfed in a manly hug, and he welcomed the familiar scents of sweat and leather and horse before they both stepped back.

"Hey man, good to see ya. Welcome home," said Nick. "Sal was getting worried. Where you been?"

"Sleeping off pain meds at the cabin," he said.

Nick raised his eyebrows, looking from Jeff to Faye. "I guess you didn't expect to find a sitting tenant, huh?"

Faye ignored him and carried on preparing the meal.

"Yeah." Jeff glanced at her. "It would've been nice to have been asked, or even told what the old man was doing."

"We thought he'd told you," said Nick. "If I'd known he hadn't, I'd have let you know. So would Sal. But we didn't have a clue, man." He walked over to the Frigidaire and pulled out a couple of bottles. "Beer?"

"Probably not a good idea on top of your medication," said Faye as she continued to work at the stove.

"What are you, my damned nurse?" Jeff snapped. "I'll have a beer if I want one." He reached out for a bottle from his brother-in-law.

Nick pulled a face and handed it over. "I guess you two are getting acquainted, huh?"

Neither Jeff nor Faye bothered to reply. Nick shrugged,

opened his beer and took a long slug. "Well, I guess Sal's getting the kids ready for bed. I need a shower. See you guys at dinner?"

He headed out of the kitchen as though the hounds of Hell were after him. Jeff took his beer and sat back down at the table. As he drank, he rubbed his thigh. He probably should take some pain meds, but he was sick of feeling woozy and out of control. He decided he'd see the doc in town about getting some meds that weren't so strong. He hated feeling like this. He only hoped the family lawyer wasn't going make things worse when he revealed what his dad's final wishes were.

A bark from Bear warned them of an approaching car. Jeff got up slowly and limped out to the front door. By the time he got there, Tom was standing there, his battered briefcase in his hand.

"Jeff, welcome home, son." He put out his free hand and the two of them shook. "I'm sorry about your dad. Damn shame the old boy couldn't hang on for a few weeks until you got home."

"Tom. Thanks. Come on in. Sal will be down in a moment."

"Maybe I should set up in the office," he said.

"Don't you want a drink?"

"Can you bring me a coffee?"

Jeff shrugged and raised a hand to indicate Tom should go into his father's study. He went back into the kitchen to find Faye already spooning coffee into the pot.

"I heard him," she said. "Go and talk to your guest and I'll bring it in."

"Thanks," he said and turned to go.

In the hallway, he thought about yelling up to Sal to tell her Tom was here, but he decided against it. She'd get mad if the kids were just dropping off to sleep and he woke them up again. Instead he went into the study, to find Tom sitting in his father's chair and trying to organise a pile of paperwork in front of him. Jeff sat down opposite the desk, straightening out his leg and sighing with relief as the ache subsided a little.

"Good to see you back in one piece, son," said Tom. "Too many of our boys are coming back from 'Nam in body bags or crippled."

"Yeah. It's a shit-show out there," he said. "I guess I've been lucky."

"Let's hope Nixon gets his head out of his ass and puts an end to it soon, eh? Jackass has been spreading us too thin. While our boys are dying in 'Nam, he's swanning off to China and Russia and kissing their asses. Never thought I'd live to see the day when an American president sucks up to commies."

Jeff shrugged. He didn't want to get into a debate about politics or war, or how Nixon could kiss someone's ass when he had his head up his own. He was just glad to be home.

Faye came in with a tray. She greeted the lawyer and poured his coffee.

"I've let Sally know you're here. She won't be long," she told him. "I'll leave you to—"

Tom stopped her. "No, Faye. You need to be here as well."

She handed him his coffee, then poured another and handed it to Jeff. "Help yourself to cream and sugar," she said before turning back to Tom. "Jefferson … Senior, that is, assured me he wouldn't leave me anything in his will, so I don't see why I should be here. If he lied and has left me something, I'm telling you right now I don't want it."

Tom sipped his coffee and smiled. "He kept his word, Faye. He hasn't left you a cent. But you're mentioned in the will. It's only right you're here to answer any questions that might arise."

She stilled. Jeff could swear she'd stopped breathing.

"He didn't," she whispered.

Tom looked both embarrassed and sympathetic at the same time. "He did. He wanted them to know."

"Know what?" asked Jeff, just as his sister came in and closed the door.

Tom stood and shook hands with Sally, ignoring his question.

"Good to see you, Sal. Time to get this done." He looked at the two women. "Please, take a seat."

Jeff watched Faye. She'd looked strange just before Sal had

come in, like she was horrified or scared or both. Now, in the space of a few seconds, she'd wiped all expression from her face. It was like looking at a mask. He had no idea what she was thinking.

"Can I speak to you in private first, please?" she asked the lawyer.

Tom shook his head. "Sorry, Ma'am. I've got my instructions. My client thought it was for the best."

"Bloody old fool," she muttered, crossing her arms over her chest and sitting stiffly in a chair. "I told him to let sleeping dogs lie."

Chapter Nine

Faye's jaw was clenched so tightly she thought she might break it. She couldn't believe Jefferson Senior would betray her like this, but judging by the look in the lawyer's eyes, that was exactly what was about to happen. Out of the corner of her eye she could see Jeff and Sally looking at her, but she kept her gaze fixed on Tom and his paperwork, wishing the pages would burst into flames. No good would come of this.

What the hell was he thinking? Ooh, if he wasn't already dead, I'd bloody kill him myself.

Tom cleared his throat, took another sip of the coffee and picked up the first paper. Faye noticed Jeff had put his cup on the desk in front of him. She only hoped he wouldn't throw it at her when he heard what the lawyer had to tell them.

She felt her heart thumping in her chest. Her whole body began to tremble. Her instinct was to run, but she knew it wouldn't help. She had to get through this, so she did what she always did. She lifted her chin, took a deep breath and waited for the axe to fall.

"What I have here is the Last Will and Testament of Jefferson Andrew Mackay…"

As he began to read, Faye tuned out. This was nothing to do with her. They had had an agreement. Now it was over. There was nothing to be gained by letting his children know about it now. It was just going to complicate matters. She really should get up and walk out. But she stayed, frozen in place.

She closed her eyes, and immediately she was back in the courtroom. She hadn't wanted to be there either. But it had been important that she stick it out, that she play her part in the proceedings. She had no part in the Mackay family. Yet duty compelled her to stay. She felt the trembling in her body and did her best to control it, welcoming the chance to focus on something other than what Jefferson's lawyer was saying.

In the distance, she was aware of the words being spoken gifts to loyal employees, the transfer of the Mackay lands to Jefferson's son and daughter, with various provisions regarding the management of the ranch and the supplementary businesses and investments that the old man had built up over his lifetime. All as expected. No nasty surprises. Until...

"Finally, I wish to record that Faye Elizabeth Evens Mackay—"

"What the fuck?" Jeff burst out of his chair and leaned over the desk as his sister gasped and covered her mouth with her hands, her eyes wide.

Faye remained immobile, an odd feeling of calm descending upon her. It was as though speaking those words had released a weight from her shoulder.

"Now, Jeff, son. Sit yourself down and I'll finish this, okay? It's all right. Nothing to worry about. Let me read what your papa wanted to say."

Jeff turned to his sister. "Did you know about this?"

Sally shook her head. She didn't look at Faye. Jeff did, though. His angry gaze seared her, and it was all she could do to remain cool and collected under his scrutiny.

"Listen to the man," she said. "Though it's beyond me why he thinks it's a good idea to bring this up now."

"So it's true? You were married to our Dad?"

She sighed. "Just let the man do his job. I'm sure it will all become clear."

Although she couldn't help thinking that the only thing that had happened was that everything had become much, much more complicated.

Jeff glared at her for a few more moments, but when she raised her eyebrows at him he huffed out a breath and sat down heavily in his chair.

"Okay," he said, waving a hand at the papers on the desk. "Let's hear it."

Tom cleared his throat and began to speak. "Finally, I wish to record that Faye Elizabeth Evens MacKay," he repeated, "has, in accordance with the pre-nuptial agreement – which was her idea, by the way…"

Faye wanted to smile. She wasn't sure if those exact words were written in Jefferson's will, but it sounded just like him.

"Anyway, as per the agreement, she will inherit no part of my estate."

Well, that's a relief, she thought.

"However…"

She was aware that Jeff sat straighter in his chair and Sally wiped a tear from her eye. Faye was aware that this was a shock for them. *An unnecessary one. He promised me this would all remain a secret.*

"…my children will not be aware of the fact that Faye married into the Mackay family, but that doesn't mean that now they know, they can ignore the fact that she is a legitimate member of the family. We kept the marriage a secret for our own reasons. But I promised that I would keep her safe. To that end, I request that she be allowed to continue to live at the cabin in which she was residing in prior to my death for as long as she needs or wishes to."

"But that's my house!" yelled Jefferson. "Dammit, I knew you weren't a real tenant," he sneered at Faye. "You even made up that shit about paying rent."

Faye raised her chin. "Check the accounts. I have been paying rent. I didn't take a cent from your father in his lifetime, just as I won't now."

Jeff looked at Sally, confusion written all over his face. "Is this true?"

Sally nodded. "She paid a year in advance. If I'd known…" She shook her head. "How could Dad get married without telling us?"

"Were you blackmailing him?" Jeff demanded.

Faye met his angry gaze with cool eyes. "Do you realise how ridiculous that sounds? Was I blackmailing him and paying him rent and bringing my surplus produce here? Tell me, Jeff, what on earth could have been in it for me? What deep, dark secret could he have had that I might use to have my evil way with him?"

Jeff ran a hand over his face. He looked like he was ready to explode. "Well, hell, lady, it just don't make sense. Why the hell would the man marry a girl younger than his own kids if she didn't have some kind of hold over him?"

Faye did smile then, although it didn't reach her eyes. "Darling, do you need a diagram?"

He closed his eyes. For a moment, she wondered whether she'd gone too far and she wished she could take it back. But then she remembered why she was here and why she still needed the protection of the Mackay name. If she told them the truth, it would be all over and she'd be left out in the cold again. She didn't have the energy to run right now. If she could just hold on until Grainger could find her somewhere else to go, then she could walk away from here and never look back.

"Why didn't you live here?" asked Sally. "I don't understand."

Faye shrugged. "You and Nick have been running the ranch for a while now and this is your home. Your father didn't want to upset you by bringing another woman into the house."

"No, but it was okay to give you my house?" snapped Jeff. "He knew I was going to come home. What the hell was he thinking? That we could be room-mates and I'd turn a blind eye when he came over to fuck you?"

Sally gasped and Tom coughed. Faye refused to react. She remained stony-faced.

"If you think for one moment that's how your father would behave, then you didn't know him very well at all," she said.

Jeff stood up again, towering over her. "Listen, Princess, don't you ever tell me I didn't know my dad. He was a good man. A damned fine man who served his country and built a good life for his family. But sometime in the last few months you came into his life, and he suddenly does something that makes no sense at all." He turned to the lawyer, who was sitting red-faced, watching him. "Did you know about this marriage?"

Tom nodded. "I did, son. I have copies of the pre-nup and marriage certificate for you here." He tapped a pile of documents on the table.

"You've been his friend since high school. Why the hell

didn't you talk him out of it?"

"Now, Jeff, I know it's a shock. But your dad assured me he knew what he was doing, and I respected that. As Ms Faye wasn't going to benefit financially from the marriage or from his will, I figured I should trust my friend. I never saw anything to make me think he'd come to regret his decision."

"What? Are you crazy? There's nothing right about this situation. How can you say that?" Jeff glanced from Faye to Tom. "She giving it to you as well, old man?"

As the lawyer paled, Faye stood up, facing Jeff who stood his ground. Without saying anything, she pushed her chair back and moved towards the door.

"Where the hell d'you think you're going?" he yelled.

She stopped with her hand on the door handle and looked over her shoulder at him, contempt in her gaze.

"I don't intend to stay here and listen to you ranting like an idiot," she said. "I'm going to the kitchen to rescue the dinner. Even if everyone else has lost their appetites, I expect your brother-in-law will be hungry after a long day's work. In the meantime, I suggest you think before you open your mouth again… Oh, and maybe think about other people for a change." She nodded towards Sally. "Your sister has also had a shock and looks like she needs your support. Shouting insults isn't helping anyone, least of all her."

She closed the door quietly behind her and leaned against it, taking deep breaths. After a few moments, she raised her head, squared her shoulders and went into the kitchen.

Chapter Ten

Jeff watched her go, not knowing whether he wanted to kill her or admire her *chutzpah*. She hadn't flinched. She hadn't fought back. She was ice-cold while he felt like a volcano about to erupt – hot and angry and out of control.

Sally crumpled in her chair, sobbing quietly. Jeff went to drop to his knees beside her chair, but then he realised if he did that he wouldn't be able to get up. Instead he leant over his sister, gathered her in his arms and let her cry.

"I'm sorry, Sal. It's just... I don't know... Why would he do that?"

She shook her head. "I don't know. I don't understand why he didn't tell me. I was right here, dammit. He didn't even invite me to his wedding!"

They'd forgotten Tom, who now cleared his throat. "I'm sorry, folks. I know it's a shock, but I can assure you it doesn't affect the Mackay lands and your inheritance."

"No? Yet he's left us the legacy of a step-mother who's younger than both of us," said Jeff.

"Can you at least tell us he loved her?" asked Sally. "He must have loved her, to ask for her to stay. I just wish he'd told us they were married."

The lawyer shook his head. "I truly don't know. I'm sorry. He said they had a good reason to marry – and it wasn't about money or babies or blackmail, I made sure of that. I guess the only person who can tell you now is Faye, if she chooses to."

"She damn well will," Jeff growled. "She owes us that much."

"Well, son, I'll tell you something my daddy taught me – you get a lot farther using honey instead of vinegar. You go round yelling at her, likely she'll clam up for good. Talk to her.

But if she don't want to tell you, there's nothing on this earth can make her."

Sally mopped her face and nodded. "He's right. She's strong, Jeff. She keeps herself to herself and don't trust folk. I've been friendly, but she's been like a skittish colt. I... I thought we were starting to get along. It was nice to have another woman around the property, you know?" She sighed.

Jeff felt bad for his sister. She was always busy, what with the kids and the ranch business and cooking and cleaning for everyone. He doubted she got into town to see her friends very often. He didn't even know if any of her old high school friends were still around. A couple had gone to college and not come back. Were the others married and busy with their own families and jobs? Now he was back, he needed to take some of the burden off her, to give her time to relax and spend time with her friends. But now wasn't the time to talk about that.

"We done here, Tom?" he asked.

"Yeah. I'll leave the copies of the papers here for you to check over. I'll need to get some signatures from you in the next few days to transfer ownership and give you access to your dad's personal accounts. Sally already deals with the ranch accounts, so that's been functioning without any problems."

Jeff stood up and faced the man. "Thanks. And I'm sorry about—"

"No problem, son. You've had a shock. I told your old man he should've told you, but you know what he was like. He'd made up his mind and that was that."

Tom was right. But Jeff would never in a million years have imagined his dad would have kept a secret like this. Maybe Faye was right – maybe he didn't know his dad as well as he thought he did.

The thought hurt – like really, physically hurt him. He felt like a weight was bearing down on his chest and he could hardly breathe. Losing his dad so suddenly had been hard. Being forced to miss his funeral while he recovered from more surgery when he got Stateside had been hard. Coming home, knowing his dad was no longer there, had been hard. But finding that the woman who had taken over his cabin had been his dad's secret wife felt like it had broken him.

It wasn't as though he'd been against his father remarrying. He'd been widowed ten years ago and both Jeff and Sal had encouraged him to start dating again. Trouble was they were thinking of him meeting up with some nice elderly lady who would help him enjoy their final years in comfortable companionship. *Not some cold, young, beautiful witch who didn't even live in the same house as her husband.*

Chapter Eleven

Dinner was a strained affair. Nick had taken one look at his wife's distressed face and demanded to know whether they'd lost the ranch. When Sal had told him no, but they'd discovered that Faye was their father's secret wife, he'd bombarded them with questions – the answers to which neither Sal nor Jeff knew and which Faye refused to give.

"Why won't you tell us?" Jeff asked.

"Because it doesn't matter any more," she said. "He should never have told Tom to tell you. It was pointless and cruel."

Faye noted that Jeff agreed with her last statement, even if he wasn't happy that she refused to say anything else. She had a feeling he wouldn't give up asking, but there was no way she could tell him the truth, so rather than lie she chose to say nothing. Instead, she concentrated on dishing up the dinner – Sally had been thrown so off-balance she didn't seem capable of doing anything – then she focussed on eating the meal she didn't want. When she'd eaten a small portion of everything, she gave up.

It looked like no one was very hungry. There was no suggestion of a dessert or coffee after the plates of the main course had been cleared away. Faye started to fill the sink to wash the dishes and was surprised that Jeff came to join her, a tea towel in his hand. Behind them at the table, Nick coaxed Sally to get up and he led her upstairs to bed.

"We'll talk tomorrow," he told Jeff as he wished them goodnight. "Will you turn out the lights when you leave?"

Faye's heart sank. She'd half-hoped that Jeff would arrange to stay at the ranch. But apparently not. She sighed as she placed the last pot on the drainer and pulled the plug to empty the sink. She busied herself, wiping down the surfaces and putting away things that Jeff didn't seem to know where to put.

She'd been here for meals quite often, although she'd never made a habit of it. For a while, she thought she and Sally might actually become friends, although of course she could never have been one of those friends who bares their soul, so maybe not. Now that Sally knew about the marriage, Faye doubted if she'd ever trust her again.

I don't blame her. I'd feel the same. Damn Jefferson for putting us all in this position. If he'd kept his word, the family could have gone on in blissful ignorance and wouldn't now be looking at me like I was some monster who had stolen their sainted father from them. Not that I did. Far from it. But I liked him and trusted him, idiot that I am!

They finished the clear-up in the kitchen in silence, both lost in their thoughts. Eventually, she turned to him.

"Ready to go, or do you want to stay here?"

"Good try, Princess, but I'm going home, and as I don't want you upsetting my sister again, you're coming with me."

"I didn't upset her. You and your father managed that all on your own."

He shook his head. "You really are a piece of work. Are you incapable of taking responsibility for anything, or is that you just don't care?"

She fought to keep her expression calm, but she felt the sharp jab of his words. He knew nothing about the responsibilities she had been forced to accept, or about what she'd lost or given up in order to do the right thing. If she hadn't cared, it would have been so much easier. But she couldn't tell him that, because she couldn't tell him anything. She couldn't afford to take on the responsibility of revealing her secrets to him. They were hers to guard, all on her own. All she could do was keep calm and carry on. Then, when Grainger found her a new place, she'd walk away from the Mackay family and they could get back to normal. She knew they'd be glad to see the back of her. Most people were. She was a bad penny, rolling through people's lives and hurting them. That's why she had created a solitary life. It was simpler and safer that way.

"Right. I'll just collect my baskets and will meet you at the truck." She turned away, not know how long she could maintain her composure.

The journey back to the cabin took just a few minutes. As before, Bear sat between them. The dog had enjoyed his own dinner and a play date with the ranch dogs out in the barn, but he was happy to jump into the truck when he saw them leave the ranch house. Faye concentrated on driving, aware of Jeff's brooding presence on the other side of the dog. Bear was trying to snuggle into him, licking his face until Jeff brushed him away. It was as though the animal sensed the man's turmoil and was trying to cheer him up. Faye wondered whether she'd be able to take Bear with her when she left. She hoped so; he was a wonderful companion. But she was also aware that he had belonged to the Mackay family before she'd got him. If she felt he'd be happier with them, she'd have to leave him behind. Maybe she'd get another dog. They were much more trustworthy than humans.

When she parked beside the cabin, Jeff got out immediately and limped his way up the steps to the front door with Bear at his heels. They'd left the door unlocked, at Jeff's insistence. She wasn't happy about that, but there wasn't much she could do about it. However, when they entered, she locked and bolted it behind them.

"Why'd you do that? No one's going to break in here. We're miles from town."

"Force of habit, I suppose," she said, going through to the kitchen and checking the back door was secure.

"Just don't lock me out again," he snarled.

"I won't, so long as you don't give me any reason to," she said.

He laughed, although he didn't look amused. "You know you've just locked us in here together?" He moved closer. She stood her ground, unwilling to show any weakness. He leaned towards her, his face just an inch from hers. "I could snap your neck and hide your body out in the mountains," he whispered, "and no one would ever know what happened to you."

She felt his warm breath on her cheek but still she didn't back down. "Go ahead," she said, her words strong and precise. "You'd be doing everyone a favour."

He froze. She smiled. "Got cold feet? I thought you were a trained killing machine. You could do it, couldn't you? A man with your skills would be quick. I wouldn't feel a thing, would I?"

"Who the fuck are you?" he asked.

"No one," she said, softly. She knew he thought she was playing with him, but right now she was telling him the absolute truth.

When he didn't move, she sighed and stepped back. "You could get away with it, you know. If you decide to kill me. But it looks like you have more of your father's honourable character in you than either of us thought. Good night." She turned away and headed into the living room.

"Where are you going?" he asked.

She looked over her shoulder and pointed to the ladder resting at the side of the stone fireplace. He followed her into the room and watched as she moved the ladder towards the open attic hatch.

"There's a day bed up there," she said.

"It's just a storage area," he said.

"It was when I moved in. But I've had it fitted out so that it's a useable room."

"With just a ladder for access?"

She shrugged. "I never got round to getting anything else. It seemed silly to lose space down here, putting in a staircase. This is fine." She began to climb but paused half-way up. "If you think you can trap me up there by taking the ladder away, think again," she said.

"For fuck's sake!" he snapped. "Will you stop with the killing and the trapping?"

She smiled. "All right. Good night."

And then she was through the hatch. He heard a click as she turned on the light, then she lowered the hatch cover, leaving him in darkness.

Chapter Twelve

Jeff sank onto the couch, his eyes on the thin line of light he could see around the hatch in the ceiling. She'd not only moved into his house, but she'd begun remodelling? He closed his eyes, feeling bone-weary, despite having slept away the past couple of days.

He couldn't understand why his dad had brought this woman into his life, only to pack her off to this cabin and let her plant a garden and make changes to the building. This was Jeff's home. His grandfather had left it, and a small parcel of land, to him. He had always intended to come back here when his army career ended – *Dad had known that.*

Did he think I wouldn't make it? Or did he think I'd be away so long I wouldn't notice he'd installed his secret wife here? So many questions raced around his head, each one creating another and another, until nothing made sense and he felt his grasp on reality slipping away.

His leg throbbed. He turned and rested it on the couch and lay back, an arm over his head as he tried to figure out what this all meant.

Okay, so his dad had married Faye in secret and decided to reveal it to his family after his death. He guessed that if Faye wasn't going to talk about it, they'd never know why. That didn't mean he would stop asking her. Maybe if he kept on, he'd finally break her stubborn ass and she'd tell them what they wanted – maybe needed – to know. But judging by how she'd been with him the past couple of days, he didn't hold out much hope that it would be easy. But that was okay. He was stubborn too. She'd tell him eventually.

In the meantime, he could only assume that his father hadn't expected to die so suddenly and maybe thought his son would be away in the army for much longer, or that Faye would eventually move into the ranch house. But he didn't like the idea of her there. It was Sally and Nick's house now. They had their own family filling it. No. Faye couldn't be allowed to upset what they had.

So, she was here, and so was he. Jeff refused to contemplate leaving, and it seemed that old Jefferson had expected his kids to take care of Faye after he was gone. If she'd been a middle-aged widow, grieving the loss of her beloved husband, Jeff would have understood that.

But Faye was young. She was feisty and independent and tough and cold and… *dammit*, she was beautiful. He could understand why his dad might have been smitten. But to marry her? Then not even live with her? It just didn't make sense. And she sure as hell didn't need anyone to take care of her. She'd had that shotgun aimed at his heart and he'd been in no doubt she had been ready to pull the trigger.

So what did a woman like her want from his dad, if she didn't want his money? *It couldn't have been a love match. That cold bitch didn't seem capable of love. Yet… despite her icy demeanour she'd been gentle when she'd patched me up… and she'd fed me… and she'd stopped little Pete from barrelling into my leg… She'd even noticed Sally's distress when I was too angry to see it.*

None of this made sense. It was like she was a reasonable human being hiding behind a cold façade. What the hell was she hiding?

He shook his head, trying to clear his thoughts. He'd come full circle again and he was none the wiser. He thought about getting up and going to bed, but he wasn't sure he could be bothered to move. His mind might be going crazy, but his body was exhausted. The couch wasn't really long enough to take his six-foot frame, but it was okay. It wasn't cold. Maybe he'd just lie here. He doubted he'd be able to sleep anyway…

He was so hot he felt like he was melting inside his clothes. The sun beat down, sucking the energy out of him. What he'd give to be at home in Montana, snowed into this cabin with a sweet gal. He'd heard rumours that the President was aiming to get them all home by Christmas, but he'd heard that rumour every year since the US army had arrived in Vietnam, so he didn't hold much hope that Nixon would deliver.

Their patrol was nearly over. They were heading back to base where there was a cold beer with his name on it. They entered the village. The people there were friendly – probably because the soldiers usually dispensed candy to the kids as they passed through. There was usually a crowd of them, waiting for their treats. But today everything was eerily quiet. He looked across at Greg, the patrol leader. He was frowning.

"Something's off," he said quietly. "Be on your guard, men."

They nodded and proceeded along the street on full alert. The doors and windows of the houses were closed. None of the villagers were around. When a scrawny chicken ran across their path, a couple of the soldiers jumped and swore.

"Calm down," Jeff told them. "Keep your eyes open."

In the centre of the village, he thought he heard the sound of a woman weeping, but it was quickly stifled. He felt a chill run up his back. A door opened and the whole patrol spun around towards the sound, weapons raised.

A child – a little girl of no more than three – ran out and headed towards them. She had something in her hand.

"Shit!" someone yelled. "Drop it! Drop the damned grenade!"

But she didn't understand the words. So she smiled and carried on, holding out her hand, as though she was offering them a present. The guys scattered behind Jeff. All except Greg, who ran towards the kid.

"No, Greg!" Jeff yelled, knowing Greg was aiming to grab the grenade and toss it before it blew up in her hand. But they didn't know when the pin had been pulled. It might have been just before the spooks had pushed her out of the door, or they could have waited a few seconds, in order to stop the soldiers from lobbing it out of harm's way.

Jeff started after Greg, acting on instinct. But as he did, a window opened to his left and he saw the flash as a weapon discharged. He felt the impact as a bullet tore into the flesh of his thigh, and he fell to the ground just as the grenade exploded... Jeff saw the child and Greg – his friend, his comrade, his brother-in-arms – disintegrate before his eyes.

"No!" he screamed, as blood and bone and shrapnel rained down on him.

Chapter Thirteen

Faye awoke, unsure what had disturbed her. She sat up, her senses immediately on full alert. She heard a deep murmur coming from the room below. Was it Jeff? Or Bear? Or had they found her? She'd known that leaving the cabin unlocked was a damned stupid risk. What if they'd been inside when she locked up? It would serve that stupid sod right if they were hiding in the main bedroom when he went to bed.

But if that was the case, she thought, *they'd have slit his throat and immediately come for me.* These people didn't hang about.

She heard the voice again, but this time it was louder and more urgent. Was he fighting them off? She got up and crept towards the hatch. Leaving the light off, she quietly opened it, peering into the moonlit room below.

"No, Greg!"

She gasped as she saw that Jeff was alone down there, his tall frame stretched out on the sofa. He seemed to be having a nightmare. This was confirmed when he screamed, the sound making her blood run cold. Within seconds, she'd climbed down the ladder and was at his side.

"Jeff!" she said. "Jeff, wake up."

Bear appeared at her side, whining. She put a hand on his head. "It's all right," she said, not sure whether she was trying to reassure the dog, the man or herself. "It's just a dream."

Jeff writhed, swiping at whatever was covering his face, his body, his arms. He was covered in sweat, and his teeth gritted as he fought to escape from whatever terror had made him scream.

She reached out and touched his arm. "Jeff, wake up," she said, trying to keep her voice calm and clear.

He lashed out, catching her in the stomach. She fell backwards with a gasp. A moment later he was on top of her, straddling her body, his hands finding her throat. She didn't have time to scream before his fingers tightened, closing her airway. She scratched at his hands, trying to loosen his grip, but he was still in the throes of his nightmare and her vision began to swim as she was starved of oxygen. With one last effort, she brought her knee up and caught him in the balls just as Bear leapt on him. The pain in his groin and the weight of the dog made him loosen his hold on her and he slumped to the side.

She lay there, dragging in deep breaths as he rolled away, groaning. Bear licked her face and she put up a hand to stop him.

"It's all right, Bear. He's just having a dream," she whispered, her voice sounding raspy. She coughed, trying to ease the pain in her throat.

"What the fuck?" Jeff sat up, pain etched on his face. "What just happened?" He winced as he registered where she'd kneed him.

Faye coughed again and slowly sat up. "I think you were having a nightmare," she said.

He looked dazed, as though he couldn't work out what was real and what was a dream. She knew that feeling.

He frowned when he saw that she was on the floor, watching him with caution. "Did I hurt you?"

She turned away and got to her feet. "Nothing serious," she said.

"What are you doing down here?" he asked.

"I need a drink." She headed into the kitchen, Bear at her heels.

She heard him groan in pain as he got up. He came into the kitchen limping badly. She didn't turn to look at him, but pulled a couple of glasses out of a cupboard and stood at the sink, filling them with cold water. She put one on the table and turned back to the window and drank hers down, trying not to gasp as her throat protested.

She heard him move, and watched his reflection in the dark

window as he got up and limped over to the light switch. Brightness flooded the room and she flinched, closing her eyes against the glare. When she opened them again, he was standing next to her.

"I hurt you," he said, his fingers lifting her chin. "Damn! I'm sorry."

She stepped away from his touch. "It's all right. You were having a nightmare."

He ran a hand down his face. "Yeah. I guess. I thought I was back in 'Nam."

She filled her glass again then sat at the table. He sank into the chair opposite her and stared at her, frowning. In a reflexive action, she lowered her head and combed her fingers through her hair, pulling it over her left shoulder.

"Why'd you do that?"

She looked up. "What?"

"That with your hair. You always cover your left cheek."

She shrugged. "Habit, I suppose."

He reached towards her but she sat back out of his reach. "So you're not covering anything?" he asked, his gaze narrowed.

She glared at him. This wasn't about her. "What was your nightmare about?"

He sat back and closed his eyes. "When I got shot."

"Have you had it before?"

He was silent for a while, as though considering what to say.

"It's quite common," she said softly.

"What is?"

"Having nightmares after a trauma. I expect you saw more than your fair share of horrible things in Vietnam."

"What are you, a psychologist?"

"No." She took another sip of her water then put the glass down and stood up. "I could do with a real drink. Scotch?"

"You drink whisky?"

"I certainly do," she said, disappearing into the pantry. Seconds later she was back, a bottle of twenty-year-old malt in her hands.

He whistled. "That's good stuff."

"I know. What's the point of drinking paint-stripper when you can savour a wee dram of the amber nectar?"

She got two more glasses from the cupboard and poured them both a generous measure. "Just don't suggest putting ice or water or any other abomination in this," she told him as she sat down again, the bottle on the table between them. *"Slàinte mhath."*

"Say what? *Slan ge var?* What is that?"

She laughed. "Near enough. It's Scottish Gaelic for *Cheers*."

"Oh. Okay. Cheers." He raised his glass and took a sip. "Damn, that's good."

She savoured the whisky on her tongue, then swallowed slowly. It still hurt. She would probably have bruises on her throat as her skin was so pale. She kept out of the sun – not for vanity, but because she didn't want to expose her scars. She always kept them hidden by her hair and clothing. It had become normal for her to cover up not just her scars but all of her body. Gone were the days when she would wear the skimpiest skirts and tops, displaying her flesh for all to see. She would cover up the bruises with one of her scarves. She wore them a lot, so no-one would think anything of it.

"I don't understand. I could have killed you in there. So, why aren't you freaking out and running like hell?" he asked, bringing her out of her reverie.

"But you didn't," she said.

"Only because you and Bear managed to wake me up."

She laughed. "Yes. Sorry about the knee. It seems I'm not so keen on the idea of dying after all." She took another sip of the amber liquid, letting its warmth flow through her.

"You're apologizing?" he raised his eyebrows and shook his head. "You could have hightailed it out of here and brought the Sheriff back to arrest me. I can see the bruises from my fingers on your throat." He took a gulp of his drink. She winced. It really was too good to be knocked back like that. "Why the fuck are you still here?"

"I live here," she said.

"And now so do I. What if I have another nightmare and you can't wake me up?"

"I'll leave you to scream," she said.

"I'm serious," he snapped.

"So am I. You're not the only one in the world who has nightmares, Jeff. I'll leave you to wake up by yourself and keep well out of your way."

He studied her for a while. "You have nightmares?"

"Doesn't everyone?" She looked him in the eye, challenging him. "You're not special, you know."

He sighed and rubbed his temples. "So what do you dream about?"

She looked down at her glass. It was starting to relax her, but nothing on this earth would make her drop her guard enough to tell him the truth. "Nothing like yours, I'm sure. Have you told anyone about them?"

He shook his head.

"Maybe you should. Bottling it all up won't help."

"So why don't you talk about your nightmares?"

Because I deserve them. She shrugged and took another drink. It was getting easier to swallow, thank goodness. "I can live with them," she said. "And I don't tend to try and kill anyone."

He leaned his elbows on the table and rested his head in his hands. "I've never done that before."

"I assume there was no one around the other times you've had a nightmare?"

"No." He looked up. "You really need to move out. It's not safe... I'm not safe."

She narrowed her eyes and studied him as she took another mouthful of whisky. When she'd swallowed it, she put the glass down and rested her hands on the table.

"Are you using this as an opportunity to get rid of me?" she asked, raising a hand to stop him when he went to respond. "Nice try, soldier, but you're wasting your time." She sighed. "Anyway, you don't have to worry, so save your breath. As soon as a suitable place is found, I'll be leaving."

"How long will it take?"

"I don't know. How long is a piece of string? But I won't leave until it's…" She stopped. What the hell was she doing? She had just been about to say 'safe.' If she had said that, he'd know there was a threat and it would make things ten times worse. She'd insisted to his father that no one, not even the lawyer, was to be told. It would put them all in danger, and she wasn't prepared for anyone else to be hurt because of her.

"Until it's what?" he asked, looking suspicious.

"Ready for me to move into," she said with a small smile. "Want a top-up?" She picked up the bottle and held it over his glass. He looked at it, then at her, no doubt wondering whether she'd spill her secrets if she got drunk enough. Her smile widened. It would never happen. She could drink him under the table before she gave anything away.

He nodded and she poured him and then herself another. She held her glass up.

"It looks like we're going to be room-mates for a little while longer. Here's to harmony and no more bruises."

He didn't look happy as he raised his glass and clinked it with hers before he drank. She relaxed back and enjoyed her drink, having no desire to make small talk. Jeff, on the other hand, was obviously thinking things through, and eventually just had to break the silence.

"Are your nightmares the reason you didn't live at the ranch with your husband?"

"Not all married couples live in the same house," she replied. God knows, her parents were rarely in the same county, let alone the same house. They came together to host dinners and country weekends to keep up appearances, but otherwise lived totally separate lives. Even when they were forced together, they never slept in the same bed. Faye sometimes wondered how on earth they'd managed to produce two children. She couldn't imagine a time when they'd fancied – or even vaguely liked – each other.

"My parents did," he said, his chin jutting forward. "They hated being apart. It nearly broke Dad when Mom died."

"Then they were very lucky," she said. She knew he'd think she was being sarcastic, but she meant it. There had never been a time when she'd imagined a love like that for herself. Even before, she had assumed she was damaged goods simply because of her parents' coldness. And after… Well, now she definitely didn't expect to find that elusive fairy-tale ending. *Maybe I shouldn't have fought back when Jeff throttled me. This would all have been over now. I might actually have found some peace. But then again, I'd probably end up in Hell with Percy and James and all those other nasty bastards who littered my past.* She shivered.

He looked so lost she almost felt sorry for him. Maybe it was the whisky, but she felt the need to offer some crumb of comfort. "He never stopped loving her," she told him.

"He talked about her?"

She nodded. "She sounded nice. I'd like to have met her."

He looked even more confused. "So why try to replace her?"

She scoffed. "I never tried to replace her. Why would I do that?"

"Then why marry my dad?"

She rolled her eyes. "Because he asked me. I liked him. The arrangement suited me."

"That's it? You marry a guy, take over his son's house – and dog and truck—"

"Don't forget Ebony," she said.

"Right, and my damned horse. Jesus, do you have to look so smug about it?"

She put a hand over her mouth to hide her smirk. Maybe she should lay off the whisky. She was getting far too relaxed. It was quite fun, winding him up. She cleared her throat and remembered his hands squeezing her windpipe. *Maybe I shouldn't rile him.*

"Sorry. Go on."

He huffed and ran a hand through his hair. "Yeah. So… what exactly was this 'arrangement'?" He made quote marks in the air. "And what did my dad get out of it?"

"If that's your not-so-subtle way of asking about our sex life, you can sod off," she said. "It's none of your business."

"So you had a sex life," he said, his narrow-eyed gaze

pinning her to her chair.

She met his gaze, refusing to be rattled by him or to say anything else. They sat there in silent combat for a minute or so, neither giving way. Eventually he looked down at his glass and picked it up. He knocked back what was left of his drink and stood up. He went to the sink, rinsed the glass and put it on the drainer to dry.

When he turned around, Faye was sipping her drink, watching him.

"I'm going to bed," he said.

"Good idea," she said. "Better make sure you use the bed this time, or your leg will be sore in the morning."

When she didn't move, he picked up the water glasses and took them to the sink.

"Leave those," she said. "I'll do them."

He put them on the counter and turned around. "Aren't you going back to bed?"

She shrugged. "Probably not. I'll finish my drink and see how I feel."

He peered up at the clock on the wall. "It's the middle of the night."

"I know. I don't sleep much, anyway."

"So what are you going to do – sit there and drink?"

"Maybe. Or maybe I'll get my knitting out."

"You knit?"

She laughed. "God, no!" When he still didn't move she went on: "Look, if we're going to be sharing this place, you need to learn to give me some space. I don't sleep much. I keep busy most of the time and like to relax when I want to. If you're going to stand over me and question what I'm doing every minute of the day, you and I are going to fall out pretty quickly."

"Do you have friends over?" he asked, emphasising the word 'friends' with a sneer.

"If I did, would that be your business?" she asked.

"Depends on how much noise you're likely to make. Are you a screamer?"

She put her glass down carefully on the table and poured

herself another, smaller, drink. "The only screamer around here is you, darling," she said.

For a moment, she thought she might have gone too far. She braced herself for his anger. But instead he shook his head.

"You're a piece of work, Princess," he said, and walked out of the room. A couple of seconds later, he slammed the bedroom door behind him.

Faye felt the tension drain out of her. She felt a little mean. That last dig at him had been cruel. But if he was going to make assumptions about her like that, she needed to let him know he couldn't get away with it.

It's better he hates me, she thought. *I'll be gone soon, and the family will be safe and they can all forget about me.*

She didn't want to admit to herself just how lonely that thought made her feel.

Chapter Fourteen

Jeff lay in bed, staring at the ceiling. Bear snored beside him.

He didn't know if it was his flashback nightmare, or the fact that he'd found out something about his father that he'd never in a million years suspected, that left him feeling so unsettled. He wished both of them would go away, but they both haunted him.

He kept trying to imagine his dad married to Faye, but he couldn't do it. It didn't make sense. The woman was younger than Jeff and Sally, he was sure, and was nothing at all like their mother. *And where the hell had he met her? She sounded like she belonged in Buckingham Palace, not a ranch in Montana.*

He rolled over, trying to get comfortable. Bear was almost as big as he was, so he took up half the bed. The dog had never been allowed to sleep on a bed before, but Jeff figured Faye had let him get away with it and now he refused to budge. With a sigh he rolled back to his original position. The dog's breath was not something he wanted to have in his face while he tried to sleep.

He heard Faye moving quietly around the kitchen, the sound of the tap as she rinsed the remaining glasses, the soft thud of the cupboard door as she put them away. He couldn't work her out. She didn't belong here. Her accent and attitude were all wrong. If he hadn't already clashed with her, he might have considered that she was an attractive woman who might, just might, have turned his dad's head. *Maybe the old man had been lonelier than we thought,* he considered. *She could have been one of those mail-order brides – prepared to marry someone for security, no matter how incompatible they were as a couple. But if that's the case, why insist on paying rent for the cabin and refusing to take anything from his estate? Where'd she get her money from? Nothing makes sense! If she's not a gold-digger, what the hell is she doing here?*

He sighed and rested an arm across his eyes. He wished like hell he'd been able to make it home before his dad passed. He really needed to talk to him. About Faye, about his time in 'Nam and the nightmares he was having, and about his future. For the first time in his life, he couldn't go to his father for advice. He knew that at thirty he should be able to work things out for himself, but right now he was feeling as uncertain and lost as a teenaged kid trying to navigate his way through the turmoil and craziness of adolescence. He needed his dad to guide him through it all.

He lay there for hours, unable to sleep. He ached all over and was desperate for some rest. But his mind wouldn't let up, going round and around, trying to make sense of everything. He couldn't admit to himself that maybe it was fear that stopped him sleeping. The dream tonight had been the worst yet, and he couldn't bear the thought that he'd attacked a woman while he was in the throes of the nightmare. What if she hadn't fought back? Could he have woken and stopped himself from killing her? He didn't think so. It had taken an agonising blow to his manhood and the weight of Bear to get his attention away from the terrors he had been fighting in the dream.

Maybe I need to move out – to keep myself from ending up in jail for murdering her.

He doubted a jury would accept that he hadn't known what he was doing. They'd look at the fact that he'd just discovered his unwanted house guest was in fact his damned stepmother and figure he'd killed her in anger. He wouldn't blame them.

But, if I'm not safe to be around in my own home, where the hell can I go? Not the ranch – what if it was Sally, or one of her kids, who got in the way next time? He shuddered, horrified by the thought.

As the sun rose, he was still no nearer to a solution. But his exhausted body finally overruled his mind and he slipped into a deep sleep.

Chapter Fifteen

Long after Faye had heard Jeff settle into bed she remained in the kitchen. She should have felt threatened by this tall, well-built man. He was a soldier – trained to kill – and he'd very nearly succeeded in ending her life tonight. But with Bear's help she'd managed to fight back, and she realised that, despite her earlier words, her instinct for survival was still strong.

Jeff had been appalled when he realised what he'd done in the throes of his nightmare. It made him a bit more human. Up until now, she'd simply regarded him as the enemy – the angry man who had invaded the space she'd claimed as her sanctuary. But seeing him at his weakest, she was beginning to realise that in his own way he was as haunted as she was. That made her feel a bit better about having him around, and possibly even a little bit safer than she usually felt.

He's more honourable than I am, though, she thought. *If he had any idea of what I've done, he wouldn't be apologising for hurting me and he sure as hell wouldn't let me stay here.* She sighed. *I really have to move on before he finds out.*

Realising she couldn't do anything about that now, she got up, washed the glasses and put away the bottle of Scotch. It was less than half full now. She made a note to buy some more next time she went into the city. It wasn't the sort of thing she could find in town. Around here they all seemed to drink beer or Bourbon.

She realised she needed to buy more groceries if she was going to be cooking for two for the time being. There were steaks in the freezer she could thaw for their dinner, so they would have to do. Planning the dinner menu made her smile. In her former life she had been more interested in eating out than cooking, even though she'd been taught to *Cordon Bleu* standards. In the life she had now, she'd cooked the occasional meal for Jefferson Senior, but they were usually impromptu events when he popped over with a message or to check that she was okay.

She missed the old man. She'd never been able to think of him as her husband, even though they were legally married. Despite knowing everything about her, he didn't judge.

"It's what you do with your life now that matters, Faye," he'd told her. "Don't let the past drag you down."

He was right, of course. But that didn't mean she could forget what she'd done and how she'd ended up here. Nevertheless, she'd surprised herself how well she had settled in Montana, into a life so far removed from what she was used to. So much so that she didn't want to leave. And that might be a problem, now that Jefferson Senior was gone and his son had arrived. Not forgetting the fact that both Jeff and Sally now knew that Jefferson had married her without telling his family.

She was still angry that he'd chosen to reveal their secret like that. What was the point, now that he was dead? He'd probably thought it would ensure his children would let her stay, but all it had really done was upset them when it hadn't been necessary. They could have gone on quite happily, not knowing their father had lied to them. So she would have to leave anyway.

It was still dark outside. There weren't any chores she could do in the house without making a lot of noise, so she turned off the kitchen light and went back to her room in the attic. But she couldn't sleep. She tried to read, but the words swam in front of her eyes, not making any sense. Eventually, she put the book aside and got up and went to the small desk under the window. There was only one thing left she could do. She picked up her sketchbook and pencil and began to draw.

A couple of hours later, the sun had risen. Faye closed her sketchbook and stretched. She knew Bear would be wanting to be let out any time now, so she quickly washed and dressed and went downstairs.

As expected, she heard the dog scratching at the bedroom door to be let out. She opened it and petted him as he wandered out towards the back door. She let him out and went back to shut the bedroom door before she disturbed Jeff. She needn't have worried. He was sprawled across the bed, snoring softly.

She took a few moments to study him. He was a handsome devil. In other times, she'd have set her cap at him and probably propositioned him within a short time of meeting him. She'd been fairly free with her favours in those days. But not now. She'd learned hard lessons in a series of humiliating ways. There was no way she was going back to that.

With a sigh she closed the door quietly and went to fill Bear's food and water bowls. As she watched the dog wolf down his breakfast, she decided she couldn't sit around waiting for Jeff to wake up. She had to get on with her life. And the first thing she needed to do was to go back to the ranch and call Grainger again. Now that the Mackays knew about the marriage, it was more urgent than ever for her to move on.

At the ranch, Sally came out the house when she heard the truck.

"Where's Jeff?" she asked.

"Sleeping. I need to use the phone again, if that's all right?"

Sally didn't look happy about letting her in the house. Faye felt a pang of regret that the easy friendship they'd been developing had been wiped out by Jefferson's revelation. Not that she blamed her. If their positions were reversed, she'd probably be spitting mad about it. But the difference between them was that Sally was Jefferson's daughter and he'd brought her up to be polite and respectful of others, even if they didn't deserve it.

"Okay," she said.

"Oh, and Jeff forgot to collect his things last night," she said. "Do you think I could take some of his clothes back for him? He can get the other stuff when he's ready."

"He's staying at the cabin, then?"

"Yes. And I'll be leaving. As soon as I can arrange it. But it might take a little while. Can you put up with me until then?"

Sally stared at her, obviously wanting to ask questions, or maybe throw accusations. But instead, she merely nodded and said, "It's what Dad wanted."

"Thank you. I'll go and make that call."

"And I'll find Jeff's stuff," Sally replied.

Faye noted she didn't offer her a cup of tea and a chat, as she usually did. She was surprised how much that hurt. But there was nothing she could do about it. If they knew the truth behind her marriage to Jefferson, it would make things a hundred times worse. So she simply nodded and headed into the ranch house and made her way to the study to use the phone.

Chapter Sixteen

Jeff awoke to find Bear missing from his bed and three boxes of his clothes stacked outside his bedroom door. After he'd showered and dressed, he went in search of Faye and the dog. They were outside, Bear lazing in the sun while Faye was working in the vegetable garden. She looked up and saw him when Bear alerted her to his presence by lifting his head in Jeff's direction as he stepped off the porch, a cup in his hand.

"I see you found the coffee. I hope it isn't too stewed. I made it an hour or so ago."

"It's fine," he said. "Thanks. Did my sister bring my stuff?"

"No. I went over and got it. I opened your door to let Bear out this morning and you looked like you were dead to the world, so I decided to leave you and go and get it myself. I needed to use the phone again, anyway."

"She okay?" he asked.

Faye shrugged. "A bit brittle, perhaps, but I understand. I'd be the same in the circumstances."

"Yeah, it's not every day you find out you have a stepmother who's younger than you," he muttered into his cup.

He knew she'd heard him because she rolled her eyes, but she didn't say anything. Instead she went back to digging. Jeff sat on the porch steps and watched her.

It was a beautiful day – warm, sunny, cloudless. He could hear the birds singing in the woods and the soft rumble of Bear's snores. Faye was planting out a tray of lettuce plants in a neat row, between rows of what he thought were peas and carrots.

"That's an awful lot of produce for one person," he commented.

She paused and looked up. "What I can't use or preserve, I

take to the ranch. In return, I get fresh meat."

"Sounds good. I know Sal wanted to make a vegetable patch but she never has the time to tend it, what with the kids and the running the ranch."

Faye planted the last lettuce and stood up, rubbing her back. Her face was pink and sweaty. He frowned.

"You should be wearing a hat. The sun's strong, even this early in the season. And you'd probably be more comfortable in shorts and a tank top. You'll overheat in those jeans." He would have mentioned her long-sleeved shirt, which was buttoned up to her neck, and the scarf she had wound around her throat, but he realised he sounded like he was criticizing her.

"I'm fine," she said. She watered the new plants, then collected her tools and returned them to the barn. He sat on the back steps, turning his face to the sun. He heard Ebony nickering in the paddock. Jeff would love to be able to saddle him up and take a ride, but he knew he wasn't capable right now. He needed to fix some physical therapy appointments at the clinic in town and build up his strength before he could swing himself onto a horse and control the animal with his thighs.

Something to aim for, he decided. *It will be good to get out on the range again.*

It would also mean he could make himself useful at the ranch. He didn't want to take over, but he wanted to pull his weight and take some of the pressure off Sal and Nick. He wasn't going to be a freeloader.

"Do you want some lunch?" Faye stood in front of him. She still looked hot, but she hadn't so much as rolled her shirt sleeves up to expose her forearms. As usual, she'd styled her long brown hair so that it flowed over her left shoulder. This time, it was braided, but it was still loose enough to cover most of her cheek.

"Well?" she said, raising her eyebrows.

"What?"

"Food," she said, walking around him and onto the porch. "You're too late for breakfast but I'm ready for lunch. Ham and eggs okay?"

The low rumble of his stomach answered for him. She laughed.

"Ten minutes," she said and disappeared into the kitchen.

Chapter Seventeen

Faye made quick work of preparing the meal. She didn't bother asking him how he liked his eggs but instead scrambled half a dozen, adding chives and fresh dill. She added slices of home-grown tomatoes to the plates alongside the thick slices of ham, and cut some bread to go with it.

She found it soothing, creating a decent meal to go on the table. It kept her mind busy. But eventually everything was ready and Jeff was coming through the kitchen door.

"That looks good," he said as he washed his hands at the sink.

"Eat it while the eggs are hot," she said.

He sat down and they ate in silence. She was aware of his thoughtful gaze on her, but she didn't look at him. She had no desire to enter into a conversation with him. She knew it would only end in frustration for both of them, as he would ask questions that she would refuse to answer. At the moment, they were existing in relative peace. She wanted it to stay that way.

"For someone who said she didn't need a phone, you seem to be mighty busy making calls," he said eventually.

She looked at him then. He didn't seem angry, just curious. "You want me to move out, don't you? I can't do that unless I call people."

"So, you're talking to realtors?"

She should have just said yes, but when had she ever taken the easy option? "No. My people are."

"And who are your people?"

"No one you know," she smiled, turning her attention back to her food. She put the last of her scrambled eggs into her mouth and put down her fork, satisfied. There had been a time when she'd been incredibly fussy about what she ate and how much – always conscious of her weight, not wanting to look fat in her fashionable mini-dresses. But now she ate what she liked, when she liked. The amount of physical work she did, as well as taking long walks with Bear, meant that she was in better shape than she'd ever been.

Her thoughts were interrupted when Jeff stood up and took his plate and cutlery to the sink.

"Leave it," she said. "I'll do it. Aren't you supposed to go to the ranch to talk to your sister and brother-in-law?"

He looked over his shoulder and frowned. She sighed.

"Don't worry, I won't lock you out again," she said. "It's not practical for us to go around like we're joined at the hip. We'll just have to trust each other. Anyway, you'll all be able to speak freely and bitch about me much more effectively if I'm not there."

"Yeah, I appreciate that," he said, turning round. "But if the car is out of action and I can't drive the truck…"

She wanted to slap her forehead for being so stupid. Of course he'd need a ride.

"How about I take you and the car battery over there? I'm sure they'll have the means to recharge it. Then one of them can drop you back here when you're ready."

He nodded. "Okay. Sounds like a plan."

She dropped him off at the ranch and went straight back to the cabin. It was good to have the place to herself again, even if it was only for a little while. She washed the dishes and cleaned the bathroom, noting the addition of male toiletries and shaving gear on the shelf over the sink.

It had been a long time since she'd shared her living space with a man, and she wasn't sure how she felt about it now. Part of her wanted to get the hell out of there and find somewhere else to call her own. But another part was quietly enjoying having a man around, even if he quite possibly hated her guts.

Since his nightmare, she'd found that she wasn't quite so afraid of him as she had been before. It was crazy, really, considering he'd nearly strangled her to death. But… she didn't know why she was feeling like this. Maybe it was because she understood how real and terrifying nightmares could be, and she realised that in his own way he was as vulnerable as she was. His injured leg was healing. But his mind was another matter.

She remembered staying at her grandparents' house in Scotland when she was a child. Her grandfather's younger brother lived there too. He'd been in the trenches in the First World War and had come home a broken man. *He had nightmares, too. The whole house would be woken by his screams. He was usually all right during the day, but the slightest noise would spook him, and they had to move him to London during the grouse-shooting season because the sound of the guns made him think he was back on the Somme.*

Faye knew he'd been diagnosed with shell shock, and judging by Jeff's behaviour last night, he might be suffering with something similar. She only hoped he could cope with it better than her great-uncle. He'd ended his days in an asylum.

She found it hard to imagine this tall, strong, vital American giving in to his fears. But who knew? She'd never expected to live out her days in fear either, but here she was. Not cowering in a corner, certainly. But not taking any chances, that was for sure. That's why she had to move now. Before Jeff asked too many questions.

She'd been lucky with Jefferson Senior. He'd worked with Julian Grainger in the Second World War, and maintained a working brief with him through agencies they'd work for in peacetime. He knew her story and hadn't judged her. Instead he'd given her a safe haven and the chance to start again.

But now that he was gone, his son wanted to know who she was and why she was there. There wasn't anything she could tell them that would satisfy them, so the sooner she left, the better.

Chapter Eighteen

Jeff sat in the same chair he'd occupied during the will reading. His sister sat in what he still thought of as his dad's seat, and Nick leaned against the bookcase.

"I still can't get my head around this," said Sal. "I mean, she was around here for over six months and Dad said nothing." She shook her head. "At his funeral she sat at the back of the church, and when anyone asked her who she was she said Dad had been her landlord."

"So how did she end up here?" Jeff asked. "She's a long way from home."

Sally nodded. "She came with Dad's English friend. You know, the guy he met in Italy."

"Grainger? Julian Grainger?"

"That's the guy. And I talked to Tom about who was at the wedding and he said he didn't attend the ceremony. Dad told him they'd wanted to keep things low-key, and he had an old English friend as a witness."

"Grainger? He was here at the ranch?"

"No. We thought Dad was visiting friends in New York, but it seems he arranged to meet up with Grainger and Faye in Billings and Dad married her there."

Jeff shook his head. *Damn! Could it get any more tacky? A secret wedding? Come on, man!* He blew out a breath. "Do you think they're related?"

"Faye and Julian? Maybe. I don't know. Her maiden name was Evens."

Jeff leaned forward. "You got Dad's address book in there, Sal? Maybe we should talk to Graingcr."

She nodded. "Sure." She opened a drawer and brought out a book. She flicked through the pages and found the number.

"Here it is. D'you think he's who she's been calling?"

Jeff shrugged. "Maybe. Probably. She sure don't seem to have any friends round here." He laughed. "Let's face it, she's a cold bitch. I can't see her calling her girlfriends to gossip about her life as a recluse."

While Nick laughed with him, Sally frowned. "I don't know, Jeff," she said. "I know she's a tough nut to crack, but I thought she was warming up a little in the last month or so. When Dad died, I pretty much fell apart. She came over every day, made sure we had hot meals on the table, washed our clothes, and kept the kids occupied while I got myself together."

Her husband nodded. "Yeah, I guess she did step up to the plate for us. I had so much to do on the ranch, I couldn't be in two places at once. She helped a lot. But you've gotta agree, Sal darlin', she ain't exactly oozing love and friendship."

Jeff looked back and forth between them. He was sort of surprised to hear what Faye had done when Sal had needed help. But then again, he had seen her gentleness and thoughtfulness himself. While she might talk like she didn't give a damn, her actions were the opposite. He sighed and rubbed his forehead, trying to ease the tension headache that just wouldn't quit.

"So it looks like our newly-discovered step-mom is a puzzle. I guess we'd better talk to Grainger and see whether he can shed some light on what the hell is going on."

"Agreed," said Sal. "Let's call him."

As she picked up the phone there was a crash upstairs and a kid started to wail. She jumped up and handed the phone to Jeff.

"I'd better see to that," she said.

"And I've got to get back to work," said Nick. "We're expecting a delivery of new steers in an hour. I need to make sure the hands have got the paddock ready."

"Okay. I'll talk to Grainger and let you know," said Jeff. "Go."

He waited until they'd closed the door behind them before he moved into the seat Sal had vacated and dialled the number.

It seemed to take a long time to connect, but eventually someone picked up.

"Grainger."

"Er, yeah. Mr Grainger? Julian Grainger?"

"Yes. Who's calling?"

"My name's Jeff Mackay Junior."

"Ah, Jefferson's boy. How are you? I'm sorry to hear about your father."

"Thank you. We're holding up. I just got back from Vietnam a few days ago. We – that's my sister and me – are hoping you'll be able to explain something to us."

"I'll do my best," he said. He sounded cautious.

Jeff took a deep breath. "We need to know why our dad married Faye Evens."

Grainger was silent for a moment. Jeff was about to check he was still there when he spoke.

"Who told you?" he asked.

"Dad did. Well, sort of. He left a message in his will, asking us to take care of her. Until his lawyer read the will, we had no idea she was his wife. It's been a shock."

"I imagine it was. What has Faye said about it?"

"Nothing. She was mad about us finding out, and she refuses to explain. It doesn't make sense."

"Well, I suppose she felt that now that your father has passed, it was irrelevant."

"That's what she said." Jeff sighed. "But we know about it now, and we want to know why. I mean, they didn't even live in the same house, and, well, we just can't believe our dad would fall for a girl who was younger than his own kids."

"She's a beautiful girl."

"Yeah. But let's face it, sir, she's not exactly sweet or huggable, is she?"

Grainger let out a bark of laughter. "No, she certainly couldn't be called that," he agreed. "But she and your father were fond of each other in their own ways."

Jeff grimaced. *What the hell did that mean?* "That's as may be, but why didn't he tell us? Why keep her stashed away in the cabin like a dirty secret?"

On the other side of the Atlantic, Julian Grainger sighed. "I'm afraid I can't tell you, Jeff. All I can say is that your father knew what he was doing. He wasn't a man who could be persuaded to do anything he didn't want to do."

"I guess not," said Jeff, acknowledging the truth of the Englishman's words. "But who the heck is she? I mean, it's clear she doesn't belong here."

"Some people don't necessarily belong where they come from," Grainger said, frustrating Jeff even more. "But that doesn't mean they can't adapt to somewhere new and eventually fit in."

"How can she fit in if she avoids people? How can she fit in if she won't answer even the simplest question?"

"She's a very private person. I think it would be easier if you could just take her at face value – concentrate on the person she is now, not where she came from."

"But why? It's crazy. I could meet a guy in a bar and get more of his life story over a beer than this woman will give up. I could have an axe murderer living under my roof."

"She's not a murderer, I can assure you."

Jeff could hear the smile in Grainger's voice, but he wasn't comforted. "But you won't tell me who or what she is, will you?"

"Other than to confirm that she is Faye Evens Mackay, I'm afraid I can't, dear boy. Look, I know this is difficult for you and your sister on top of losing your father. But please, trust in your father's judgement. Give her a chance."

Jeff ran a hand through his hair. He was getting nowhere. "My dad said she needed to be protected. Can you tell me why?"

"All I can tell you is that she went to America to make a fresh start because her life was in danger in Britain."

"So she's on the run from someone?"

"No. So long as she stays in your country there is no reason to believe she is in any danger."

"Well maybe you should tell her that. The first time I met her she was pointing a loaded gun at me."

"Oh dear. I'm sorry about that."

"Yeah, me too. Look, thanks for talking to me, sir." He wanted to ask more, but he knew in his gut that this guy wasn't going to tell him any more, even though Jeff was sure that Julian Grainger knew everything he needed to know about the mysterious Faye.

"You're very welcome, Jeff."

He hung up and sat back. He stared up at the ceiling and blew out a long breath.

Well that was a damned waste of time.

Chapter Nineteen

Jeff didn't come home until late. Faye had made a steak pie for dinner, but when he didn't show up, she put in the freezer and had a cheese sandwich instead. She was annoyed at herself for thinking they'd share a meal. No doubt he had enjoyed dinner with his sister and her family. Why would he want to sit at a table and eat with the woman he regarded as an interloper?

Even if he did, he'd probably start interrogating me again and I'd end up with indigestion, she thought as she cleaned the kitchen and fed Bear. By the time Jeff got back to the cabin, she was up in her attic room with the hatch closed. She wasn't in the mood for another encounter with him.

She heard him moving around below, greeting Bear. She knew he would see her light from around the edges of the loft hatch, but she made no move to open it. She focussed on the book she was reading, ignoring the noise of the television in the living room. It sounded like he was watching an American baseball game. Faye rolled her eyes. She had tried to watch it, but thought it was just a glorified game of rounders, which English schoolchildren played. She hadn't been impressed with American football either. She had thought it would be like rugby and had looked forward to it. She'd often enjoyed a good rugger match. The players were always so well-built and fearless. She'd been out with a few of them in her time. But this American game – well, she couldn't take to it. So much padding and posturing, and half the team were dragged off to be replaced with the other half whenever the direction of play changed. Old Jefferson had tried to explain about offense and defence players, but she'd mocked him, saying rugby players could run both ways.

When someone apparently scored, Jeff whooped and Bear

barked. Faye gave up trying to read and turned out the light. She lay there in the moonlight, listening, and wondering why she felt so lonely when the cabin was overflowing with the presence of Jeff bloody Mackay Junior.

She was up early the next day, but not before Jeff, who was outside, fitting the recharged battery to his car.

The cabin was filled by the aroma of coffee. Faye wrinkled her nose and made herself a cup of tea. She was debating whether to cook some breakfast when the front door slammed and Jeff limped in with Bear at his heels.

"Morning," she said, sipping her drink while leaning against the counter. "I see you've got your car working again."

"Yeah. I've got a physical therapy session in town later. At least now I can drive myself."

She nodded, breathing a quiet sigh of relief. If he'd needed her to take him, she would have done. But she didn't like going into town. She'd tried a few times. It was a small place where everyone seemed to think they were entitled to know your business, and she got tired of their endless questions – *What's your name, honey? Where you staying? What brings you here? How long you staying?* – God, she got sick of it. At least in London or New York no one was interested.

These days she just took herself off to a larger town about fifty miles away when she needed anything. It was still nerve-wracking, but at least it was a big enough place that she didn't stand out quite so much. She'd also perfected enough of an American accent to be able to get by without anyone going daft when they heard her speak. It was ridiculous how people would act if they realised she was English. She'd lost count of the number of times she was asked if she knew the Queen when she first arrived in the US. It occurred to her that she didn't even think about changing her accent when Jeff had arrived. She supposed it had all happened so quickly she didn't have the chance to think about it.

"I also called the phone company. They should get a line out here in the next couple of weeks."

She shrugged. "I don't need a phone."

"But I do," he said.

"Fair enough."

"You can give Julian Grainger the number when we get it."

Faye felt her heart miss a beat, but she kept her expression neutral.

"Who?" she asked.

"The guy who witnessed your wedding," he said, watching her.

"Oh, him." She took another sip of her tea, not looking at him. "He was a friend of your father."

"He seems to know a lot about you. I called him yesterday." His tone was mild, but when her startled gaze met his, she knew he was playing with her, fishing for information.

She didn't know how he'd made the connection between her and Grainger, but that didn't mean she was going to give him any more ammunition to use against her. She didn't for a minute believe that Grainger would have told Jeff much at all. He was a man of secrets, and she knew she could rely on him to keep hers.

"So what?" she asked, refusing to give anything away.

He turned away to fix himself a cup of coffee from the pot on the counter. She moved out of his way and headed towards the back door.

"Don't go anywhere," he said.

She halted and looked back over her shoulder. "I beg your pardon?"

"We need to talk."

"I can't think why," she said. "But if you're that desperate for my company, I'll be outside. The smell of that coffee is giving me a headache."

She shut the door behind her and crossed the porch to sit in her favourite spot on the steps. From here she could see her garden, the chicken coop, the forest beyond and the mountains in the distance. She sighed. She could never get enough of this view. When she'd first arrived here, she'd been sure she would go mad in the silence, but it had soon worked its magic on her troubled soul.

The door opened behind her and Jeff came and sat beside

her. Bear pushed his way in between them, but not before Faye had felt the warmth of Jeff's big body against her shoulder. She shuffled her bottom over towards the post to create more space between them as Bear ambled down the steps and lay down in a patch of warm sunlight.

"He assured me you weren't an axe murderer," said Jeff, watching the dog as it scratched itself with its back paw.

"Huh. Not yet, anyway," she said, her tone dry.

He laughed. "Thanks for the warning."

She smiled, though it didn't reach her eyes. "You're welcome."

""Don't you want to know what else he said?"

She shook her head. "Nothing to do with me." She put down her cup and stood up. "I've got things to do."

"Sit down, Faye. We're not done yet."

She raised her eyebrows, her eyes cool. "I'm not interested in hearing about your conversation with a man I hardly know."

"He said you're safe."

She frowned. "What do you mean?"

"He said no one was after you and you're safe here."

She shook her head. Of course she wasn't safe. Hadn't this bloody man invaded her sanctuary just a few days ago? If Bear had co-operated, she'd have been in the truck and out of there before Jeff had had the chance to register what was happening. She'd have driven as far as she could and then started all over again, because one day it wouldn't be a good guy who turned up at three in the morning, and she would have to either run or die. She had thought she wanted to die, but now she knew she wanted to live. So she had to keep running.

"Faye?"

She blinked and looked at him. She'd been so deep inside her head that she'd ignored him.

"What?"

"Who did you think was after you?"

She whirled around and walked away without answering him. She knew that he was watching her as she went into the barn, and he was still watching when she came out a few moments later with a bucket and headed for the chicken coop.

She didn't look in his direction, but she could feel his gaze on her as she entered the enclosure and fed the chickens. They gathered around her, clucking and pecking, and she concentrated on making sure each of the dozen birds got their fair share.

When the bucket was empty, she walked around the henhouse, opening hatches and collecting the eggs.

"Faye." Jeff stood outside the coop, looking at her through the chicken wire.

"Shouldn't you be on your way to town?" she asked.

He looked at his watch and swore. "Damn. Yeah. I'd better go."

"See you later then," she smiled.

He scowled at her before he turned and limped away. She stayed in the chicken coop until she heard his car drive away.

She took the eggs into the kitchen and packed them into egg boxes. She needed to take most them over to the ranch. Sally fed them to the ranch hands with their morning bacon. But Faye didn't feel like facing anyone at the moment, so she left them there and called Bear.

She needed to think. She didn't know what Grainger had actually said to Jeff. But it was clear that Jeff wasn't likely to give up trying to get her to spill her secrets. If she wanted him to stop, she needed to give him something. But what? She didn't know how far she could trust him. He was an unknown, and that frightened her.

With Bear at her side, she headed towards the forest. A good, long hike would help her clear her head. At least, she hoped so.

Chapter Twenty

His first physical therapy session meant he was answering lots of questions about his injury and what he wanted to achieve in terms of physical activity from now on. His army career was over, so he didn't need to maintain the levels of fitness he had during his service, but now he co-owned the family ranch and he wanted to pull his weight. That meant long hours in the saddle, working with the cattle, hauling feed and fixing fences. He needed to be strong. He was also sick of limping. It made him feel like an old man when he was barely thirty.

The therapist, Teddy, had been in his year at high school and they'd played on the football team together. Jeff had gone out with his sister, June, in his senior year, but it hadn't been anything serious. Teddy had come back from college and married his high school sweetheart, and was now running the clinic while his missus stayed at home with their two kids.

"Got another one the way," he grinned.

"Congratulations, man. Wow, three kids." Jeff shook his head, smiling. He couldn't imagine himself settled with a wife and babies. He'd joined the army straight out of high school and had intended to make it his career. He'd wanted to see the world beyond Montana.

"So, how was 'Nam?" asked Teddy.

Jeff shrugged. He knew there was a growing anti-war movement in the US, and he could see their point. But that didn't mean he would take abuse for being a veteran. He'd enlisted a long time ago, wanting to serve his country. He had nothing to do with the politics of war, and didn't intend to get into any debates about it now he was home.

"I hear it's a shit-show out there" Teddy went on.

"Yeah. It's tough."

He nodded. "I'm damned glad I never got drafted. A few guys from school went, but not all of them have come home." He stood up. "Anyways, let's see what we can do to get your leg back to strength. I'll bet you're hankering to get back on a horse, eh?"

Jeff nodded. "Do I ever," he said, getting to his feet. "Let's get on with it."

"You know it's gonna be tough, right? It's important to keep moving to build up the muscles again, but you've gotta be careful not to overdo it and cause more damage, you know?"

Jeff pulled a face. It had been weeks since he'd been shot. At first, he'd been worried that the bone had been shattered, but by some miracle the bullet had just nicked it rather than broken it. He knew he was lucky. A broken thigh bone could have left him with permanent problems. But he hadn't thought it would take so long to heal the damage to his muscles. He'd thought the MASH doctors had patched him up good, but when he'd arrived Stateside, the docs at the veterans' hospital had insisted he needed more surgery – hence his relatively new stitches.

"So long as I can ride and maybe get rid of this limp, I don't care how tough it is," he said.

"Okay. Get changed and we'll hit the gym. I'll give you a program of exercises to do regularly, and I'll see you every few days to check on your progress. How does that sound?"

Jeff nodded. "Let's do it."

He was aching and light-headed by the time he left the clinic. He regretted that he'd promised his sister he'd drop by and tell her how the session had gone. All he wanted to do was go back to the cabin and crawl into bed with a couple of painkillers.

He arrived at the ranch entrance just as his nephew Pete got off the school bus. Jeff stopped and wound down his window to call the boy.

"Uncle Jeff! Hi!"

"Hi, kid. Want a ride?" It was half a mile from the gates to the ranch house.

"Okay." The boy got in the car, tossing his school bag into the footwell.

"So, how was school?" Jeff asked as he put the car into Drive mode.

Pete shrugged. "Okay, I guess."

"Don't you like school?"

"Nah. Mama says I've got to work hard and graduate. But I wanna be a rancher when I grow up, like Papa, so I don't need to know all that stupid stuff they make us do at school, do I?"

"I know it seems stupid, Pete, but your mama's right. How you gonna do all the paperwork and make sure you're not getting cheated when you sell your cattle if you don't have no school learning, huh?"

Pete sighed. "I guess. But it don't mean I have to like it."

Jeff laughed as he pulled up outside the ranch house. He reached over and ruffled the boy's hair. "Do your best, bud. That's all your mama wants you to do."

Pete nodded. "Yeah. Thanks, Uncle Jeff."

Jeff found his sister in the office, little Amy playing on the floor with her dolls. His niece would be starting school next semester, which would give Sally a little more free time.

He limped in and dropped into a chair opposite the desk.

"Hey," said Sal.

"Hey yourself. I met Pete and gave him a ride from the bus stop."

Sally rubbed her face. "Oh God, I forgot the time. He's had to walk from the road on his own too many times lately."

"He's okay. He wasn't worried."

"I know, but I feel bad. But I keep getting bogged down with paperwork and I hate to let him down."

"Well, Nick was just coming in when we got here and he's taken him to see the new calf you've got in the barn."

Amy sat up. "Can I go and see it, Mommy?"

Sally nodded. "Go straight to Daddy and do what he says. Remember, the momma cow won't want you getting too close to her baby."

The little girl nodded and ran out of the room, her dolls

forgotten on the floor.

"So how was your physical therapy?"

Jeff laughed. "Painful. But it will get better. Teddy's good."

"Yeah. I didn't think he'd come back to town after he finished his training, but Cindy wanted to so that her family could help her with the kids."

"Did you know they're having a third? Man, I knew he was sweet on Cindy in high school, but I never thought they'd have so many kids by now."

"Why not? They've been married as long as Nick and me." She rubbed her temples. "Which reminds me, it's our anniversary in a couple of weeks. I'd better see if we can get a babysitter."

"Planning something special?"

She laughed. "No. Just our annual date at the drive-in. Hope there's a decent movie showing this time. Last year was some horrible slasher movie."

"Well, I can watch the kids for you if you want. You and Nick deserve a break."

"Really?" She looked sceptical.

"Hey, if I can run a platoon in a war zone, I can manage to keep a couple of kids safe and happy in their own home."

"Okay, you're hired."

He smiled. "Good. I wanted to talk to you about how I can help on the ranch as well. I know I can't do much of the physical work right now, but how about we share the load of paperwork and accounting? It would give you more time with the kids."

He hadn't expected his sister's eyes to fill with tears, so he worried that he'd said the wrong thing. "Look, I'm not trying to take over or anything, Sal darlin'. But I know you're always busy and I want to help. It's only right."

She rubbed at her eyes, wiping her tears away. "It's okay. I don't think that. I've been hoping you'd want to help, but I didn't want to ask. You're barely out of the hospital. You need time to heal."

"Well, I can heal just as well sitting at a desk. I'll go stir-crazy if I don't have something to do."

She nodded and smiled. "I need to start working on dinner now. Why don't you come into the kitchen and we can work out a schedule?"

Jeff grinned. "Sounds like a plan."

As they left the office, something else occurred to him. "Hey, maybe we should try to find out a bit more about our surprise step-mom as well, don't you think?"

Sally paused and looked at him. "I don't know, Jeff. I've been thinking about that, and... it's just... well, if Dad was okay with what was happening with her, maybe we should trust him and just let it go." When Jeff opened his mouth to respond, she held up her hand. "I mean, it's not like she's making any claim on the ranch or Dad's money, is it?"

"No, but she's taken over my house, my dog..."

"I can't imagine Bear preferring her to you now you're back. And she'll be moving on soon, won't she? Is it worth trying to dig up all her secrets?"

"So you're happy to just let it go?"

She nodded. "If it was okay with Dad, I think it should be okay with us."

He wasn't convinced, but he kept quiet. He wasn't ready to just roll over and give up. The woman was hiding. He wasn't sure he could rest easy until he knew what she was hiding from. One of his old army buddies had gone to work with a detective agency out of Denver, and now ran his own business. Maybe he'd give him a call.

Chapter Twenty-One

Jeff had been back in Montana for a few weeks now, but Faye hadn't seen much of him. She knew he was there at night – her own nightmares woke her just as he was screaming out his own pain. But she didn't go to him. Bear usually woofed and growled until Jeff awoke. She would hear his low murmurings as he spoke to the dog, then his quiet wanderings around the cabin as he sought out the whisky and a clean glass, which he took back to bed with him.

He got up early. On the days he wasn't going into town for his physical therapy sessions, he worked out on the makeshift gym equipment he'd set up in a corner of the barn. After a quick shower and breakfast, he'd take himself off and leave her in peace. Only then would she descend the ladder and begin her own day.

She knew he was working in the office at the ranch, because she'd seen his car there on the days she'd delivered eggs and produce from the garden. She soon learned not to expect him back for dinner, which – after the initial irritation that she'd cooked extra in order to be polite – she began to welcome. The less she saw of him the better. It was almost like it was before he'd come home, but not quite.

She had moved her clothes and personal items to the attic room, storing them in boxes as there wasn't a set of drawers available. She could have bought one, but didn't relish the thought of getting new furniture up the ladder to the loft hatch. The daybed and few bits of furniture that were there now had been hauled up by old Jefferson and one of his ranch hands. While she was relatively strong for her size, she wasn't an idiot. Nor did she think she could ask anyone at the Mackay Ranch to do the job for her now. She would make do. *After all, it shouldn't be long now before Grainger comes up with a new place for me.*

The lack of communication from Grainger bothered her. He had usually been quite prompt, especially when she had needed to move on. Last time, when she'd needed to get out of New York, he'd arranged it within a couple of days. She shivered when she thought about it. She'd been there for over a year, happily working in an art gallery in Manhattan, when at an opening she'd spotted someone she knew.

At first, she hadn't been able to place him. Then she'd heard his voice, and she realised she'd met him at the roulette tables in London. He'd been a high-flyer – winning a lot, laughing when he lost. She remembered James had hated him because the game had been far more serious for him – and the cause of his downfall when he couldn't pay the casino bosses what he owed. Faye had chatted him up a couple of times, just to annoy James. It hadn't gone any further than that, but seeing him in New York had shaken her. What if he recognised her?

He hadn't, of course. She wasn't the same blonde slut she'd been then. Now, she wore demure clothes and her natural brown hair was longer. But she'd been careful not to speak when he was within hearing range, and had feigned a headache and made a swift exit from the gallery, even though she was supposed to be working. As soon as she'd reached her apartment she'd called Grainger and begged him to get her out of the city.

She'd tried a couple of other cities, but hadn't been able to settle. She had lost her nerve and become paranoid – sure that someone from England would show up and recognise her. That's when she'd tried to blend in with an American accent. But having a British passport had made it difficult to explain. In the end, she'd stopped talking to people and rarely went out, and that was when Grainger had suggested the move to Montana.

At first, she'd thought he was mad. She couldn't live in cowboy country! But then she'd started to think about the school holidays she'd spent with her grandparents – on the farm in the Cotswolds with her mother's parents, and the estate in the Highlands of Scotland with her paternal grandparents. She remembered how happy she'd been then, loving the wide open spaces, and she'd agreed to give it a try. Within a couple of weeks, she'd been introduced to Jefferson Mackay Senior and they'd married just after she arrived in Montana as a means of her obtaining an American passport. It had all seemed so simple then. Grainger had arranged the paperwork, and she'd just gone along with everything. But now that Jefferson was gone and his son was home, she was back to square one – looking over her shoulder and preparing to run again.

Bear raised his head and she stilled, waiting. Within seconds she heard the faint rumble of an engine. She recognised it as Jeff's car and relaxed. It was the middle of the day, so she didn't expect he'd stay for long. She stayed where she was on the porch and carried on sketching, even though the urge to run and hide in her attic room grew with every second.

He pulled up in his usual spot by the paddock fence. She didn't look up when he slammed the car door. It was only when he stood over her that she looked up.

"Is that Ebony?" he asked, pointing to her drawing.

"Yes. And now you're blocking my view," she said. "Could you move, please? Aren't you supposed to be at the ranch?"

"Not today. Just had my session with Teddy." He stepped to the side and sat down on the chair beside her. She sighed and went back to her sketching. She didn't ask why he wasn't working today. She didn't want to know. She just wanted him to go away.

"You're good," he said after he'd been watching her for a few minutes. "Did you go to art school?"

"No." She'd had private lessons, but she wasn't going to tell him that.

"Why not? I'll bet you could've got in."

"My father didn't approve," she said without thinking. She blinked rapidly, trying to gather her thoughts.

"I thought princesses were all taught to paint and embroider and stuff, so they could keep busy while their servants did all the chores and the princes went hunting and grabbing taxes from the peasants."

She looked at him. "Are you serious, or are you taking the piss?"

He laughed. "Am I right?"

She shook her head. "Not at all."

"So, why didn't your dad approve of you going to art school?"

Faye rolled her eyes. She should have kept her mouth shut. "He thought I'd end up pregnant and living in a garret with some hippy artist," she snapped.

"So instead you end up in a garret," he pointed upwards, "with a soldier with a gammy leg." He rubbed his thigh, stretching his leg out in front of him. "Who also happens to be your step-son."

"But not pregnant, thank God," she said.

He seemed surprised by her vehemence. "Don't you want kids?"

She laughed. "Why would I? I've got two step-*children.*"

"Don't forget the step-grandkids," he smiled.

"Of course – one big happy family," she sneered. That wiped the smile off his face. She stamped down hard on the twinge of regret she felt.

"We were – we are," he said.

"Well, isn't that nice? But let's not pretend I'm part of it, whatever your father said." She looked away, trying to focus on the horse grazing in the paddock.

Before either of them could say any more, a truck turned onto the drive. Faye was on immediate alert. Jeff got to his feet.

"Phone company's here," he said as he walked down the steps to greet them.

Well that explains why he's here, bothering me, she thought as she closed the sketch book.

Faye didn't wait for the truck to stop. She picked up her stuff and slipped into the house. By the time Jeff came looking for her, she was up the ladder and in her attic with the hatch closed.

She stayed up there for the rest of the day as an engineer worked in the room below, and others arrived to erect telegraph poles along the drive and string the phone wire from the road to the house. She hoped Jeff had had the sense to move Ebony out of the paddock and away from the noise, but she wouldn't go down and check.

She was hungry, thirsty and dying for a pee by the time she heard the ringing of a telephone and the sound of laughter and back-slapping. She waited until there was silence in the cabin and the phone company trucks had driven away before she went down. She was coming out of the bathroom when she walked into Jeff's chest.

"Oof! What are you doing there, you big oaf?" she snapped. She was more annoyed with herself, not realising he was so close.

He had put out his hands to stop her and now held her shoulders. "Are you okay?" His thumbs moved over her skin and she shivered.

"Of course. I just didn't think you'd be loitering outside the bathroom, that's all."

"Loitering? Hmm. That's a good word. I must remember that."

"Did you want something? Because holding me prisoner isn't going to help, you know."

He let go of her and stepped back. "No one's holding you prisoner, Faye," he growled. "It's your choice to be here."

She wrapped her arms around her waist, wishing he'd just go away. "Don't worry, I won't stay any longer than I have to. Now, I'm starving. Do you want something to eat?"

"I had a sandwich earlier. Why didn't you come down?"

She turned away, heading towards the kitchen. He followed her.

"You could've had lunch with me and the guys," he went on. "I thought you'd gone for a walk or something."

"No, I was in my room."

"So why didn't you come down?"

"I don't like strangers," she said, opening the Frigidaire and pulling out the makings for a sandwich. "If you've warned me they were coming, I'd have gone out for the day."

"Is this something to do with what Grainger said about you being safe?"

"No. I just don't like people, okay?" She could feel her ire rising. He seemed to have a talent for winding her up. "Why does every conversation I have with you turn into a bloody interrogation?"

"Because what you tell me doesn't make any sense," he said, watching her with narrowed eyes.

"That's your problem, buddy," she said, slapping a slice of bologna onto some buttered bread. She spread some mustard and slices of tomato and cucumber on it before topping it with the second slice of bread. "If you don't like my answers, stop asking so many questions."

She sliced the sandwich into quarters and put it on a plate with some cookies (*so much nicer than boring digestive biscuits*), poured herself a glass of water, and took it all back up the ladder to the attic. She closed the hatch behind her, catching a glimpse of Jeff leaning on the door jamb between the kitchen and the living room watching her and shaking his head. She was tempted to throw the glass at him, but thirst prevented her from doing that. She didn't want to go downstairs again anytime soon.

After she'd eaten the food and slaked her thirst, she settled down to work. The sketches she had done of Bear and Ebony were preliminary pieces she wanted to use for a painting. She might even include the chickens. If she was going to have to leave them all behind, she decided she wanted something to remember them by.

That thought brought her head up and she stared at the sloped ceiling. She'd never been sentimental about anything before. She'd turned her back on her old life with no mementoes, taken nothing that would link her to a place or people. It wasn't as though she could forget – she'd been cursed with a photographic memory. That's why she'd managed to wreak such devastation when she had taken the witness stand. She forgot nothing. So why was she feeling sentimental enough to want to a painting of the animals?

She shook her head. She was getting soft. It wouldn't do. She needed to speak to Grainger and get this next move out of the way. It didn't matter how much she wanted to stay here. Her sanctuary had been breached.

As if to underline that thought, she heard Jeff in the room below, talking to someone on the phone. With a direct line to the outside world, she was no longer able to ignore it.

Chapter Twenty-Two

Six weeks after his first physical therapy session, Jeff was feeling stronger and more optimistic about the future. His pain was almost gone, so long as he didn't overdo his workouts, and he was off the meds. Teddy had finally given him the green light to get back on a horse.

"But no wrangling cattle just yet, man," he warned. "Just take it easy, ride the range and get used to being in the saddle again. Don't push it, okay?"

Jeff nodded, although he was keen to mount up and gallop into the distance and reacquaint himself with the land he'd grown up on. Up to now, he'd had to make do with short walks, building up his leg strength again. The urge to go further, into the mountains that had stood sentinel over their valley for centuries, had been building in him since the day he'd arrived home and found his cabin occupied by Faye and her shotgun.

His first ride was as tame as it could get. He'd gone back to the ranch, keen to saddle up, but Sal was ready for him. He'd ended up trotting across the close pastures in the company of Pete and little Amy and their mother on their own mounts. He'd wanted to bitch about it and gallop off, but the sheer joy on the kids' faces as they smiled at him as they rode alongside him got him right in the gut and he didn't have the heart to leave them behind. By the time they got back to the ranch house an hour later, he was glad he'd shared this time with his sister and her kids. But he was also aware that he wasn't ready for a good gallop yet because he was sore as hell after just a gentle ride.

He sighed as he dismounted and led his horse into the stable. Sal and the kids followed him, and between them they got all the horses brushed down and settled in their stalls with fresh hay. He was glad to see his sister was teaching her kids that if they wanted to ride they had to learn how to care for the horses. It brought back memories of his mom and dad doing the same thing with him and Sally. He knew she was thinking about it too when she sent him a sad smile.

"You staying for dinner?" she asked.

He shook his head. "Nah. I arranged to meet a friend tonight."

"Yeah?" Sal looked delighted. "Do I know her?"

He laughed. "Subtle, sis. No, it's not a date. I'm meeting an old army buddy in the city. I'll probably stay overnight."

"Oh. Okay. But you are thinking about dating, right? I'm getting tired of all the single women and their mommas around here calling up and inviting us over and then just mentioning the invitation includes you."

He scowled. "Do what I do – tell 'em I'm still getting used to civilian life and getting over losing our dad, and I'll be sure to let them know when I'm ready to be sociable."

The kids had raced ahead of them back to the ranch house. Sally put her hand on his arm. "It's been nearly two months since you got home, Jeff. People are starting to think you don't want to stay, because you don't go anywhere and you turn down any attempts to get you out."

He patted her hand and ran his fingers through his hair. "I know. I just need a bit more time," he said. He didn't want to admit to his nightmares or any of the other unsettling things that were happening to him. When he was around anyone he didn't know well, his gut would churn and he'd be constantly on edge, always expecting something horrible to happen. It had taken a while for him to get used to being around his own family, but he'd forced himself to do it and eventually it had got easier. Sal, Nick and Teddy had learned not to ask about 'Nam, and Faye left him alone when he woke up screaming, just as she said she would. She never mentioned it, but he'd caught her watching him with a thoughtful look on her face more than once.

He tried not to let it get to him, but it was playing on his mind. He hated that a woman, even one he didn't like much, found it uncomfortable to be around him. He wondered why it was taking so long for her to find somewhere to go to. Maybe he should call Grainger again. He was sure that was who she'd asked for help, though what a guy in London could do, he had no idea.

"How about we invite some people over here, huh? Just a few for a cookout, nothing special." Sally looked at him, her worry written all over her face.

"I guess. But not a crowd, okay? Maybe Teddy and his family and the ranch hands and their women." As he said it, he hated the idea, but he knew he had to try.

Sally beamed at him. "Great. Sunday?"

He sighed. "Okay."

Chapter Twenty-Three

Faye had resisted using Jeff's phone, apart from making a quick call to Grainger to give him the number and to check if he had found her a new place. He hadn't, but promised to get back to her as soon as he could. But that had been weeks ago, and she was getting impatient.

Living in the same house while trying their best to ignore each other was taking its toll on both of them. She was snappier than ever and he was snapping back. Not surprising, considering neither of them slept well and both of them were working themselves to the bone in an effort to distract themselves from this ridiculous situation. She supposed he resented her presence in his home, because he seemed to spend a lot of time at the ranch rather than the cabin. It didn't help that, as word spread that Jeff was home, the phone kept ringing. She didn't answer it; she didn't want to speak to anyone from around here. If Grainger called, he'd let it ring three times then hang up and dial again. That was their agreed signal. But the bloody man hadn't called yet. She needed to leave, and soon.

She was reaching for the phone to call Grainger again when she heard Jeff's car approaching. She swore and went into the kitchen, filling the kettle for a cup of tea. Her call would have to wait until tomorrow.

He strode in and went straight to his room.

She sat at the table with her drink, seething at his rudeness. When he came out again with a small duffle bag, she put her tea down and glared at him.

"It's bad enough having to share this space with you, but would it hurt for you to at least be civil? A simple hello wouldn't kill you, would it?"

He stopped and stared at her. "Why? You never talk to me."

He was right. She tried to ignore him. But this cold war was driving her mad. "If you weren't interrogating me, I'd be happy to talk to you," she said.

He raised his eyebrows. "Okay," he said and headed for the door.

"Wait! That's it? 'Okay', and then you walk out?"

He looked over his shoulder. "I'm late. I'm meeting someone in the city. I'm staying over, so don't wait up, honey."

"Oh." She stared at his back as he left. She sighed. *That went well. I finally try to talk to him and he's off on a date.*

She wondered if the woman he'd be sleeping with could cope with his nightmares. The memory of his hands on her throat brought her own hand to her neck.

Maybe he'll have sex and leave, just to be on the safe side. If I ever have sex again, that's what I'd do. She shivered. It wasn't something she'd contemplated for a long time. Now her mind was filling with images of Jeff Mackay in her bed. She'd seen him there, when she'd checked on him in the early days after his arrival. He had a good body – broad shouldered, slim-hipped. Despite the limp, he carried himself like a man who was comfortable in his own skin. She shook her head, trying to chase her thoughts away. *Don't go there. Sex just leads to betrayal. It's not worth it.*

As the sound of his car dwindled, she realised she could now call Grainger and have her conversation with him in private. The sooner she could get out of here, the better.

She got up and went into the living room. She sat in the armchair nearest the phone and dialled.

"Burgess."

"I need to speak to Grainger," she said, frowning. She knew Burgess was Grainger's right-hand man, but he'd never answered this number before.

"He's not here at the moment. Can I get him to call you?"

"Yes. No. I'll call back. When will he be there?"

"Probably not until tomorrow. If it's something urgent, I can help."

"No. I'll call back tomorrow."

"Can I tell him who's calling?"

She hesitated. She knew this man. He'd put her in handcuffs and handed her over to the police. She knew he was one of the good guys, but she still remembered the fear she'd felt as he'd held her, helpless and distraught. That was the start of her nightmare.

"No," she said and hung up.

She sat there, her whole body trembling. His voice had opened the floodgates, and she was overwhelmed by the sights and sounds that rushed into her head from the deep, dark hole where she had hidden them. The angry voices; the crunch of her car's bodywork as it hit the wall; the hushed tones at her brother's bedside on the one occasion she'd been allowed to visit him, punctuated by the beep and wheeze of the machines trying to keep him alive; blood; pain; despair; shame.

She curled up into a ball, fighting to regain control, to lock the memories away. It wasn't until Bear nudged her and licked her hand that she broke down and the tears came.

Chapter Twenty-Four

The drive to the city wore him out, but he felt his energy return when he spotted his buddy, former US Army Captain Steve Baldwin, waiting for him in the bar of his hotel.

"Hey man, good to see ya," he said as he was engulfed in a bear hug.

"Mackay, what's up? They told me you was a cripple."

Jeff laughed. "Just a limp. It's temporary. Working with a physical therapist. I'm already back in the saddle."

"That's good. Damn shame it earned you a discharge."

Jeff shrugged as they sat down. He signalled a waiter before he replied. "It is what it is. We lost my dad a couple of weeks before I got home, so my sister needs me to help with the ranch. I wouldn't be much use to her if I was still in 'Nam."

"Good point. Sorry about your dad. That sucks."

"Yeah." The waiter arrived and took their drinks orders. As he walked away, Jeff leaned forward. "He left a widow none of us knew about. That's why I called you."

"Say what?"

Jeff recounted the story of his first encounter with Faye and then the bombshell that exploded at the will reading, pausing only when the waiter brought their drinks.

"So, let me get this straight. Your pa marries a woman younger than his kids but doesn't tell anyone. She lives in your cabin, pays rent and signed a pre-nup which ensured she didn't have a claim on the estate?"

"That's about it."

"It don't make sense. What does she want?"

"Apparently, nothing. She insists she'll move on as soon as she finds a place. She won't discuss where she came from, or her marriage to Dad. She tried to stop the lawyer from telling us. If Dad hadn't mentioned it in his will, we'd never have known."

They drank their beers, each lost in their own thoughts.

"And she's English, you say?"

"Yeah. Sounds like the Queen of England and is cold as ice."

"Maybe the marriage was to get round the need for a green card."

Jeff shrugged. "She doesn't work, so why would she need a green card?"

"Okay. Maybe she wanted an American passport."

"Maybe. But it's not like she's trying to fit in – she's like a damned recluse. Never goes into town. I tell you, man, she's hiding. Why else would she be prepared to shoot me when I showed up?"

"She shot you?"

He shook his head. "No. But she had a loaded shotgun pointed at my head. If I hadn't been bleeding and woozy with pain, she probably would have taken me out and claimed self-defence."

Baldwin whistled. "Damn, Mackay. Sounds like you've met your match."

"Not funny, man. She was married to my dad. That makes her my step-mom. I have no idea what the old man was thinking."

"She ugly?"

Jeff frowned. "No. Just too damned ornery. Even the most beautiful woman turns ugly when she's always snarkin' and bitchin'."

"Beautiful, huh?" his friend grinned.

"Don't go there, man. You gonna help me or not?"

He took a drink of his beer, his eyes never leaving Jeff's face. "Okay. What do you need?"

"I need to you find out everything you can about Faye Evens Mackay."

Jeff decided to go straight to the ranch when he got home the next day. After the long drive, he knew he should just go back to the cabin and take it easy for a few hours, but he didn't relish another round of verbal combat with Faye. So he took the turn to the ranch and decided to give his sister a break and do some more of the ranch book work. Maybe that would get his mind off the crazy thoughts he had going round and around his head about his mysterious step-mother.

He and Baldwin had talked for hours, trying to think of all the possible scenarios that would bring a high-class British woman to a log cabin in the middle of Montana. None of them sounded right. He just hoped his friend would be able to dig up the real story before too long. He wondered whether he should take Sally's example and let it go – trust that Dad had known what he was doing and just wait it out until Faye moved on. But he couldn't. He needed to know.

So much of his life hadn't made sense lately – the fear, the pain, the regret. Maybe this situation with Faye was helping him redirect his energy away from the shit-show that his life had become in the months he'd been in 'Nam. He knew he should feel grateful he'd come through it alive, but even all his fretting about the woman in his house couldn't erase the nightmares that gripped him every night.

He had barely opened the car door when Sally came running out of the house.

"Thank God you're here!"

"What's up?"

"It's Amy. We can't find her anywhere," she sobbed. "I was on the phone to the feed store and she was playing with her dolls. Then when I looked, she was gone and the kitchen door was open."

"Okay. She can't have gone far. Have you checked the barn?"

"Of course I did. Nick and the hands are out looking for her."

"How long has she been gone?"

"About an hour. Oh, God, Jeff. What if something's happened to my baby?"

He took her in his arms and held on tight.

"Nothing's going to happen to her. She's probably playing hide and seek and thinking it's a great game."

"But there are snakes and coyotes out there. What if she falls in the creek, or meets a bear?"

"Stop it, Sal." He wanted to tell her none of that would happen, but he couldn't lie to her. The area was full of wildlife, some of which could easily kill a small child. All he could do was join the hunt and pray one of them found her. "Go back in the house. Keep calling her. She might have crawled into a closet and fallen asleep. I'll head out and join the others."

Sally wiped at her tears. "Okay. You'd better take a gun. The others said they'd shoot in the air if they find her. If you hear a shot, head that way."

"Okay." He followed her into the house and waited while she unlocked the gun cabinet. A few moments later, he was on foot, heading into the woods between the ranch and his cabin, calling his niece's name.

Thirty minutes later, he came out into a clearing and froze. Faye was on the other side of the sun-filled glade, her focus on the child in front of her. Amy was holding a wriggling bundle of fur.

"Look, Faye. Isn't this kitty pretty?" she asked.

Faye nodded and walked towards her. "She's very pretty, darling. But I think you need to put her down now. Her mummy will be looking for her, and she might be cross if she thinks you're trying to keep her."

"But she likes me, and her mommy has left her here, so we've been playing."

"That's nice. But playtime is over now. I expect your mummy is wondering where you are, and the kitty's mummy will be looking for her too."

"Oh, but…"

"Amy," said Jeff, keeping his voice low. "Put. It. Down."

As the little girl turned, surprised by her uncle's urgent tone, her grip on the kitten loosened and the animal leapt out of her arms and disappeared into the undergrowth.

Amy began to cry, her arms scratched by her escaping playmate. As he moved towards her, he saw Faye raise her gun. He lunged for his niece, hitting the ground as the mommy cougar broke cover and Faye fired.

Jeff felt the blood spatter against his cheek as he sheltered Amy under his body.

Chapter Twenty-Five

Faye's knees gave way as the cougar dropped to the ground next to Jeff. Underneath him, Amy screamed and tried to get out from beneath him. But he wasn't moving.

For a moment, Faye thought she'd shot him too. There was blood on the side of his head. But then she realised it was splatter from the dead animal.

"Jeff!" she said, crawling towards them. "Are you okay?"

He didn't move, despite the crying child pushing at his belly, trying to get free. His face was screwed up in a grimace of horror, his body was rigid and he was breathing heavily. As she reached him, she realised his eyes weren't focussed and there were beads of sweat on his forehead. *Just like after his nightmare.*

She was trying to decide what to do when Nick and a couple of ranch hands crashed into the clearing from different directions.

"Amy? Where is she?" asked her frantic father.

Faye pointed. "She's okay. Jeff sheltered her," she said. "Jeff, it's okay now. You can let her go."

He still didn't move. As Nick approached, Faye waved at him, frantically shaking her head. "I think it's triggered some sort of memory," she said quickly. "Be careful. He thinks he's back in Vietnam."

Nick frowned and motioned for the other men to approach slowly.

"Jeff," said Faye again, her voice firm and clear. "It's all right. It was a cougar. You saved Amy. Get up now. Let her see her father."

Jeff started, staring around, clearly not seeing what everyone else could see. He flinched when he saw the carcass of the cougar. "Sarge?" he asked.

"No. It's a cougar. It's not a man." Faye shouted. "Get up. Let Amy breathe."

He turned his head to look at her. He blinked and shook his head. "What are you doing here?"

"Same as you. Saving Amy. You did it, Jeff. Get up now. You're squashing the little mite. Let her father see her. The poor man's been frantic."

He looked away from her and saw his brother-in-law and the hands staring down at him with worried eyes. The child's wriggles finally got through to him and he rolled off her. Nick immediately jumped into action, snatching the child up in his arms, unashamed of his tears as he covered her face with kisses.

"It's okay, baby. Daddy's got you. You're safe. Let's go and see Momma, yeah?"

A moment later, Sally came running through the trees. "Where is she? Where's my baby? I heard a shot. Did you find her?" She let out a cry as she spotted the dead cougar, and her brother lying on the ground next to it.

Faye stepped forward and grabbed her by the shoulders. "It's all right," she said, turning her away from her brother and the carcass and towards her husband and daughter. "There she is. She's had a fright, but she's safe."

Nick held out an arm and Sally went to him, hugging their daughter between them. While the family reunited, Faye spoke quietly to the hands, letting them know the animal had at least one kitten, possibly more. They assured her they'd deal with it and dispose of the body.

"What about Jeff? Is he okay?" one of them asked.

She turned to look at him. He lay on his back with an arm over his face. "Yes. He just needs a moment to catch his breath. Leave him to me."

They looked sceptical, but nodded and jogged off to get what they'd need to deal with the carcass and search for the kittens. Nick and Sally were talking quietly to little Amy, who'd stopped crying and was showing them her scratched arms. Faye approached them, pasting a smile on her face.

"Why don't you head back to the house?" she suggested. "I expect Pete will be home from school soon, won't he?"

Nick nodded. "What about Jeff? Is he okay?"

Sally looked over at her brother. "What's wrong with him?"

Faye sighed. She suspected he would hate them seeing him like this. But she also felt sure they should know that he had a problem. "I had a great-uncle who fought at the Somme in the First World War," she said softly. "When he came home he had nightmares, and could never cope with the sound of gunfire without thinking he was back in the trenches."

"Oh God," breathed Sally as she made the connection to her brother. "Is he going to be okay? How can we help?"

"Carry on as normal. Don't whatever you do treat him differently. He'll hate it. Just give him time and let him work it out."

"But—" Nick started to speak, but Faye held up a hand to stop him.

"Take Amy home and patch her up. I'll stay with Jeff and we'll be over soon. Okay?"

They both looked like they wanted to argue, but, as she had hoped, their concern for their daughter won. They nodded, and left Faye and Jeff alone in the clearing with the dead cougar.

Faye picked up her gun and the one Jeff had been carrying and emptied them, before putting them down and lying down next to him.

"You still with us, soldier?"

"Yeah."

She snorted. "Barely. You haven't insulted me yet, so I know you're not yourself."

"I don't insult you."

"No? It must be some other fellow then. Nasty chap. Keeps asking questions that aren't any of his business and telling me what a cold bitch I am. Let me know if you see him, won't you?"

He sighed. "What are you still doing here? Why don't you go back to the cabin?"

"Can't," she said. "I promised your sister I'd take you over to the ranch. For some reason she thinks little Amy will want to see you to thank you for saving her."

"I didn't save her. You did."

"Not quite. If you hadn't tackled her to the ground, I wouldn't have got a clear shot of this old pussy cat." She lifted up a lifeless paw and dropped it again. "So I suppose we could call it a team effort."

Jeff moved his arm away from his face, turning to look at the dead animal. "You got it right between the eyes," he observed.

"It's the only humane way to kill an animal. She wouldn't have felt a thing. Much better than a sloppy shot that takes ages to kill it. And let's face it, an animal in pain is far more dangerous."

He turned to look at her. "Like me, you mean?"

She laughed. It was forced and she doubted he was convinced. "Well, you're no pussycat, darling. But not that dangerous. You Mackays are far too honourable."

He ran a hand over his face, and his fingers came away with specks of blood. He swore and wiped his hand through the dirt.

"Here." She picked up some dried leaves and handed them to him. "Scrub it off, then we'll follow everyone back to the ranch. Your sister's worried about you, and you need to reassure Amy that you're still her favourite uncle. You frightened her almost as much as that bloody cat did."

"Jesus, I can't. She'll be terrified of me."

Faye sat up, hugging her knees. "It'll be worse if you don't go. Leave it too long and she *will* be scared of you."

"Maybe it's better if I stay away for a while…"

"No. That's not acceptable," she countered. "You must go there now, smile and joke, give her a hug. Let her see the Uncle Jeff she knows and loves."

He shook his head, but she poked him with her boot. "Yes. Get up and let's go."

"What if she screams when she sees me?" he growled.

"She won't. Not if you act normal. Now stop being such a girl and get up."

He glared at her. She stood up and stared down at him, her

eyebrows raised, hands on hips. With a sigh he scrubbed the blood off his face and hands with the leaves before throwing them down and getting painfully to his feet.

Without another word, he turned and started limping down the path back to the ranch. With a smile, Faye picked up the guns. With a last glance at the dead cougar, she followed him.

Chapter Twenty-Six

It was safe to say that Jeff was more scared of facing his four-year-old niece than he'd ever been in a dozen years in the army. He wasn't quite sure what had happened back there in the woods – it was as though he'd been transported back to that village in 'Nam. It had been so real. At first sight, that dead cat had been the mutilated body of his comrade. The squirming child underneath him was the sweet little girl holding out a live grenade like she was giving them a gift. The echoes of the gunshot became the explosion that took their lives.

He swallowed hard as they cleared the woods and the ranch buildings came into view. He slowed his steps, but a nudge from his side pushed him on. That damned Englishwoman wasn't letting him get out of this.

"Hey, Uncle Jeff!" It was Pete, jogging up the drive with his school bag rattling on his back. "What'cha doin'?"

He raised a hand and waved at his nephew. "Hey, buddy."

They met at the front steps of the ranch house. "You missed all the excitement," Faye told him. "Your sister tried to make friends from a cougar kitten."

"Say what?" he said, his eyes wide. "Is she okay?"

"Yeah, buddy, she's fine," Jeff ruffled his hair as he glared at Faye over the boy's head. *What are you trying to do – scare the kid?* Faye just smiled back at him, ignoring his anger.

"Let's go and see, shall we?" she said, walking quickly up the steps. She was through the front door with Pete at her heels before Jeff had limped up onto the porch. She waited for him in the hallway while the boy ran ahead.

"Don't forget. She doesn't need any more trauma," she told him. "She needs a happy, light-hearted Uncle Jeff right now.

Don't let her down."

He opened his mouth to tell her to get out of his face, but she turned and walked towards the kitchen. He stood there for a moment, wanting to yell at her. Before she went into the room, she looked at him over her shoulder, her raised eyebrows again, challenging him.

He scowled at her then nodded his head. She smiled and disappeared into the room.

Half an hour later, Faye took pity on him and suggested they get back to the cabin.

"I left Bear inside. I thought he'd be more of a hindrance than a help," she explained.

He nodded and hugged his niece and sister, ruffled Pete's hair and shook hands with his brother-in-law.

"Thanks, man," said Nick. "Glad you were there."

"Yeah, me too," he said with a grim smile. He still felt like he was shaking inside, even though he'd put on the performance of his life in front of the family.

"Hang on," said Sal. "I just need to talk to Faye about something." She tilted her head. "Outside."

Faye shrugged and got up, sauntering after Sally as though she'd just been strolling through a park instead of hunting down an angry cougar.

"I'll meet you at the car," he called after her.

She waved a hand, which he took as agreement as the two women went out onto the porch.

He followed them out five minutes later, to be greeted with the sight of his sister hugging Faye, and the Englishwoman looking like she'd been poleaxed.

Chapter Twenty-Seven

Faye hadn't known what to expect when she followed Sally outside. She hoped it wasn't going to be more gushing thanks – it was embarrassing.

"I'm so pleased Amy is all right," she said. "Let's hope she's learned her lesson about kittens."

"Yeah. She's already asking if we can find it and take care of it now her momma's dead."

Faye laughed. "It did look cute," she said. "But I don't think it will be for long. Not the ideal house pet."

"No," she sighed. "God, I don't know what I'd do if—"

"Stop it, Sally. It's over and done with. Tell her the kitten had to go to a home for orphaned animals where it'll be looked after with other baby cougars."

"D'you think that'll work?"

"It did for me," she said, remembering the deer her father had hit with his Landrover in Scotland. She'd wanted to take its fawn home – her very own Bambi. But her mother had told her the lie about the sanctuary as they drove away. It was only later that her brother had laughed at her and told her the fawn had been killed as soon as she was out of sight as there were too many deer on their grandparents' estate that year and they were culling them anyway. He'd delighted in describing it in graphic detail, the bastard.

"Oh. Okay, I'll try that. But I'm never letting that child out of my sight again."

"She'll be fine, and so will you."

"I guess. Anyway, I need to talk to you about Jeff. Do you really think he's got shell shock?"

She nodded. "I don't know what they call it these days – combat fatigue? But whatever it's called, it sounds like the same thing my uncle suffered with after The Somme."

"So, he's having nightmares?"

"Yes."

"Does he talk about them?"

"No."

"Have you asked him?"

"Look, I think you should be having this conversation with your brother," said Faye. "It's none of my business."

"Of course it is. You live with him."

She smiled, her eyes cold. "We share a house. Separate bedrooms. And we don't interfere in each other's lives."

Sally frowned at her, her frustration evident. "But you know enough about him to see what the problem is."

Faye rolled her eyes. "It's not rocket science. The man has bad dreams. The one time I got close enough to try and help him, he jumped me and tried to throttle me, thinking I was an enemy soldier. Now I keep out of his way and let him get on with it."

Sally covered her mouth with her hand, her eyes distressed. Faye shook her head. "Don't get hysterical. I kneed him in the balls and Bear pushed him off me. No harm done." She wasn't about to mention the bruises on her throat that she'd covered with a scarf until they faded.

Unable to help herself, Sally started to giggle. "You kneed him? Oh my God! I'll bet that woke him up."

Faye couldn't help the smirk that spread across her face. "It certainly did."

The other woman laughed out loud, then she was crying. "I'm sorry. I shouldn't be laughing. This is a horrible situation. Should we have him move into the ranch house so we can take care of him?"

"God, no. Leave him alone. Let him work it out of his system. I'm sure he'll be all right." She wasn't about to reveal that her great-uncle had ended up in an asylum – a dirty little family secret, never to be discussed again. She didn't think Jeff would be so feeble as to have a total breakdown, but forcing him to move in with the family wouldn't help. It might make things worse.

"What can we do?"

She shook her head. "I'm not an expert. But I really think you just need to carry on as normal. Don't treat him like an invalid; he won't appreciate that. If he wants to talk, listen. But if he doesn't want to talk, don't push him."

They were both silent for a few moments, each lost in their thoughts.

Eventually Sally nodded. "Okay. But can I ask a favour?"

"What?"

"Will you stay until he's okay? I don't want him being alone while he's going through this."

Faye backed up, shaking her head. "I'm the last person he wants around."

"I don't care. You're good for him. You saw what none of us saw, and you're taking care of him in your own way. He needs you."

What about what I need? she wanted to shout. But she kept that thought to herself. "He hates me."

"You're distracting him. Please, Faye. Stay. Don't let him go through this on his own."

She stared out over the pastures, the foothills and the mountains that sheltered the valley. This had been her sanctuary. She hated the idea of leaving and starting again. But she was also realistic. Jeff Mackay wanted her gone. Sooner or later he'd get his way. In the meantime, she didn't have anything else to do. She could carry on, but she didn't have to turn into Florence bloody Nightingale. Just be around so that his sister didn't worry so much about him.

"Look, I can't promise anything," she said. *He's not the only one haunted by the past.* "But I suppose I could hang around a bit longer."

"Thank you!"

Before she had time to react, Sally had engulfed her in a hug. She stiffened, preparing to push the other woman away. That's when she saw Jeff come out of the front door and start walking towards them. He looked bemused. She could imagine the look of horror on her face as she endured his sister's hug. *I can't help if I don't like being touched. Does he have to find it so funny?*

"You ready to go?" he asked as he reached them.

"Yes. Definitely," she said as she extricated herself from Sally's arms. "Let's go."

Sally stood back and turned to hug her brother. He was more receptive to her gesture. He kept his eyes on Faye, as if to say: *This is how you do it. It's just a hug.*

Faye turned away and walked over to the car. She wasn't going to let him see how such displays of affection unnerved her. She couldn't remember the last time anyone had hugged her. Probably one of her many nannies. Certainly never her parents or her brother. Or even any of her lovers.

If she had wished for anything else – for some small gesture of affection from someone, anyone – she would never, ever admit it.

Chapter Twenty-Eight

A few days later, Jeff was in the kitchen when the phone rang. Through the window, he saw Faye straighten up from the vegetable beds, her face cocked to the side as though she was listening. When the phone carried on ringing, she shrugged and bent back to her work.

With a frown, Jeff went to answer the call. It was Greg.

"Hey, man. How's it going?"

"Good," Jeff replied. "You got anything for me?"

"Well, here's the thing. I can't find a record of a Faye Evens in England. It's like she never existed until she got to the US."

"What? Nothing?"

"Not a thing. I tried different spellings, possible names that would be shortened to Faye. The only woman I could find with the same name was ninety years old and she's been in a home for the last ten years."

"Could she be a relative?"

"Don't think so, bud. She never married, and hell, she'd be too old to have a daughter under thirty."

Jeff couldn't take it in. He'd been suspicious of Faye, but he'd never thought she'd be hiding behind a false name.

"Anything else?"

"Yeah. I tried to be discreet, but I attracted some attention. I got a visit from someone who suggested I stop investigating Faye Evens."

"Who was it?"

"Not sure. He flashed a badge, but not long enough for me to check it out. He suggested I could lose my licence if I kept on with the case."

"Damn! I'm sorry, man. What the hell? I don't know what to say."

He could imagine his friend shrugging. "Can't be helped. But it looked like your mysterious step-mom has some powerful friends. He wanted to know who I was working for but I claimed client confidentiality. He wasn't happy, but he let it go for now. But he warned me he'd be back if I didn't drop it."

Jeff sighed. "I guess you'd better close the case. Send me a bill for the work you've done."

"Forget it, man. I'd rather not have a paper trail back to you. The beers are on you next time I see ya, okay?"

They talked for a little longer. Greg had picked up Faye's trail in the US a couple of years ago, when she'd worked in an art gallery in Manhattan for a few months, then she disappeared again for a while before surfacing in Chicago. Not long after that, she moved to Montana and married Jefferson Senior.

"But Dad hardly ever left Montana. How the hell did he meet her?"

"It looks like getting married sped up her application for US citizenship," said Greg. "Which points to your dad agreeing to a marriage of convenience. D'you reckon she paid him?"

"No. I haven't found anything in the accounts. Although she paid rent on this cabin – a year in advance."

"Maybe it was disguised as rental," suggested Greg.

"It doesn't make sense, man. Dad didn't need to do this for money. Did you find anything about that guy called Julian Grainger? I reckon he's the link."

"I couldn't find much. He worked for the British Government, although it wasn't clear what his job was. He's retired now, but is a director of an organisation in London. It's a successful business, but there's not a lot of information about what it actually does, beyond personal security. I don't know."

"Personal security? Bodyguards?"

"Mmm. I think so. But they're high on privacy, so your guess is as good as mine. I can keep on digging, but I guess you'd have to go to London if you wanted to find out any more."

Jeff thanked his friend and ended the call. He was no closer to finding the truth about Faye. But he was sure that Grainger was the key. He needed time to think.

The back door slammed as Faye came into the kitchen. He turned towards her, watching her through the doorway from the living room. She was standing at the sink, washing her hands. As usual, her hair flowed over her left shoulder. He saw the delicate line of her jaw on her right side, the shell-like ear, and the graceful sweep of her neck. She bent down and drank cold water from the running tap before she turned to grab a cloth to dry her hands. She froze when she saw him there.

"What?" she asked, moving to the table, using the cloth to wipe the moisture from her fingers and chin.

"You'd be cooler if you tied your hair back," he said.

She dropped the towel on the table and raised an eyebrow at him. "I'm fine," she said. "I like it like this."

"There ain't no one round here that cares about fashion."

"What has that got to do with anything?"

He pulled out a chair and joined her at the table. "Just saying."

She got up and hung the cloth on a hook by the sink. When she didn't say anything else, he went on.

"You know, my dad was a soldier."

"So he told me."

"He met Julian Grainger in Italy in 1944."

"Really?" she opened the Frigidaire, inspecting the contents. "Have you eaten?"

"No."

"Do you fancy an omelette? The chickens have been laying well. I've got some eggs for the ranch, but there's plenty left over."

He nodded and watched as she brought out the ingredients and started to cook. When she didn't say anything else, he went on. "Dad also worked for the government after the war. Just like Grainger."

"I wouldn't know," she said, keeping her back to him. "I thought he was a rancher."

"Born and bred. But he didn't take over the ranch full-time until Mom died. She'd run the show while he was away."

"Just like Sally."

"Yeah."

"So, are you going to take over now you're home?"

"Hell no. Sal's a great manager, and Nick has worked here since he graduated from high school. It wouldn't be right to take over."

"So what are you going to do? Live off the fat of the land? Now that you're a war hero, no one will mind."

"I'd mind," he growled. *Damn, how does this woman push my buttons?*

"That's good to know. So, what are you going to do?"

"Maybe I'll ask Grainger for a job. I hear he's operating in the US these days."

He watched her back, noticing that she seemed to catch her breath before she carried on breaking eggs into a bowl.

"Hadn't you better get that gammy leg of yours fixed first?

He smiled. "Do you think I'll need to pass a fitness test for that kind of work?"

She paused again. *Gotcha!*

"What kind of work?" she asked, still not looking at him. "He's pretty ancient, so I don't suppose he does much physical labour."

"I hear he's into a lot of stuff. I'd sure like to find out more about it."

She laughed. "Good luck with that," she said as she tipped a fluffy omelette onto a plate and placed it in front of him. "Do you want some bread and salad with that?"

"No, this is fine, thanks."

"You're welcome. Have a nice day." She gave him an insincere smile, picked up a tray of eggs and turned to leave.

"Where are you going?"

"To deliver the eggs."

"I can take them. Aren't you going to eat?"

"No thanks. I'm not hungry. I'll let them know you'll be over soon."

And then she was gone.

Jeff paused with a forkful of eggs halfway between his mouth and his plate. He'd been sure she was going to eat with him, but she had clearly been spooked by his words. It reinforced his conviction that Julian Grainger knew who she was and why she was here. With a shake of his head, he brought the fork to his lips and took a bite of the perfect omelette she'd cooked for him before she ran away.

Chapter Twenty-Nine

Faye drove away from the cabin, furious at herself for letting him get to her. He was like a dog with a bone – constantly biting and mauling, trying to get to the marrow inside. She didn't know who he had been talking to on the phone, but it had obviously got him thinking again about her and Grainger.

Damn! Why the hell can't he just leave it alone?

She hadn't heard from Grainger, nor had she tried to call him again after her conversation with Sally. She realised it was silly to feel as though she owed the woman something. Jeff was a grown man. He was coping in his own way. But she knew from bitter experience that nightmares were a fact of life, something to be endured. Her being there might be distracting him during the day, but they were both plagued by their memories in their dreams. Who could say whether he might have more chance of getting over them if she wasn't around, forcing him to wonder why his father had secretly married such an unsuitable woman?

She knew her nightmares would never stop. She accepted that. It was her punishment. It was only right. She had messed up everything – not just her own life, but others' too. But Jeff's problems were different. His trauma was borne out of his service to his country. He was a good man, no matter how much he irritated her.

She pulled up at the ranch and collected the tray of eggs from the seat beside her. No doubt Sally would want to talk about her brother, but Faye really wasn't in the mood. She'd been a fool to agree to stay around. He wouldn't give up trying to discover her secrets. She'd been so close to screaming at him today, to pulling her hair aside and exposing her physical scars to him, to telling him what an evil woman she was. If he knew the truth, he'd want her gone – that was for sure.

After all, who would want to share their home with a criminal who had been responsible for the deaths of her brother and her lover?

Chapter Thirty

By the time Jeff had finished his meal and driven over to the ranch, Faye was gone.

"I didn't pass her on the lanes," he said.

"No, she took the main road. Said something about going into the city."

He wanted to ask why, but his sister was already talking about the ranch accounts and asking for his opinion on plans for expansion of the herd that she and Nick were working on.

Faye didn't come home that night. He called Sally, who told him she usually took a couple of days when she went to the city, but no, she didn't know where she went or why. But she was sure Faye was okay and would turn up again sometime soon.

In frustration, he made the painful climb up the attic steps so see if he could work out where she'd gone. As he went up the ladder, he wondered why he cared so much. He should be celebrating that she'd taken off. He should be hoping she never came back. But he couldn't help thinking that his questions about Grainger had set her running, and he wanted – no, needed – to know why.

When he opened the loft hatch, he'd expected to find a bedroom. But this was something else. New windows had been cut into the rear slope of the roof, flooding the room with light. Along one wall, under the eaves of the roof, was a day bed, barely big enough for a child. He supposed Faye would fit it quite comfortably as she was so short and slim. But his long legs would hang over the edge, and he'd never get any sleep in there.

Next to the bed was a small table with a lamp and a pile of

books. Her clothes were neatly folded into boxes at the end of the bed. But it was the rest of the room that took his breath away.

Under one window was a table and chair, and under the other was an easel with a cloth draped over it. Next to it were shelves, cluttered with jars filled with paintbrushes, tubes of paint, pastels and charcoal. Along the other walls were stacks of canvases. He recognised some of the landscapes as the same style as the framed artwork on the walls downstairs. They were accurate renderings of various places around the valley and up into the mountains that sheltered it. There were studies of Bear and Ebony, and even the cattle and chickens. In another stack were portraits of his father, his sister and her family, and the ranch hands. At the back, he found his own face scowling back at him.

He turned to the easel and lifted the cloth. Leaping out of the canvas was the cougar she'd shot. He felt chills down his spine as he realised this is what Faye had seen in the moment before she'd pulled the trigger. The animal had been in full attack mode, its teeth bared, its eyes… *God, its eyes.*

He dropped the cloth back over the canvas and took a step back. He turned slowly, trying to make sense of the room.

Okay, so she was an artist. A damned good one at that. But she'd never said. No one had. The poses of the subjects were natural, unaware. She hadn't asked anyone to sit for her. Instead, she'd just watched and recorded what she'd seen. The level of accuracy was incredible. She must have a photographic memory.

He turned back to his own portrait. He was sitting on the porch, glaring out at her. His injured leg was stretched out in front of him, and he had a bottle of beer in his hand. Pain was etched on his face and he looked tired as hell. He remembered the moment. She had just returned from riding Ebony. He'd been snarky about her exercising his horse, and she'd shot back that he should stop feeling so sorry for himself and get on with his physical therapy.

"When you're fit enough to ride Ebony, you can have him back," she'd said. "But don't think whining about me riding him in the meantime is going to stop me. If you weren't so full of self-pity, you'd know that a good horse needs regular exercise."

She had been more concerned for the horse's welfare than his. And she'd been right. That's why he had scowled at her. She had captured the moment – his annoyance and frustration – perfectly. He felt exposed. Yet he couldn't help admire her skill as an artist.

He looked through the rest of the canvases, hoping to find something about her life before Montana. But there was nothing. It was as though her art – and her life – had begun when she got here.

Chapter Thirty-One

Faye spent a couple of days in the city, staying at a nondescript motel chain and stocking up with fresh art supplies and essentials, including a case of her favourite single malt Scotch whisky, so that she didn't need to visit the town nearest the ranch. She wondered whether she ought to call Grainger to see if he had found a new place for her, but she decided to wait until she got back to the cabin.

Much as she would love to be able to just head off and make a fresh start, she knew she had to go back to the Mackay ranch. It wouldn't be fair on Sally if she were to just disappear. No doubt it would confirm everything Jeff had been thinking about her, but she couldn't do it. For some stupid reason she wanted to say a proper goodbye to the rest of the family before she moved on. It worried her that she was getting soft. She couldn't afford to drop her guard.

She arrived home in the middle of the day, confident that Jeff would be either at his physical therapy session or working in the office at the ranch. Sure enough, his car was gone. Only Bear was there to greet her.

She unloaded the truck and put everything away, all the while making a fuss of the dog. She'd even bought him a new squeaky chew toy which she was sure would annoy the hell out of Jeff. She was sitting out on the back porch half an hour later, beginning to regret the choice of dog toy, when the phone rang. Her head came up and she listened and counted. One ring, two rings, three rings, silence. She stood up, her breath catching in her throat as she moved into the cabin and stood by the phone. A few seconds later the phone rang again, and Faye picked up the receiver.

"Hello?" she said, her voice breathless.

"Faye, my dear. How are you?"

It was Grainger. She breathed a sigh of relief. "I'm fine. Have you found me a new place?"

"Not yet, I'm afraid."

"Then why are you calling?" she asked, frowning.

"I have some news. Are you alone?"

"Yes. What's going on?"

"I'm sorry to have to tell you, my dear, that your father died a few days ago."

She had been standing by the telephone. At those words she felt her knees crumple and she slid to the floor. It happened as though in slow motion while her mind was racing, filled with thoughts and memories, with anger and regrets.

"Are you still there?"

She took a deep breath. "Yes. I'm still here." She swallowed hard, trying to control her thoughts. "I don't really know why you told me that. I've been dead to him for years now. Why bother telling me he's gone?"

"Well, I thought you had a right to know, my dear."

"All right. Thank you for telling me. I assume I won't be expected at the funeral. After all, it might embarrass my mother, and that would never do." She was proud of the cool, polite irony in her voice. Her father would have been so proud.

"Actually, the funeral was yesterday. It's about your mother that I'm calling."

"Oh?" She couldn't imagine what this would have to do with her. Her mother had made it quite clear that she blamed Faye for everything and that she'd washed her hands of her.

"She wants to see you, my dear."

"Why? So she can blame me for Daddy's death as well?"

"Of course not. Look, I know this has been a shock. Should I call back later?"

Though she was tempted, Faye didn't want to drag this out any longer than necessary. "No," she said. "Tell me now."

"I think she's had a lot of time to think, and, well, you're all she has left now. I believe she wants to make her peace with you."

"But you told me I couldn't go back. That if I returned to

Britain I would be in danger."

"That's right, and I still believe that to be the case. However, your mother has suggested that she take an extended round-the-world trip so that she can meet with you wherever you are in the world. I think New York would be a good place to meet, don't you?"

Faye rubbed a hand over her face, trying to decide what to do. "I don't like New York. What if someone who knows us spots us?"

"It's very unlikely, my dear. Out of the millions of people in the city, the odds of such an encounter is miniscule."

"You said that last time. Yet I had to escape again."

Grainger sighed. "I know. But I really don't think it's likely to happen again. It's a big city. And wouldn't it help you to make your peace with your mother?"

"Probably not. We've never had what you might call a warm relationship." That was why she had been such an evil brat – if she couldn't get her parents to love her, at least she'd been able to grab their attention whenever she broke the rules. But even that had backfired in the end. She didn't for a moment think that her mother would be any different towards her, even though Faye had changed beyond recognition. "I really don't see the point."

"You know it was your mother who arranged for your trust fund to be made available to you in your new life, don't you?"

She hadn't. She'd imagined Grainger had organised an income for her from some clandestine fund he had access to.

"Oh." She wondered why her mother had done this. It couldn't have been because she cared. The last time she'd seen her mother, the woman had screamed at her to get out and never come back.

"I know some harsh words were exchanged," Grainger went on, as though he could read her thoughts. "But when it came down to it, she wanted you to be safe and not have to worry about money."

"Maybe that was her way of making sure I didn't come back from the dead."

"You won't know unless you meet her, will you?"

Faye sighed. She was so confused. *Why now? Why, when I need to start again and need all of my strength to do that?*

"Will you at least think about it?" he asked.

She suddenly felt so tired. All she wanted to do was curl up in a ball on the floor and sleep. But she knew she would get no rest. "When?" she asked.

"There's a liner leaving Southampton on Friday. It'll dock in New York the following Wednesday. Is that too soon?"

"No. Better to get it over with," she said wearily.

"That's the spirit. I'll make arrangements for you to meet for lunch on Thursday. Any preferences for a venue?"

Faye rolled her eyes. "She'll expect nothing less than the Waldorf. Tell her I'll meet her in the restaurant at midday on Thursday week. At least if we're in public, she shouldn't scream at me."

Grainger chuckled. "I'm sure she won't."

"I hope I don't regret it," she said. "But once that's done, will you please find me somewhere to go?"

"I'll do my best, my dear."

"Thank you." She hung up and stayed on her knees on the floor, staring into space. She had a bad feeling about this.

***

Outside on the porch, Jeff listened. He'd walked home from the ranch, needing to exercise his leg. He'd seen Faye through the window. She'd answered the phone, then seemed to slide to the floor. She'd looked shocked. He'd intended to rush in to the house to see what was wrong, but as he approached, he'd caught the end of the conversation through the open window. Something about her coming back from the dead and meeting someone at the Waldorf next week. By the end of the call, he'd decided it might be best if she didn't know he'd heard her side of the conversation.

When Faye got up and went into the kitchen, he quietly left the porch and walked back the way he'd come.

Chapter Thirty-Two

When Jeff returned to the cabin an hour later in his car, he found Faye in the kitchen nursing a glass of whisky, the half-empty bottle in front of her. Bear sat at her side, his head on her lap.

"You're back," she said, raising her glass to him and drinking.

It was clear to him she'd hit the bottle not long after she'd hung up the phone. Her eyes were half-closed, her lips a thin line. The fingers of her free hand were stroking Bear's head, as though soothing the dog would make her feel better.

"Where did you go?" he asked, sitting opposite her. He stretched out his leg. The extra walk, back to the ranch, had left him sore and tired.

"Needed supplies," she said, raising her glass again, as though that would explain everything. "If you want some, get yourself a glass. I'm too pissed to move."

He got up and found a glass. When he was back in his seat, sipping his drink, he asked, "Are you okay?"

She was silent for a while. He waited.

"I've got a photographic memory, you know," she said at last.

"Yeah? Sounds like a good skill to have." He was thinking about her paintings.

She shook her head. "It's not. It's bloody awful. I. Can't. Forget. Anything."

"I guess that sucks," he said, his tone gentle. "But whisky won't help."

She laughed. "I know. But right now, I don't care. I'm going to drink until I pass out. At least then I won't have any bloody dreams. I'm sick of them. Every night, every bloody night. I can't remember the last time I had a decent night's sleep." She pointed at him, a few drops of Scotch spilling from her glass. "Every bloody night. You know what I'm talking about, don't you? I hear you. You and your screaming."

He felt rage at her words. He hated his dreams, and did his best to work himself to exhaustion in the hope they wouldn't surface. Yet every night, he was back there, in hell, watching his friend and the little girl explode in front of him while he writhed on the ground in agony.

"Fuck you," he said.

Again she laughed. "Yeah, fuck me. Maybe that's what we need, eh? A good old rutting session. Angry sex. Get all that frustration out in the open. Use all that pent-up energy we've been trying to ignore."

He stared at her in shock. "Are you serious?" His anger grew as his body responded to her words. He did not want to go down that road. It would bring nothing more than trouble.

She took another long drink then refilled her glass. "Yes, so long as you've got some rubbers handy. I never let anyone near me without one. It might work. I don't suppose either of us have had any for a while, what with you being off fighting a war and me hiding away like a scared rabbit. Did you find any local girls? I hear there's a lot of your comrades coming home with Vietnamese wives and babies."

He shook his head. He was no angel. He'd stayed away from the local women, but he'd had a brief fling with a MASH nurse last year. "None of your damned business."

She smiled and raised her glass. "*Touché*," she said. "Flinging my own words back at me. Clever that." She took another sip and licked her lips. "Good stuff this. Too bloody good for a piss-up. But then again, I didn't know, did I?"

"What didn't you know?" he asked.

She rested her head on the table. "Doesn't matter. I was dead before he was, anyway. And he never fucking liked me. Always sneering at me. No matter what I did, I could never please him."

"Who?"

She looked up, peering at him with bleary eyes. "Mind your own bloody business," she hissed. She dropped her head again. "Are we going to have angry sex or not? Because if we don't do it soon I'm going to be too drunk."

"Maybe we should wait until you're sober."

"Hell no. If I'm sober I won't touch you with a barge-pole. No offence, darling, but if I haven't had a drink, I'll talk myself out of it. I decided. No men. Ever. That's my motto now. Not worth the bother. The only way you'll get into my knickers is if I'm too pissed to care."

He drank some more and watched her. "I assume by 'pissed' you mean drunk?"

She opened one eye and looked at him. "Of course."

"In these parts, pissed means angry."

She giggled. "Separated by a common language. So strange. Anyway, I can be very angry when I'm pissed. Are you one of those sickeningly happy drunks?"

"I guess you'll have to wait and see."

"All right. Bottoms up." She raised her glass to him, then raised her head to pour what was left in the glass down her throat.

They sat in silence for a while, Faye drinking steadily, clearly determined to keep going until she was senseless. Jeff watched her, taking the occasional sip of the rich malt. She was right. It was too good to waste on a drunken binge.

"Who died, Faye?"

She looked at him and shrugged. "Everyone." She refilled her glass, emptying the bottle. "Percy, James, me, your dad, my father. All dead."

"You're not dead, Faye."

"No? Huh! Shows what you know." She pointed a finger at him. "I might be sitting here, but she died in front of the whole world. I've got the scars to prove it." She swept the hair off her left cheek and pulled the neck of her t-shirt aside. "See?"

He gasped. There was a long white line running from her temple, down her cheek to her ear. The bottom of her ear was missing. Another line ran at a different angle below her ear, down her neck to her collarbone.

"Stupid bastard missed my jugular," she muttered. "But I died anyway."

"Who did this?" he asked, anger replacing his shock.

She shrugged. "A rather inept assassin," she said. "Got it all wrong. Too late, too stupid, didn't make any difference." She peered at him. "Why am I telling you this?"

"Because you're drunk."

"Hah! I could drink you under the table, soldier. They don't even brew a decent beer in this country. I know how to drink prop– proper booze."

He smiled as she stammered over her words and sipped his drink. "Okay, Princess. I believe you."

"You shouldn't. I'm a liar. Always lying. If you knew… But you already hate me, don't you?"

"I don't hate you. I don't think you're a liar, either."

"Why not?"

"Because a liar would have spun a yarn about why you married my dad. Instead, you say nothing. In your own way, you're as honourable as Dad was."

She shook her head. "I'm not hon– honourable. I'm a h– horrible person." Her eyes filled with alcohol-soaked tears. "I didn't deserve him." She sniffed. "He was a good man, your father. Too good for me. I'm sorry he died."

"Yeah, me too," he said, his throat tight. "So why *did* you marry him?"

"New name. New life."

"Because you died," he said, trying to make sense of her drunken ramblings.

"Yes. I died. Now I'm Faye Mackay and they can't find me."

"Who?"

"My assassin and his friends."

"Why do they want to find you, Faye?"

"Not Faye. The other one. The one who died," she mumbled as she dropped her head to the table and passed out.

He watched over her for a while, wondering whether she'd wake up. But when she began snoring softly, he decided she was out for the count and would be better off sleeping it off. He cleared away the glasses and the empty bottle, and made sure Bear had some food and water.

She still hadn't moved, so he gently picked her up and carried her through to the bedroom. He knew he wouldn't be able to manhandle her up the ladder to the attic, so he laid her on his bed. She rolled away from him and curled up in a ball and carried on snoring. Bear followed them in and got on the bed beside her.

"Good dog," he whispered. "You mind her for me, okay, buddy?

Jeff fetched a bucket and left it by the bed in case she woke and needed to throw up. On the bedside table he left a couple of aspirin and a glass of water.

He went outside to check on Ebony and the chickens. He'd taken over caring for them while she'd been away, and it felt good to be responsible for the welfare of the creatures. After he'd mucked out the horse's stall and collected the eggs, he checked on Faye again. She hadn't moved, but her breathing was deep and even.

The rest of the day passed slowly. He called Sally to explain why he wasn't coming back to the ranch today. His sister was surprised to hear about Faye drinking in the middle of the day, but he played it down as best he could, suggesting she might have just been over-tired from her trip to the city.

He'd learned a lot about the English woman in the past few hours, but none of it made sense. She'd been attacked and left her own country to escape. It sounded like she'd faked her own death. But he still didn't know why. He didn't really want to share this new information with his sister until he'd figured out what it all meant.

By about ten o'clock, Jeff was ready to turn in. But Faye was still deeply asleep on his bed. He remembered what she'd said about not getting a good night's sleep, which made him reluctant to wake her. In the end, he pulled off her sneakers, socks and jeans and pulled the covers over her. Bear was exiled to the floor and he stripped to his boxers and lay down beside her.

He just prayed he wouldn't have a repeat of his first night here. He didn't want to hurt her.

He was beginning to see that she wasn't as tough as she pretended to be. She wanted the world to think she was cold and uncaring, but he'd seen how she nurtured the animals and the garden; how she protected people – him included. She wasn't the hateful bitch he'd imagined her to be. She was just plain scared. And judging by the scars that she wore, she had reason to be.

He lay there for a long time, listening to the woman and dog snoring softly. He knew that once she was sober she wouldn't give him any more information. She'd be back to her usual guarded self, keeping her secrets hidden. In the darkness, he realised that, if he wanted to get to the bottom of this mystery, he needed to follow her to New York.

Chapter Thirty-Three

It was an explosion that woke her. She sat up as another bang echoed through the valley. She put her hands to her head, feeling as though the noise was going to blow her brain to pieces. Another ... *Was that gunfire?*

She looked around her in confusion. She was in the downstairs bedroom, under the covers. Her head throbbed and her throat felt dry. She ached all over and felt as though her stomach was about to erupt. She took a deep breath, trying to calm herself. It didn't matter how bad she felt, she needed to move, to act. Someone was shooting nearby. Had they found her? Who or what were they shooting?

Her jeans were at the end of the bed. She quickly pulled them on. As she stood up she noticed a bucket by the bed. She didn't remember putting it there, but then again, she didn't remember going to bed either. Her socks were by her sneakers. Once she was dressed she crept to the window. She couldn't see anything. The sunlight burned into her brain and she flinched.

What the bloody hell did I do last night? She wondered. She recognised her hangover, torn between trying to remember why she'd got drunk and her need to escape whoever was out there shooting. There'd been a short pause, but then more shots rang out.

She opened the bedroom door with a shaking hand. The living room was empty. She crept through the cabin to the kitchen, peering out of the window. Over by the barn, behind the chicken coop, Jeff was standing with his back to her, firing a pistol at tin cans lined up on top of the fence.

She rolled her eyes, which hurt. "Bloody man," she muttered. She grabbed a cup from the drainer and filled it with water. She drank it down, hoping she wouldn't throw it all back up again as soon as it hit her fragile stomach. She waited a few moments. When the water stayed down and the firing began again, she pulled open the back door and stormed out of the house.

"What the hell are you doing?" she yelled.

He didn't seem to hear her. He kept on shooting until the gun was empty. Then he broke it open, emptied the shells onto the ground and reloaded.

"Don't you dare," she shouted as he took aim again.

He spun around, pointing the gun at her. His face was grey but he was sweating. His hand shook.

"Faye? What are you doing here?"

"Put it down, Jeff."

He frowned and looked at the weapon in his hand. He closed his eyes and lowered the gun. "Don't worry. I'm not going to shoot you. But you should know better than to surprise an armed man."

"Right now, I've got such a god-awful hangover I'd be grateful if you'd put me out of my misery," she said. "But if all you're going to do is shoot at tin cans and waste perfectly good ammunition, then I'll say it again. Don't."

She stood her ground, hoping he'd listen to her. Something was off. His pallor, his shaking hand. He'd had a melt-down when she'd shot the cougar. Why the hell was he doing this?

He sighed and lowered his hand again. "I've got to do this," he said, as though he'd read her mind.

"Why?"

"You know why," he snarled.

She was right behind him now. She could feel his tension; it was coming off him in waves. "Can't you at least wait until I've got rid of this bloody headache?"

He looked at her over his shoulder. She didn't like the smirk on his face. "Can't hold your liquor, Princess?"

"I seem to be out of practice," she said. "So what?"

"Not as tough as you think, huh?"

She glared at him. "What has this got to do with you shooting the place up?"

He sighed and ran his free hand over his face. He turned slowly to look at her. "A man who can't shoot, or be around when others are shooting, is useless on a ranch."

Suddenly the sweat on his face, the shaking, his clenched jaw, all made sense. "You're trying to get used to it so you don't freak out."

He nodded, looking at the gun in his hand. "I've been practising for three days now. Still makes me feel like I'm gonna throw up every time."

"But you haven't," she pointed out. "And you're not cowering on the floor, either."

He laughed. "I did the first time. I was mighty glad you were out of town."

"Then you've made progress. Well done."

He raised his eyebrows, probably surprised by her encouraging tone. The truth was, she was impressed. To fight your demons like that took a lot of courage.

"But can you stop it now? I can't stand the noise when my head's this fragile."

"You do look a little green," he observed, opening the gun and emptying the bullets.

"Thank you," she said. "Yes, I'm green, I'm nauseous and have a killer headache. I need a fry-up to settle my stomach, and some painkillers."

"I left aspirin by my bed," he said.

"Thanks. I didn't notice. I was too busy wondering why someone was shooting and who they were after." She turned away, not in the mood to ask how she'd ended up in his bed. At least she'd had her underwear and t-shirt on, so it unlikely they'd had sex.

In the bedroom, she took the pills and drank the water. She noted the dent in the pillow next to hers. Bear never bothered with pillows, so it wasn't the dog who'd left that impression. *So, Jeff slept there too. So what? I was hardly in any condition to do anything about it.*

She wouldn't admit to herself that part of her wondered what it would be like to have big, bad Jefferson Mackay Junior in her bed when she was fully conscious.

She got busy, cooking bacon, eggs, mushrooms and tomatoes. She also fried some bread as well as making toast.

"Hungry?" he asked as he watched her.

"Not really, but if I'm going to be good for anything today, I need a lot of fried food. It's the perfect hangover cure."

He shook his head and poured her some orange juice. She took it and drank deeply.

"Thanks."

"You're welcome. Want coffee?"

She pulled a face. "No. I need strong tea. So strong the spoon stands up in it."

He laughed. "I'll pass. Some of us don't have a hangover."

"Lightweight," she sneered as she turned back to her cooking.

Five minutes later she placed two full plates on the table. They ate in silence. The first few mouthfuls were the worst, but she kept on chewing and swallowing until she started to feel better. She worked her way through the food on her plate and two large cups of strong tea before she sat back with a sigh.

"Better?"

She nodded. She closed her eyes, enjoying the quiet and the fact that she wasn't go to die of a hangover after all.

"I guess you got your wish."

She opened her eyes. He was watching her intently. "I'm sorry?"

"You said you wanted a good night's sleep. You didn't have a nightmare."

She frowned. "Neither did you."

"How do you know?" he asked, his expression unreadable.

"I didn't hear you scream. As you were lying right beside me, I definitely would have heard you."

He shook his head. "Your snoring kept me awake, Princess."

"I don't snore," she snapped.

"No? Must have been Bear. But I could have sworn it was both of you."

"What the hell was I doing in your bed anyway?"

He grinned. "You don't remember asking for some angry sex?"

She stilled, wracking her brain to try to remember. She vaguely remembered suggesting they needed to have angry sex, but she couldn't for the life of her remember whether they'd actually done anything. And she'd had clothes on when she woke up. Why would she have sex and then get dressed, only to crawl back into his bed again?

"I don't believe you," she said, sounding more confident than she felt.

He laughed, enjoying her discomfort far too much for her liking. "Don't worry, Princess. I don't kiss and tell."

"That makes a nice change," she muttered. She'd got heartily sick of the world lapping up the details of her private affairs.

"Say what?"

She gave him a cool smile. "Nothing," she said. But she couldn't resist saying, "But it couldn't have been very satisfying, seeing as how I don't remember a thing. Perhaps you're used to getting women falling down drunk before you can get between their legs."

"I thought you had a photographic memory, Princess."

She had a vague recollection of telling him that. Stupid. What was she thinking of?

"It seems that downing the best part of a bottle of thirty-year-old malt acts as an effective eraser," she said.

"I suggested we should wait until you were sober. But it seemed like you really wanted us to have some angry sex right away."

Angry sex. Angry sex. Why does he keep going on about it? She wanted to cringe. In her experience there was only one kind of sex, and that was very angry. It might have been gentler and more fun in the early days, but angry was the only way to describe any physical encounters she had in the months before her world had collapsed around her. Yet she couldn't imagine that he would have indulged in it with her. He was far too controlled most of the time. The only time he had been seriously out of control had been when she'd woken him from his nightmare and when she'd shot the cougar. Yet he hadn't responded directly to her dig about getting women drunk in order to have sex with them. She shook her head. She might not like him much, but she didn't really believe he would do that.

When she didn't reply, he went on. "Don't worry, Princess. I like my women to know when I take them to bed. Humping a drunk doesn't do it for me."

She burst out laughing. "Humping a drunk? How nice to know."

He joined in her laughter and she felt the tension ease from her spine. That was until he spoke again. "What did Grainger call you about?"

"Excuse me?" *How the hell does he know about that?*

He shrugged. "You said someone had died. I figured you must have gotten a call. And as Grainger seems to be your only friend outside the ranch, it seemed like the logical conclusion."

"Well, aren't you a regular Sherlock Holmes?"

"So I'm right?"

She looked at him, so eager to stick his nose in her business. What would he say if she told him her father had died? How would he react to the fact that she hadn't had any direct contact with him since Burgess had handed her over to the police in handcuffs nearly four years ago? What would he think about the fact that he would be buried in the family plot, next to an empty grave that represented her useless, wasted life? She turned her head and stared out of the window, feeling the comfort of the mountains that guarded this valley.

"I don't know what you're talking about," she said.

Without waiting for him to respond, she got up and walked out of the cabin.

Chapter Thirty-Four

Jeff watched her go, wishing he could call her back. He hadn't meant to scare her away. He'd been determined to be gentle, to tease out her secrets, but he'd blown it. He got up and filled his cup from the coffee pot.

The only way he could tell she was nervous was when her fingers touched her hair, smoothing it down over her cheek and neck. Even with a killer hangover, she'd taken the time to fix her hair so that her scars were covered. Now he knew why, he understood her reluctance to be touched. *It must have been a hell of an attack,* he thought. *What the hell had happened to her, and why? Did Dad know about it?* Thinking back to what his father had written in his will, he guessed he had known Faye's secrets. He'd hinted that she needed protecting.

But it hadn't been a recent attack. Her scars were pale – not like Jeff's red, angry scars. The medics had told him it could be a year or more before they faded.

He ran a hand over his face and rubbed his eyes with his knuckles. *Damn, I'm tired.* He might have lied to her about her snoring, but he really hadn't been able to sleep with her in his bed. She'd been so fragile, so brittle in her drunken state, he hadn't been able to relax. He'd lain beside her for hours, trying to make sense of the pieces that made up the puzzle that was Faye Evens Mackay. In the end he'd given up and left the room. He'd watched the sun rise over the mountain tops from a chair on the back porch. But he hadn't been able to relax or sleep.

He stood up and looked out of the window. She was cleaning out the chicken coop. He thought he ought to go and offer to help, but she didn't look like she'd appreciate company right now. Her back was straight and her movements angry.

With a sigh, he left her to it and went into the living room to call his sister to tell her he wouldn't be over today. He assured her he was okay, just tired, and he'd be over the next day. In his bedroom, he pulled off his shirt and jeans and got into bed. He could smell her fruity shampoo and lavender soap on his sheets. He wondered whether he should change the sheets to get rid of her scent. But the combination of his long walks yesterday, his sleepless night, and the effort it had taken to practice shooting without freaking out, were just too much. Within moments he was asleep.

In his dreams, he kissed her scars and told her she was still beautiful.

Chapter Thirty-Five

Faye kept herself busy over the next few days. Anything to keep her away from Jeff. She didn't for a moment believe they'd done anything physical when she was drunk, but she couldn't help feeling that she'd revealed far more to him that she should have. Had she shown him her scars? Or was that just a drunken dream?

He hadn't mentioned it – mainly because she didn't stay around him long enough for the opportunity to arise. And she certainly wasn't going to be the one to bring it up.

Nor had she told him she was going to New York. She didn't want to explain who she was meeting and why. She didn't even want to think about it, let alone discuss it with anyone else.

It had occurred to her to just not go, to call Grainger and tell him to forget it. Didn't he realise how far away Montana was from New York? It was thousands of miles, like the distance from London to Moscow. It was a bloody epic journey that would take days. And for what? To make small talk with the woman who'd given birth to her and then handed her over to a stream of nannies and boarding schools? She'd give it an hour at the most before they ran out of things to say to each other. She should cancel.

But every time she went to call Grainger, she hesitated. God knows why, but she was sure he'd be disappointed in her. Given that he knew just about everything there was to know about her, both before and after, he'd never treated her with anything less than respect. He'd been kind, even when he was making her face horrible truths. He'd been more of a father to her than her own one had been. In the end, she knew that she would go, if only to please Grainger.

She wouldn't drive the truck there. She didn't want anyone to see her driving a vehicle with Montana license plates. It would be too easy to track her back here if she did that. So she either had to get a plane, bus or train, or a combination of these.

A direct flight was too risky, even though that was the shortest journey time of about seven hours. But in order to feel safe, she'd have to make her way to New York in stages. She spent an afternoon in the city library in Billings, checking bus and train schedules. In the end she decided to get Greyhound buses as far as Chicago, then fly into New York. She then plotted a different circuitous route back to ensure no one would know where she'd gone. The whole trip, for the sake of a lunch meeting with her mother, would take her a week.

She'd better leave Jeff a note rather than just disappear for that long. She would tell him she'd gone house-hunting in the Yukon or something. *After all, I did have a reputation for being a very successful gold-digger.* She smiled at the thought, then began to pack what she'd need to take with her.

Chapter Thirty-Six

The note said she'd gone house-hunting in the Yukon, but he knew it was a pile of bullshit. He arranged for one of the hands to take care of Ebony and the chickens, and left Bear with Sally before he headed to the airport. Her meeting was scheduled for Thursday at noon at the Waldorf in New York. And Jeff intended to be there.

A couple of old army buddies were New Yorkers, so he decided to go early and hang out with them on Wednesday night. It was good to catch up, to remember the years they'd been brothers-in-arms. They had a few beers and watched a baseball game in a sports bar. He didn't explain why he was in New York. "Just some family stuff," he told them. But it was good to have a few hours when his dad, the ranch business and Faye's secrets weren't messing with his head.

He booked into a decent hotel – nothing like the Waldorf's standards, but he didn't need anywhere fancy to lay his head. On Thursday morning he dressed in his good suit and headed for the Waldorf. He'd had enough foresight to book a table for lunch. He didn't want some jumped-up maître d' stopping him from getting into the restaurant.

He had no idea what he was going to find. He knew Faye was meeting a woman and she wasn't happy about it. But beyond that, he didn't have a clue. He knew Faye was going to be pissed at him for crashing her party, but he reckoned she wouldn't make a scene in a place like that. Would she?

No matter. She can scream like a banshee, but I'm looking for some answers. If this is the only way I can get them, that's how it's gonna be.

He didn't want to show his hand too early, so he booked his table for twelve-thirty, hoping she hadn't had her meeting and split by then. With luck, by that point she and the woman would be tucking into their entrées, and it wouldn't be so easy for her to just up and run. But he didn't want to miss her, so he got there early. He took a copy of the *New York Times* with him, found a vacant couch in the lobby and sat down. He watched as people from all corners of the world walked in and out of this landmark hotel, only raising his paper as though reading when he caught sight of Faye as she walked in.

He hoped she hadn't seen him. She was busy scanning the area, her whole body on alert. He watched from behind his paper as she spotted an older blonde woman standing by the front desk. At that moment, Faye went from scared rabbit to confident fox. Her whole demeanor changed. Her chin went up, her shoulders went back. Even her walk was different – like she was on a catwalk. She stalked towards the woman and stopped in front of her. He couldn't see the woman's face, but they were about the same height and build. The woman put her hands on Faye's shoulders and kissed her on both cheeks. He noticed a slight tension in Faye's shoulders but she tolerated the woman's touch. They turned and moved towards the restaurant.

As they disappeared out of his sight, Jeff let out a breath he'd been holding since she'd walked through the doors. Now he just had to wait a little longer before he went in there for some answers.

Chapter Thirty-Seven

Her mother didn't say anything when she stood in front of her. She simply smiled, took her by the shoulders and kissed her on both cheeks. Faye had to stop herself from pulling away. The brief embrace lasted only seconds and left behind the lingering aroma of her mother's usual perfume. It felt like an age before Elizabeth Broughton stood back and smiled again. Without a word, Faye turned and headed towards the restaurant. She'd been here before – with her parents once, with a lover when she was twenty-one, and more recently when she had briefly lived in New York City.

They didn't speak until they had been seated at their table, her mother first, facing into the restaurant, leaving Faye to take the chair opposite, facing the window. Faye didn't like it. She always made a point of being able to see anyone approaching. Otherwise she was vulnerable. And now was not the time to be vulnerable. But she said nothing, and sat when their waiter pulled out the chair for her.

"You're looking well, Felicity, darling," said her mother as soon as they were alone. "I like your dress. Is that Indian cotton? I love the colour. That blue suits you perfectly. Those floaty long styles seem to all the rage in London at the moment. So much better for the chubbier gals – they really shouldn't have been allowed to wear mini-skirts, although they always looked good on you."

Faye closed her eyes and shook her head. *Only my mother would be worried about skirt lengths at a time like this. And when I did wear mini-skirts, she hated it.* "Felicity is dead," she responded, ignoring the fashion talk. "She no longer exists."

"Oh darling, please. We're thousands of miles from home. Surely we don't need to keep up this charade here."

Faye laughed, the sound brittle to her ears. But before she could reply, the waiter returned to take their food and drinks orders. Tempting as it was, she refused wine in favour of a soft drink. The last thing she needed was to lose herself in alcohol. She'd save that for when she got home – to Montana, or wherever else she ended up once Grainger had made the arrangements. She wished he'd hurry up. Part of her wasn't sure she could go back. She had a feeling that leaving Montana at all had been a mistake, and her mother's opening shot had confirmed it.

Their orders taken and drinks delivered, they were left alone again. Faye studied the woman opposite her. Even in her late fifties, Elizabeth Broughton was an attractive woman. From her carefully-tinted and styled hair to the hand-made Italian leather court shoes on her feet, she presented an image of breeding and sophistication. Faye wondered what her mother would make of her digging up her own vegetables or cleaning up chicken shit. The thought made her smile.

"Widowhood suits you," she said, still unable to call her Mother.

"Thank you, darling. One must try to maintain standards."

Even when your offspring go off the rails in a spectacularly public fashion and your friends stop calling, thought Faye, but she didn't say it. They were barely fifteen minutes into their meeting. It would be crass to start the battle yet. She knew her mother would take the opportunity to start the foray soon enough.

"I must say, you're looking well. Life in America must suit you."

"Who says I live in America?" Faye smiled. "I might have popped over the border from Canada, or hitch-hiked up from Mexico."

"And did you do either of those things?"

"I'm afraid I can't say."

"Oh, Felicity, really."

Faye leaned forward, her hands on the table. "Call me that just one more time, and I walk," she hissed. "I am not Felicity. I never will be again. Accept it."

Elizabeth leaned back, her lips thinned.

"You always were a dramatic child. I'm your mother, for goodness' sake. Surely it's not too much to ask to know your new name and where you live?"

"It was explained to you at the time. The less you know, the better. It wouldn't be safe for either of us. I'm actually trying to protect you. Can't you accept that?"

"But it's all over and done with now, isn't it? You're halfway around the world. Can't we just be mother and daughter for a little while?"

Faye sat back and took a sip of her drink. She was stunned. In all her twenty-eight years, this was the first time Elizabeth had ever said anything like that to her. Her memories were of being told: *Don't do that,* or *Be quiet,* or *What have you done now, you bloody child?* "Why change the habit of a lifetime?" she asked, her tone bitter.

She expected her mother to snarl back at her, but Elizabeth closed her eyes as though in pain.

"I know I haven't been the best mother," she said after a few moments. She took a sip of her martini and put the glass back on the table before going on. "We've all made mistakes. I just don't want it to be too late before we do something about it. With your father and Percy both gone now..."

This time it was Faye who closed her eyes. "So you're not here to blame me for Daddy's demise as well as Percy's?" she asked.

"Oh, darling, of course not. I know we blamed you initially over Percy, but well, while you were in hospital for all those months, it became quite clear with all the terrible things they said in the papers that your brother was the one who led you into the situation, and not the other way around."

Faye felt her mouth drop open in surprise. Had she spent years broken under the burden of her guilt, while her parents had actually forgiven her?

The waiter arrived with their meals. A steak for Faye and a salad for her mother. Elizabeth couldn't help raising her eyebrows as her daughter sliced into the meat and ate it with gusto. Faye wasn't about to tell her mother that she'd been travelling for three days, had hardly slept, and had survived on snacks from bus stations and airports along the way.

They ate in silence for a few minutes until Faye felt human again.

"Why didn't you tell me?" she asked, her tone mild. "Why wait nearly four years before saying this?"

Her mother put down her fork and picked up her napkin, blotting at her lips in order to preserve her carefully-applied lipstick. "We didn't get a chance, darling. You were whisked away and we weren't allowed to see you. They said we had to keep up the pretence that you were dead in order to keep you alive. Then they moved you on and that was that."

She made it sound so uncomplicated, but it had been far from simple. Faye realised her mother hadn't known how long she been in hospital, or the full extent of both her physical and mental injuries. It had been decided that she needed a complete break from her past, including what was left of her family, if they were to convince her assassins that she really was dead. Even now, she couldn't tell her mother the real reason why she was moved on after a couple of months in hospital recovering from her physical injuries. *She probably thinks I was rushed out of the country just to spite her, when in fact I was in an asylum going through a nervous breakdown.*

"You could have asked to send a message," she said, stabbing at her steak. She carried on eating steadily, even though she'd lost her appetite.

"I know. But we didn't know what to say."

Faye looked up. Her mother looked genuinely sad for a moment, but then, in true Broughton family tradition, she rallied, pasting a smile on her face. "But that's in the past, all of it. I'm here now, darling, and I have a marvellous idea. I'm booked on a Caribbean cruise, starting on Sunday. I've got a suite which has two bedrooms. Why don't you come with me? We could spend the next couple of days shopping, my treat. Wouldn't it be lovely to relax and explore the islands together?"

"I can't."

"Oh. Why not? Have you got a job?"

She wanted to lie, but what was the point? "No. But I have animals and people depending on me. I need to get back."

"But where to?"

She shook her head. "I'm not going to tell you, so please stop asking." She held up a hand when her mother would have argued with her. "I know you think I'm making excuses, but I'm not. The people Percy and I got involved with weren't some tinpot gang of thugs. They were organized, brutal and evil. There were far more of them than went to prison, and they never ever forgot. If they had just a hint that I'm still alive, they'd hunt me down. If they thought you knew where I was, they'd make you talk – and it wouldn't be pretty. God, when one of them paid James a visit, he nearly wet himself."

"Of course he did. That boy was an arse," snapped his mother. "He had no backbone."

"I know." Faye laughed. "The point I'm trying to make is, he could talk the talk any time he put his mind to it, and he got away with most things. But these people don't muck around, and we all learned that to our cost. You need to accept it. Your regal bearing and no-nonsense scolding will likely irritate them rather than subdue them. They'd delight in hurting you."

Elizabeth sighed and put down her fork. "So you don't want join me on the cruise? Can you at least spend some time here in the city with me? We could still go shopping and maybe see a Broadway show."

Part of her was tempted, but she still shook her head. "Last time I was in New York, I saw someone from home. He didn't see me, thank goodness, but it's too much of a risk."

"Oh surely not. How many millions of people live here? It's not likely to happen again, is it?"

"I'm not prepared to take that chance. Nor should you. There might be a lot of people here, but let's face it, Mother, you'll only grace the right sort of shops and theatres, so the chances of our meeting someone we know is increased a thousandfold."

Elizabeth shook her head. "I'm sure it's not that—" She stopped speaking, her eyes trained on the entrance to the restaurant. "Oh dear lord."

"What is it?"

Elizabeth closed her eyes for a moment then opened them again. "Enid Fairbrother's daughter just walked in."

Faye froze. She wanted to look, but didn't dare. "Keep eating, act naturally. Don't draw attention to yourself. She might not see us."

Her mother did as she was told, but looked at her with troubled eyes. "I'm so sorry. You were right. I should have listened. I had no idea…"

Faye sighed. She took a sip of her drink in an effort to push her piece of steak down past her throat, which had tightened with tension. Her mind was whirling with scenarios and possibilities. With any luck the bloody girl wouldn't notice them – she'd never been that bright – and they could wait it out until she left. But her mother's gasp told her that wasn't going to happen.

"She's coming over, isn't she?" she said, her voice low.

"Yes. Oh, darling, I'm so…"

"It doesn't matter. You didn't know. Look, I need you to take your lead from me. Do not, under any circumstances, let me down, Mother. Promise me."

"Yes, of course, but …"

"Mrs Broughton?" A tall, slim brunette came and stood by their table.

"Oh, hello, Tabitha. What a surprise," said Elizabeth, her well-practised smile beaming at the girl.

"I thought it was you. What are the chances, eh? I must introduce you to Chip, my fiancé. His name's Charles really, but you know these Americans – always using such silly nicknames." She turned and waved at someone, beckoning them over. "Darling, this is a friend of Mummy's. I went to school with…" She gasped, pressing her fingers over her lips. "Oh, I'm so sorry, I'm sure you still miss her terribly. She was such fun."

Faye sat quietly, her gaze on her plate. She and Tabitha had never been friends. They'd been classmates, no more. They'd occasionally had to endure each other's company when their mothers arranged things, but they'd never chosen to spend time together otherwise. To hear her toadying up to Elizabeth now made her want to vomit. The girl was a frightful snob, and no doubt relished the idea of being able to recount meeting the only surviving member of the Broughton family to all of her cronies. *Well, let's give her something to gossip about, shall we?* Faye thought as she raised her head.

"Hi! Do y'all know my Aunt Betty?" she asked in her best hillbilly accent. She saw her mother flinch, and tried not to smile. Elizabeth always hated people shortening her name. "I guess it's a small world now with all those great big airplanes flyin' across that there pond between us and England." She grinned as though it was the greatest joke. Then she held out her hand to the girl who was looking at her with wide eyes. "I'm Mary-Beth, here in the Big Apple for the first time to meet my momma's cousin, ain't that right, Aunt Betty?"

Tabitha offered her a limp hand, which Faye took and shook like a man. She was grateful for the work that made her hands rough to touch, as the girl seemed to cringe while still trying to smile politely. "A cousin?"

"Yes, siree. My grandma was an English lady, the only sister to Aunt Betty's momma. She fell in love with my grandpa after he was wounded in France in the Great War and ended up in an English hospital. He was one of the first Americans to fight over there in 1917." She took a breath and grinned. "He came home with a chest full of medals and my grandma."

Tabitha looked from Faye to Elizabeth, clearly confused. Faye smiled. *Good!*

"So, anyways, when I heard that Momma's cousin was coming all the way from England, I just had to meet her. Momma couldn't come on account of her having to work shifts at the factory." She leaned towards the young man standing behind her old schoolmate. "I'm trying to persuade Aunt Betty to come visit the family down in Alabama, but she's got other plans. Can you believe it? My own kin, having lunch at the Waldorf and going on a fancy cruise? My momma's going to be so jealous when I tell her."

Chip didn't look impressed. He'd smiled charmingly at her

until she opened her mouth and started play-acting. Then his expression had hardened. Her hillbilly persona marked her as a peasant in his eyes. No doubt he had a pedigree going back to the Mayflower, and considered himself far above the hicks that populated most of the continent.

Tabitha, on the other hand, was staring at her openmouthed. Even though Faye wanted to scowl at her like she used to, she kept her face open and smiled like she was in the presence of royalty and still pinching herself to see if it was real.

"You okay, honey?" she said, feigning concern. "You've gone mighty pale." She leaned towards her. "You ain't in the family way, are ya?" she whispered, loud enough for everyone to hear.

Tabitha blinked and put a hand to her throat. "No! No, of course not. I'm sorry. I'm so sorry. It's just…" She looked at Elizabeth. "It's just that she looks so much like Felicity when we were at school together."

Faye cursed silently. She'd forgotten that. Although she'd had a bleached blonde pixie cut in later years, she'd had long brown hair at school. To distract the girl, she let out a loud laugh. "Well, ma'am, ain't that the nicest thing anyone's said to me since I got a compliment for my candied yams last Thanksgiving. I hear she was a real beauty. But I'm sure as cotton grows in the fields that I ain't got half her class."

Elizabeth gave a tight smile, which seemed to convince the onlookers that this Mary-Beth really was a crass and as uncouth as she appeared. Faye just prayed they didn't suggest they join their table.

She was just standing up, ready to use the excuse of needing the ladies' room to get away from them, when she caught sight of a tall figure striding towards them. She blinked, hoping she was hallucinating. This whole thing had already turned into a farce of epic proportions. But no, Jeff Mackay was no illusion. He kept on coming, wearing a half-decent suit and a 'Gotcha' smirk on his face.

With a shriek, she ran to meet him, launching herself into his arms and wrapping her legs around his behind. He caught her and nearly stumbled. *Serves him right.* She grabbed his face, pinching his cheek and jaw, and pulled his head down. She gave him a loud, smacking kiss, then nuzzled his neck.

"I don't know why the hell you're here," she murmured into his ear. "But if you value your balls, you'd better play along with me and don't, whatever you do, use our names. Just play dumb. Understand?"

A slight nod of his head was all she needed. She untangled herself from him, grabbed his hand and dragged him over to the table. Her mother was pale with anxiety. Chip looked like he wanted to laugh, and Tabitha looked horrified, yet as reluctantly fascinated as the rest of the restaurant's patrons, who were trying to ignore the display.

"Aunt Betty," said Faye, pulling Jeff to her side. "This here's my beau, Junior. He rode up with me on the Greyhound bus, but he got a little shy about coming in a fancy place like this, even though he brought his best suit with him. Ain't he handsome?" She grinned up at him. "I guess you got tired of waiting, huh, honey?"

"Uh, yeah, *sweet cheeks*," he murmured. "Pleased to meet you, ma'am." He nodded in Elizabeth's direction and reached across the table to shake her hand. He was clearly so confused by this situation that Faye felt she had the upper hand. She didn't expect it to last long.

"How do you do?" said her mother, smiling at Jeff. "I'm Elizabeth Broughton."

Faye ground her teeth together. *Why the hell did she tell him her name?*

Jeff didn't seem to notice Faye's irritation. He looked at the couple standing by the table.

"Chip Garroway." Tabitha's fiancé held out his hand. Jeff shook it, nodding, but not offering his name when Faye dug her nails into the palm of his other hand. "And this is my fiancée, Tabitha Fairbrother, from England." Again Jeff shook and mumbled.

"Would you like to join us, er, Junior?" asked Elizabeth.

Again Faye dug her nails into his hand. She did not want him sitting down with her mother, especially with Tabby bloody Fairbrother and her spineless wonder watching. Jeff looked at her, his eyebrows raised. Faye made a show of picking up his hand and turning it over so that she could see his watch.

She shook her head. "I'm real sorry, Aunt Betty, but if we don't get going right now, we're going to miss our bus. Then we'll miss our connection and end up sleeping on a bench in the bus station in some hell-hole like Wichita. Trust me. That's not a place to be in the middle of the night."

"You're leaving?" For a moment, Elizabeth's composure faltered but she quickly recovered. She looked at Tabitha and Chip, a polite smile on her face. "Do excuse me while we say our goodbyes. Lord knows when I'll see my young cousin again. Do give my regards to your mother, Tabitha, and congratulations on your engagement."

The couple nodded and moved away. Faye let out a breath and gave her mother a faint nod.

"Good to meet y'all," she called after them, grinning like an idiot.

When they were out of earshot, she moved towards her mother. "Thank you. I'm sorry I've landed you with a redneck branch of the family to explain away, but it was all I could think of at short notice."

Her mother hugged her – another first. "I'm so sorry, darling. Please forgive me," she whispered in her ear.

"Of course. It doesn't matter," she replied, her tone soft. "It was another lifetime."

"So long as you're happy."

"I am." *As happy as I ever expect to be. But I'm not going to admit to that without losing what little dignity I have left.*

They stepped back. Faye didn't know what to say. She hadn't ever expected to see her mother again, and after today she was sure she never would. She felt a lump growing in her throat. She took a deep breath and pulled on her hillbilly persona again.

"Now you have a good time on that fancy cruise ship, Aunt Betty. Maybe find yourself a good man, like I have." She beamed up at Jeff, who stood beside her, watching them. He gave her a slow smile, then indicated his watch again.

"Time to go, baby. It was good to meet you, ma'am."

"You too, young man. Look after her for me, won't you?"

"I'll do that, ma'am. For sure."

"Oh!" She turned to Faye again. "I nearly forgot. I have something for you." She picked up her handbag and took out a neatly-wrapped package. "Your grandmother wanted you to have these. You should have been given them years ago, after she died. But your father… Well anyway, they're yours now."

Faye took the package and put it in her bag. She kissed her mother's cheek and walked away. Jeff followed behind her.

Chapter Thirty-Eight

"Don't say a word," she said through clenched teeth as they crossed the lobby. "Just get me out of here."

He nodded, slipping an arm around her shoulder and pulling her close. He expected her to pull away, but she didn't. It was almost like she needed him. He looked down at her face as they emerged into the noise and confusion of New York City. She looked fragile, almost broken.

"Where we headed?" he asked. "I got a hotel room if you want some quiet time."

She glanced up at him then looked away. "I just want to get as far away from here as possible before I encounter another of bloody Tabitha Fairbrother's ilk."

He wasn't sure he understood the last few actual words she just said, but he got their meaning. With a nod he led her along the sidewalk, pulling her out of the way of the suits and skirts who rushed on by.

They were silent as they walked, each lost in their own thoughts. Jeff couldn't shake the feeling that the older woman was Faye's mother. They might not have the same coloring and they acted like they were just meeting today, but he'd seen Faye with that same fake smile and air of entitlement as Elizabeth Broughton had used, especially when she was guarding her secrets. People said he was just like his daddy when he laughed or got mad. A regular chip off the old block. Just like Faye and Elizabeth Broughton.

He didn't know why the other two had been there – they clearly weren't planning on joining Faye and her companion before the girl had spotted them. But whoever they were, whatever their reason for being there, they had the two women rattled, for sure. He'd watched their little show, and knew damned well that Faye had been putting on an Oscar-winning performance back there.

Well, today was the day she told him who the hell she was. Because if she didn't, he'd get his buddy investigating this Elizabeth Broughton woman and finding out why she was pretending that her own daughter was nothing more than a hick cousin.

He took her straight up to his hotel room. When he closed the door behind them, she sagged into a chair and rested her head on her arms on the little table that filled the space under the window.

"You okay?" he asked.

She nodded but didn't lift her head.

"You hungry?"

She shook her head. "I had a steak," she said, her voice weary.

"Mind if I order something from room service? I didn't get the fancy lunch I was planning."

She raised her head slowly and looked at him, her eyes narrowed. "Don't for one minute think I'm going to believe it was a coincidence you were there. You bloody followed me."

"Yep. Let me order food, then we can talk."

For a second, he thought she was going to jump up and leave. He was ready to stand in her way, but then she closed her eyes and dropped her head again.

"Do what you like," she said, her voice weary and defeated.

He figured he'd won that round, but this fight was gonna be a long one. He picked up the phone and rang in his order, adding an extra side of fries and a couple of desserts. Her meal had been interrupted, so maybe once he started eating she'd feel like eating with him.

They waited in silence. Jeff took off his jacket and tie and kicked off his shoes and sat on the edge of the bed, massaging his thigh. It was better than it was, but the tension of the past couple of days left him aching. Faye remained where she was, her head in her arms. It was only when he saw her shoulders moving that he realised she was weeping silently.

He got up and went to her, resting a hand on her back. "Aw, honey, don't cry," he said, his voice gentle. "Come here." He scooped her up, turning her so that she rested against his chest.

She stiffened in his arms, but he held her tight, not letting her push him away. Then all the fight seemed to drain out of her and she dropped her head onto his shoulder and wept. He held her, whispering and stroking her hair, trying to comfort her. They remained standing there in the middle of his hotel room until someone knocked on the door.

"Room service," called a voice from the hallway.

Faye stepped away from him, scrubbing at her face. She didn't look at him as she turned and walked into the bathroom. After she closed and locked the door, Jeff let the waiter in.

"Leave it on the table. Thanks," he said, handing him a tip.

Faye didn't come out of the bathroom until the waiter had gone. Her eyes were red and puffy, but she held her head high and was back in control of her emotions. She still looked damned beautiful, yet at the same time still fragile and broken.

"Want to eat?"

She shook her head. "I don't suppose you ordered any booze? Is there a minibar?"

He tilted his head. "I can do better than that," he said, walking over to his bag on the luggage rack. He delved inside and came out with one of her bottles of Scotch.

She put her hands on her hips and shook her head. "So, not only did you follow me, but you also stole from my supplies."

"Not stolen. I just had a hunch that you might appreciate it when I caught up with you."

"You're not wrong, cowboy," she said, retrieving a couple of glasses from the bathroom.

Neither spoke as they filled their glasses. Faye raised hers towards him in a silent toast before knocking it back in one gulp then pouring another.

"Woah, easy, tiger. It's meant to be savored, remember?"

"Sod that," she said. "I've had a bitch of a few days, ending in a triple ambush, so don't you dare preach to me, Junior." She knocked back the second whisky.

"Come and eat."

"I'm not hungry."

"Well, sit with me while I eat. I'll get indigestion with you hovering."

With a roll of her eyes, she sat opposite him at the tiny table. As he chowed down, she stared out of the window. He watched her, noting her perfect profile. He knew that the other side of her face was damaged, still hidden beneath her hair, but from this angle she was flawless.

"I don't think much of your view," she said eventually. They were downtown, a few floors up, looking out onto even taller buildings opposite. This hotel wasn't nearly as fancy as the Waldorf. He wondered if she meant that, or was letting him know that he was staring at her.

"I didn't come here for the view," he said.

"You could've just asked, you know. You didn't need to chase me halfway across the country."

"I did ask. You told me to mind my own business. Then you lit out of there leaving a note saying you were heading to the Yukon."

"A little joke, darling, although it's still an option. Everyone's searching for their own El Dorado," she smirked. "And yet, here you are. Nowhere near the Yukon, doing what you do best. Interfering."

He put down his half-eaten burger, his appetite gone. "I get the impression I performed a rescue operation back there. You were downright happy to see me."

"Did you enjoy my performance? I was thinking of Ellie-May Clampett. I do enjoy The Beverley Hillbillies. It reminds me of some of my more *nouveau-riche* acquaintances. They try so hard, but they just don't have the breeding to gain true acceptance in certain circles."

"Does that make me Ellie-May's dopey cousin?" He smiled, storing away more clues to who this enigmatic woman was.

"Well, he is a handsome beast. A bit dim, but it doesn't seem to hold him back." For a moment her expression clouded, as though she was thinking of someone else.

"You know someone like that?" he asked softly.

She took a deep breath. "Not any more."

"Why? Where'd he go?"

"To Hell, probably. He was no angel, the bloody fool." She

turned to look at the food on the table. "You know, maybe I am a little hungry. Can I nick some of your chips, darling?"

"Chips?"

"I mean fries. I keep forgetting that we speak different languages."

"You call fries chips?" he asked, offering her the bowl. "So what do you call chips?"

"Crisps," she said, selecting a fry and eating it.

He nodded. "A reasonable definition. But it'll never catch on here."

"And never tell a British man to straighten his pants, darling. He'll probably punch you. They're trousers. Pants are underwear." She shook her head. "That's not the worst of it. I once asked someone if I could borrow a rubber, and he handed me a condom from his wallet."

"You asked a guy for—"

"He misunderstood. I wasn't coming on to him, I needed an *eraser*. I never made that mistake again."

He laughed and took a sip of his whisky. He was getting a taste for this stuff; it was damned fine.

Once she started eating, she kept on going. She finished his burger and half the fries. Jeff ate the apple pie with cream, and Faye finished off the peach cobbler he'd ordered. He was satisfied that she'd eaten, because it hadn't looked like she'd finished much of that fancy steak back at the Waldorf before the circus had arrived. At least now there was something in her stomach to soak up the Scotch she continued to drink, and she didn't look like she was going to start bawling again. He guessed it was just the calm before the storm she would soon unleash on him about following her to New York and sticking his nose in her business.

The hell with that, he thought. *Time to go on the offensive.*

"I guess it was nice to see your mom again."

She put down her glass and went very still. "What makes you think she's my mother?"

He shrugged. "Oh, not much. Just your eyes, the way you both walk, the way you look when you don't want anyone to know what you're feeling." He paused. "You're a regular chip off the old block. Oh, and the fact that she asked me to take care of you, and you were acting crazy, trying to protect her."

She sneered at him. "You got all that from, what, thirty seconds' acquaintance?"

"I saw you in the lobby with her before you went into the restaurant."

"Dear God, haven't you got anything better to do than to spy on me?"

"My daddy said I needed to take care of you. That's what I'm doing."

"Don't give me that. You can't wait to see the back of me."

He shrugged. "Maybe. Or maybe I'm getting used to having you around. I like puzzles." *It sure keeps my mind off the mess of my own damned life.*

"I'm not a bloody jigsaw," she snapped.

"Yeah you are. A thousand pieces, all waiting for me to put together into a beautiful picture."

She shook her head, pouring another drink. "It's not beautiful. Trust me. You really don't want to solve this puzzle. It will make you sick."

"You think I can't handle the truth? After a dozen years in the army and three in 'Nam, I've got a strong stomach."

She focused her gaze on the whisky in her glass and said nothing. He waited. He had so many questions floating around his mind. He was pretty sure from her reaction that Elizabeth Broughton really was her mother. She certainly hadn't denied it. He filled his own glass and prepared to wait until she decided she could trust him.

The thought that he wanted her to trust him was a surprise. *When the hell did I decide to trust her? She married my dad in secret, has been living under an assumed name, and just demonstrated acting skills that would win her an Oscar if she was in the movies. I have no reason to trust this woman.*

But he realised he had wanted to trust her the moment he felt her trembling in his arms even as she gave the performance of her life. She'd been shielding her mom, and him, even as she was protecting herself from whatever threat was represented by that English girl and her preppie boyfriend.

Chapter Thirty-Nine

The food she shared with Jeff helped to settle her stomach. She'd been expecting to vomit since the moment Tabitha and that creep Chip had appeared. The whisky took the edge off her shattered nerves. She hadn't known what to expect from this meeting with her mother, but the reality had been a surreal nightmare that even her sick mind couldn't have summoned up.

The relief she'd felt when she saw Jeff walking towards her in the middle of that fiasco surprised her. Surely she should have wanted to rage at him. He was invading her privacy, following her, forcing her to contemplate yet another upheaval in her life. He was like a dog with a bloody bone. If she didn't leave right now, he wouldn't stop until he knew everything.

Yet he'd accepted her desperate command to follow her lead, and he hadn't given her away. He'd protected her and helped her escape an intolerable situation. He'd been her knight in shining armour.

In the midst of all of that ridiculous situation, she was aware that – for the first time in her life – she had felt love from her mother. Faye was sure the woman really cared. For once, she wasn't judging or demanding or punishing her. She just wanted to spend time with her daughter and for Faye to be happy. It was ironic that the one time they had connected was probably the last time they would ever meet. It was inconceivable that they could arrange another meeting. Faye would never come to New York again, and she doubted her mother would be able to travel to some one-horse town in the wilds of cowboy country without attracting far too much attention. She was just too damned British.

Faye felt tears well up again, but she blinked them away

and swallowed some more whisky.

"She was – is – my mother," she whispered.

Jeff leaned forward, resting his elbows on the table, but didn't say anything.

"We've never had what you'd call a close relationship, but we were actually having quite a nice time." Faye smiled even though the tears still threatened. She kept her gaze on the glass in her hand. She couldn't look at him. "Quite a surprise actually. We usually end up fighting. My fault most of the time. I was a brat when I was younger and a bitch when I got older."

"You a brat?" He pretended to be shocked. "I can't imagine."

"I know." She began to feel better under his gentle teasing. "But that's what you get when you hand your children off to nannies and servants and only engage with them when you want to display them in the right kind of company." Her lips twisted as she acknowledged the bitterness behind that statement. "Do you know, that's the first time I ever remember my mother giving me a proper hug?"

She blinked again, determined that she'd cried all she was going to. Tears wouldn't change anything. She needed to buck up her ideas, just as she'd been taught time and again when she'd ever whined about anything.

"She must miss you."

"I know. Strange, isn't it? She never did before."

He topped up her glass. She nodded her thanks and kept on drinking. If she was going to do this, she might as well drink herself numb. It occurred to her that this was becoming a bad habit. She'd worry about it all later.

"How did you know where I was?" she asked, looking at him for the first time since she'd started speaking.

"I heard you on the phone. It didn't sound like you was looking forward to the trip."

"No. I couldn't see the point. But Grainger can be very persuasive, and I didn't want to let him down. I told him it would be a mistake."

"From what I remember of him, he's a cool guy. Wise. He

wouldn't make you do something if it was a bad idea."

"I suppose so," she sighed. "Well, it's done now. I got my first and last hug from my dear mother, and then bloody fucking Tabitha shows up. What are the odds?"

He didn't comment on her language. "Who was she?"

"Her mother was one of my mother's cronies and we went to the same school. We weren't friends, but we often got lumbered with each other when our parents were partying together."

"Why didn't you want her to recognise you?"

She shook her head. "Give me a break, will you? It's like the bloody Inquisition. I've already told you more than I should."

"Got nothing better to do," he said mildly, sipping his drink. "The room's booked until tomorrow. I'm guessing you don't wanna go out on the town, so all we got is time to talk. Clear the air."

"Is that what you think this is? A nice cosy chat to *clear the air?*" she scoffed. "More like an interrogation."

"You're not a prisoner," he said, his tone mild even as his eyes frosted over. "You can leave any time. But I'm guessing you feel safe here, or you'd have split already."

She looked away. She could leave. She could walk away and lose herself in this vast country and never see him again. It would be the sensible thing to do. But she couldn't summon the energy to move.

"I just don't see why I should be the only one to bare my soul," she said. "What about you, soldier? Are you going to tell me about your nightmares?"

Even as she said it, she wanted to call the words back. She never talked about her own nightmares. What would be the point? It wouldn't change them. So why was she so interested in getting him to tell her everything? She tried to tell herself it was to get him to stop coming after her with his damned questions, but she couldn't help the treacherous little idea that what was driving her was more than that. She remembered his anguish that first time. Ignoring his subsequent nightmares had been impossible, even though she'd kept her distance. The pain in his voice as he cried out tormented her. She wanted to know what haunted him. She wanted to be able to stop it.

But there's nothing to be gained. I can't take his nightmares away. He can't take mine away. We're both hiding in that cabin, each locked in our own prisons, reliving our respective hells.

As she went to retract her words, he caught her gaze and spoke.

"I'll tell you mine if you tell me yours. Fair trade, don't ya think?"

She stilled. She hadn't expected the devil to make a deal with her. She thought she'd call his bluff.

"Are you serious?"

"Yep. I figure it's better to unload on you than my sister. She'd see it as an excuse to mother me for the rest of my life."

"She can be a bit bossy," Faye mused. "She means well, though." *God knows, she got me off my backside and into a routine that probably saved my life.*

He grimaced. "I know. That's why I don't want to dump this shit on her."

"But you'll dump it on me, if only to get me to dump my own shit on you?" She shook her head. "Forgive me, but that sounds rather sick to me."

Jeff sat back, stretching his leg out and rubbing his thigh. "I reckon we both need to let some of our poison out. Maybe you're the only person I've met lately who's strong enough to take it. Or am I wrong, Princess? Are you all smoke and mirrors? All piss and vinegar? Are you hiding out because you can't deal with it? Or are you comfortable in your little sanctuary in the backwoods?"

"I'm not so strong," she said, suddenly exhausted. "I'm just a bloody mess."

"So why not go home to Mama? Looked to me that maybe she'd like that."

"I can't."

"Sure you can."

She closed her eyes. Despite the tentative truce with her mother, she had no illusions that their relationship wouldn't still be fraught – there was too much bitterness and regret between them.

She opened her eyes and looked at him. He had no idea.

"No, I can't. Because Elizabeth Broughton's daughter is dead. She no longer exists, other than as a name on a gravestone."

Chapter Forty

Well, hell, that explains a lot. His buddy had been looking for Faye Evens when she'd been someone else. "What was her name?" he asked, as his mind whirled with a thousand other questions.

"Felicity. Usually known as Fliss," she sighed.

"So where did Faye Evens come from?"

She shrugged. "Faye is another iteration of Felicity. I thought it would be easier to stick to something close."

"And Evens?"

She smiled, yet he felt the sadness coming off her in waves. "My favourite nanny."

He nodded. The picture was beginning to come into focus. But that didn't explain why she'd had to fake her death. He opened his mouth to ask, but she raised a hand to stop him.

"Your turn. Who were you trying to kill when you were throttling me?"

He hesitated, his whole being shying away from opening that can of worms. Not just the fear and pain his nightmares evoked, but the anguish he'd felt when he realised he'd hurt her.

"Come on, Junior. Don't you think I have a right to know? What happened to our bargain?"

He looked away. She was right. He didn't have to like it, but he owed her an explanation.

"A fucking spook. An enemy soldier who had taken a family hostage and sent their two-year-old daughter out to us with a live grenade in her hand. She was killed, along with my buddy. I only survived because I got shot and was on the ground when it exploded."

"Did you kill him?"

He shook his head. "Not me. I was useless, screaming like a

baby. One of my patrol got him."

"But you wanted to."

He glared at her. "Wouldn't you?"

"Of course. I'm not criticizing. I know what it's like to want to commit murder but not be able to do so."

He took a deep breath, blowing out the tension that made him ache. "The guy who attacked you?"

"What makes you think it was a man? Maybe I got caught in a cat fight."

"Nah. I don't buy it. You'd have more scratch marks. Women fight dirty."

She laughed. "True." She looked down at her hands, which cradled her almost empty glass. "You should've brought more than one bottle," she said, nodding towards the bottle. There was just a couple of inches of whisky left in it, but she didn't pour any more. "But no, my assassin wasn't important. It was his bosses I wanted to kill."

"Why?"

"Because they were the scum of the earth. They preyed on people, and ruined them."

"Did they ruin you?"

"Oh no. I managed that all by myself. I thought I was untouchable. But I wasn't. I deserved to die."

He leaned on the table again, trying to make sense of what she was saying. "But you didn't die. You're still here. What the hell happened, Faye?"

She poured the last of the Scotch into her glass before she answered. She stood up, staring out of the window onto the street below where life was going on in New York time. He got up and joined her, trying to see what she saw – people rushing along the sidewalks; cars, trucks and yellow cabs, bumper to bumper; a kid on the corner, hawking newspapers. On the opposite corner, a hotdog stand was doing a brisk trade.

"I killed my brother and my boyfriend," she said suddenly.

He blinked, surprised by her blunt statement. "Really?"

She shrugged. "I didn't exactly slay them with my bare hands, but they died because of me."

"What did you do?"

She took a deep breath and blew it out. "I was greedy, manipulative and bloody stupid." She drained the last of the Scotch and put the glass down on the table, turning away from him. "Is it all right if I have a shower? I'm feeling grubby."

His head was reeling. *That's it? That's all she's going to say?*

"You haven't finished," he said, putting a hand on her arm to stop her.

She froze. She didn't turn around. Instead, she glanced at him over her shoulder. "I think we've both revealed more than enough for one day, don't you? Do you really want to air all your dirty laundry in one go?"

"How much more is there?" he demanded, wanting to shake it all out of her.

She smirked. "More than you can handle, big boy."

He felt his rage building at her snarky words. "What's to stop me from checking out your story? I know your real name now. It shouldn't be hard."

For a moment he caught a flicker of fear and something else in her eyes. But Faye was still the ornery woman he'd first met that night outside his cabin. Her expression went cool and she lifted her chin.

"Do what you like. If you're that desperate to know all the sordid details, it's all out there. But the moment you start stirring up that hornets' nest, you'd better be prepared for the hounds of Hell who'll come looking for you."

"What the hell does that mean?"

She rolled her eyes. "Use your brain. There's a reason I moved halfway around the world and changed my name."

"You running from the law?" he asked.

"No." She looked down her nose at him. "Do you honestly think your father would harbour a fugitive?"

"Good point. But you think someone's still looking for you."

"They might not have been up to now," she sighed. "But I can guarantee that Tabitha will be telling everyone she'd seen Fliss Broughton's double in New York, and pretty soon someone will be sent to check it out." She pulled away from his grasp. "But don't worry, I'm moving on. I'll be long gone before they get to Montana. Just be prepared for them to turn up on your doorstep that much quicker if you act like a bull in a china shop and start digging into my past."

"I can handle it."

"Good for you. But what about your sister and her family? Are you prepared to put them at risk just because you can't mind your own bloody business?"

"So don't make me go and find out for myself," he said. "Tell me."

She shook her head. "Just drop it, all right?"

"No can do, Princess. Why not just get it all out there in the open?"

She looked up at the ceiling. "Because you'll hate me," she yelled. "You'll realise what a vile specimen of humanity I am, and then I'll have to put up with your disgust and loathing and… and… I just can't do that again, okay?"

She spun around, grabbed something from her bag and rushed into the bathroom, slamming the door behind her. The click of the lock was like a gunshot. Jeff flinched.

A few seconds later he heard water running and the swish of the shower curtain over the bathtub. He closed his eyes against the images of a naked Faye standing under the hot water. There was never a good time to be thinking lustful things about that woman, but it took a hell of an effort to banish his X-rated thoughts.

He ran a weary hand over his face. He hadn't drunk as much as she had, but he could feel the effects of the whisky in his system. He looked at his watch. It was just coming up to four o'clock. He had no idea what to do. He'd casually told her they had all night to talk, but now the reality of them sharing a room with just one bed didn't appeal. He couldn't throw her out. Nor did he want her to leave.

They'd come so far. He had learned a lot more about her, and things were starting to make sense. But now she had clammed up again, leaving vital gaps in the puzzle.

He took a couple of steps and sank down onto the bed, lying on his back with an arm across his face. *Damn, I'm tired.* But he was also wired. As weary as his body was, he couldn't stop his mind going round and around like crazy. *What the fuck was she involved in? What was so awful that it got two men killed and forced her to fake her own death? Is she really still in danger?*

The water shut off and he waited for her to emerge. She took her time. He imagined her drying her body with a towel, heard the tell-tale hiss of a deodorant spray, then the whine of a hairdryer. It was a good twenty minutes before she emerged, her newly-washed hair falling around her shoulders. She wore a pair of jeans and a tee-shirt, and was folding her dress into her large purse.

"Is that all your luggage?" he asked, pointing at the purse.

She nodded. "I didn't want to carry a lot."

"But you've been travelling for a few days."

She shrugged. "I was on buses for a couple of days, so I didn't change. I dumped what I'd been wearing when I got to Chicago last night. It was old stuff anyway. I still had this change of clothes, and I brought the dress because it was the only thing I thought I could get away with at the Waldorf. I even got someone at a drugstore to put some make-up on me this morning. She thought I was going to buy all the products she was demonstrating." She pulled a face. "I gave her a generous tip instead. No point in buying stuff I'll never use."

"Don't you ever want to get gussied up and go out on the town?" he asked. "Go on a date, maybe?"

She shook her head. "No thank you," she said firmly. "I've been there and done that. No need to repeat past mistakes."

"You looked good in the dress."

"Thank you. It makes a change from jeans."

He lay with his head propped up on the pillows, wondering how they'd ended up having such an innocuous conversation after the high-tension words they'd exchanged before.

She came and sat on the other side of the bed. "I need to call Grainger," she said. "Warn him about Tabitha."

"Is he in danger?"

"God, no. He wasn't involved in my mess. He extracted me from it. I need to talk to him about what I'm going to do."

"I don't think you should do anything."

"What do you mean?" she frowned.

"Even if this woman does blow your cover, she thinks you're

headed for Wichita."

"Alabama actually, with a bus change in Wichita. If she was listening, that is," she said. "She's not the brightest spark, so I'm not even sure she was paying attention. She was too busy staring at me and thinking she was looking at a ghost."

"My point is, she'll be talking about some hick from down south, while you'll be safely in Montana."

"And my point is, once they get wind of the fact that I still exist, they'll leave no stone unturned in their efforts to find me."

"Where would you go?"

She shrugged. "Doesn't matter. They'll find me eventually."

"Then why run?"

"What?"

He sat up and took her hand and waited until she turned to look at him. Her gaze was guarded. He couldn't work out whether she was scared or resigned. "This is a big country. It's not so easy to find someone if they don't want to be found."

"Except that I've been to New York twice now, and each time I've bumped into someone I know. That's why I've been hiding in Montana."

"So let's get you back there. You don't even know if anyone will listen to the girl. She's staying in New York with that Chip guy, isn't she? It could be months or even longer before she goes back to England."

"She's close to her mother. She'll be on the telephone to her by now, gushing over the amazing coincidence of being at the Waldorf at the same time as my mother. And her mother has the biggest mouth of anyone south of Watford."

"Is Watford where you come from?" he asked.

Faye burst out laughing. "No. Good grief, no one wants to live in Watford! It's just a turn of phrase. It means she's a terrible gossip."

He shook his head and smiled. "Right. Our common language, huh?"

She nodded, looking a little more relaxed. "Anyway, I should call Grainger."

"Okay," Jeff agreed. "But I want to talk to him as well."

Chapter Forty-One

Grainger agreed with Jeff. "Go back to Montana. You're safe there. The Mackay family will protect you. In the meantime, I'll make sure your mother is safe."

She wasn't happy about it. Okay, so Jeff was a soldier with certain skills that would be useful in a fight, but he still had a gammy leg and no idea what he was likely to come up against. Her biggest worry, though, was Sally and her children. She knew that her enemies wouldn't hesitate to hurt them if it meant getting to Faye. When she said as much, neither man could reassure her that they would stay safe.

"I'm not prepared to put innocent children at risk," she said. "I must go."

"Think about it, my dear," said Grainger. "I'm having trouble finding somewhere suitable for you. If you strike out on your own, I can't guarantee being able to protect you, and you'll have to build up your own network to help keep you safe."

Jeff, who'd been standing beside her, the phone handset between them, listening to what the other man had to say, nodded. "He's right. I can keep you safe. Sal doesn't even need to know."

Faye felt a knot of tension in her stomach. The Scotch she'd drank wasn't helping, although she felt far from drunk. She felt torn. Part of her wanted to run and never stop. Yet another part of her wanted to lock herself away in the cabin in Montana and hope they never found her. With Jeff at her side, she might stand a chance. She just didn't know whether she could accept his help and put him and his family's lives at risk. She'd only agreed to the arrangement with his father because she hadn't known his family, and she selfishly hadn't cared to think about it. While Jefferson had been alive and she'd had the cabin to herself, she'd allowed herself to start to hope that she'd be safe and that none of the Mackays would be affected. But it hadn't stopped her being prepared to run – as illustrated when Jeff had turned up out of the blue. She didn't want to think about how awful she'd felt at that moment.

But if she did go back to Montana and they found her there, it could be a bloodbath. They wanted her dead, and they wouldn't leave any witnesses. She knew everyone who lived and worked on the Mackay ranch now, and they would all be in danger. Their blood would be on her hands. Could she risk it?

"You don't know these people," she hissed at Jeff. She hadn't been able to keep her brother or James alive. She'd been living with the guilt of their deaths all this time. She couldn't add any more wasted lives to her burden. It would break her for good this time.

Jeff shrugged as Grainger remained silent. "I've spend a dozen years in the army," he said. "I've evaded capture in Vietnam. I'm not about to let some low-life invade my home and hurt my family." He held up a hand. "And before you say it, you *are* family. Dad made sure of that."

"He's got a good point," said Grainger. "I trusted Jefferson to keep you safe, and I have no reason to think that his son won't do the same. Think about it, Faye. I'll keep things as low-key as I can here. If I get the slightest hint that your cover has been blown, I'll let you know immediately."

Faye searched Jeff's face. She wasn't sure what she was looking for. Doubt, maybe, or suspicion. But he seemed to sincerely want to help her. She couldn't imagine why. She wasn't worth it.

She sighed, making a decision. "Before you recruit him, Grainger, you'd better tell him the whole sordid story. He might not be so keen when he knows what I've done and what I'm really like." She handed the phone to Jeff. "I'm going for a walk. I'll be back in an hour. If you still want to help me then, I'll go back with you. If you don't, leave my bag outside the door and I'll leave immediately."

She took her wallet from her bag and left the room. As she closed the door, she heard Jeff demanding to know what the hell she was talking about.

She didn't walk far. She didn't want to take any more risks. She found a coffee shop in a side street and sat in a booth at the back, nursing a black coffee. She hated the stuff, but didn't want to draw attention to herself by asking for a cup of tea. They'd probably give her a cup of that revoltingly sweet iced tea that Americans seemed to love.

She sat quietly, ignoring the bustle of people around her and the sound of records playing on the juke box in the corner. She barely noticed when someone put on Helen Reddy's *Leave Me Alone.*

As she waited for the hour to pass, she worked out what she would do. If she had to run again, it would make sense for her to stay in the US now that she had an American passport and documentation, thanks to her marriage to Jefferson Mackay, so long as her enemies didn't find out her new name. But the further she could get from New York, the better. She would avoid Alabama and even Wichita, just in case dopey Tabitha actually remembered what 'Mary-Beth' had said. It wouldn't be fair to the Mackays to stay in Montana, no matter how much her heart was aching to stay there. But maybe another mountain state? She'd fallen in love with the peaks that protected the valley where she'd found peace for the first time in her life. When Elvis's *Blue Hawaii* came on the juke box, she took that as a sign. Hawaii had mountains and was still in the United States, but it was separated from the mainland by thousands of miles of ocean. She allowed herself a small smile at the thought. That should be far enough.

Her mind went round and round, not daring to hope that Jeff would let her stay. She was sure he'd reject her – after all, why would he want someone like her anywhere near his family? She hadn't understood why his father had accepted her. She had insisted he be told everything, yet Grainger had persuaded his friend to give her sanctuary and even his own name. She couldn't imagine him being able to do the same with the younger man. Jeff Junior was far more cynical and suspicious than his father. No doubt his time in the hell of Vietnam had shaped him.

Even as she tried to accept that she would have to start

again, she couldn't help but worry who would be around to help Jeff deal with his demons. His sister loved him, but she had no idea what it was like to relive terrible events night after night. Only someone who had their own nightmares could understand. Someone like Faye.

But I'm no good for him either, she thought. *I'm only likely to make things worse. He doesn't deserve that.*

Even as the thoughts formed in her mind, a little part of herself was screaming at her that she didn't deserve any of this either. She fought it down, refusing to listen. She *did* deserve this. She was guilty of so many vile acts that she must pay for. It didn't matter that she hadn't meant to hurt anyone, because nevertheless, people had died because of her.

Someone put another dime in the juke box, and Faye wiped her silent tears away as she listened to Mick Jagger singing *You Can't Always Get What You Want.* Would she ever get what she wanted and needed?

Before she left, Faye slipped her own dime into the juke box. Her heart wanted to select *If You Want Me To Stay* by Sly and the Family Stone. But her head led her fingers to select The Zombies' hit *She's Not There.* It seemed more appropriate somehow – and no more than she deserved.

Chapter Forty-Two

Jeff sat on the edge of the bed, trying to make sense of everything Grainger had told him. In some ways it all made a whole mess of sense. Yet the picture the Englishman had painted of Faye's old life was so alien to him that he found it hard to believe.

Okay, so he'd called her a princess and a cold bitch, but even as she'd encouraged his bad opinions of her, she'd shown through her actions that she wasn't the spoilt, uncaring monster she wanted him to think she was. She'd helped him when his wound was bleeding, even though he'd scared her half to death by showing up in the middle of the night. She'd tried to wake him from his nightmare and refused to let him wallow in self-pity, even after he'd physically hurt her. She'd protected him from everyone when he'd freaked out over the gunshot – and more importantly, she'd saved his niece's life.

She'd fed him. She'd let him reclaim his bed, even though it meant she had to climb a ladder to the attic to sleep up there. She'd taken good care of Ebony and Bear, and had shared the produce from her garden and chickens with everyone at the ranch house.

Today, she'd tried her darnedest to protect her mom. Yet, from what Grainger had told him, and a couple of throwaway remarks Faye had made, it was clear that Elizabeth Broughton had been a rather less than loving mother. He couldn't help feeling anger towards the woman who, after years of pushing Faye aside, had suddenly wanted to make contact with her daughter after all this time, and by doing so had once again put her in danger. Faye had been through enough.

He looked at his watch. She'd been gone for more than hour. Where was she? Had she just taken off anyway? He got up and looked out of the window, trying to spot her amongst the crowds on the sidewalk below. When he couldn't see her, he grabbed his key and opened the door, determined to go and find her.

Faye was sitting on the floor next to the door, her back against the wall, knees up, her head in her hands. She looked up with a gasp when he stood over her.

"What are you doing?" he asked.

"Waiting for my bag," she said.

She didn't look at him. She was pale and tense.

"It's inside."

"It's been an hour. You can bring it out."

She expects me to cut her loose. "No. You come in. We leave together, back to Montana." He held out a hand and waited.

She stared at it, not moving. "Didn't Grainger tell you?"

"Yeah, he did. And I told him you're coming home with me."

She kept staring at his hand like it was going to hurt her. She blinked rapidly. "It's not safe. You'll be in danger."

He shrugged. "I reckon we're in more danger here in a hotel hallway, or outside on the streets of the city, than we'll ever be at home. Come on."

For a second or two, she looked like she was going to argue with him. But he kept his hand out, and eventually she let out a long shaky breath, put a trembling hand in his and stood up. He hid a smile. She was as nervous as a wild mustang. He would need to be patient with her. The shit this woman had put up with had left her unable to trust. He understood that now.

He had recognised a wounded soul when he met her, but he hadn't imagined the things she'd had to endure. She was stronger than she knew. No wonder his dad had wanted to help her. And now she needed him.

It also occurred to him that he needed her too. She was the only one he'd been able to tell about his nightmares. He hadn't even been able to share them with the shrink in the hospital or any of his army buddies, and he sure as hell wasn't about to put that load on his sister's shoulders.

He followed her into the room and shut the door behind them. She turned to look at him as he leaned against the door.

"So, now you know," she said. "Are you sure you want me anywhere near your family?"

"You've been around them for the best part of a year now, and they're still okay."

"Your dad isn't."

"He had a heart condition. He wouldn't slow down. That's what killed him. Not you, not me, not any of our enemies."

"Maybe the pressure of our secret marriage got to him."

He shook his head. "A five-minute ceremony and some paperwork don't make a marriage, Faye. What he shared with my mom was the real deal. What he shared with you was for your protection."

She swallowed hard and nodded. "He was a good man. I miss him."

"Yeah. Me too."

He remembered how furious he'd been when he'd learned about the marriage. He'd been so disappointed in his father, thinking he'd betrayed his mother by marrying a woman young enough to be his daughter. But now he knew the truth, he was proud of his old man. He'd seen someone who needed help and he'd given it. He just wished he'd been around to talk to him about it, to support them.

I'm here now. Dad, if you're up there looking down, I promise I'll step up to the plate. I'll keep her and Sally and everyone at the ranch safe, just like you did.

Faye looked down at her hands. "I'm sorry," she said.

"What for?"

"You didn't ask for any of this. I've taken over your home, your animals, even your truck." She let out a huff of laughter. "I really expected to find my bag outside. You can't possibly want me around, with all my complications."

"You put up with my nightmares," he pointed out.

She raised her head. "I wish I could take them away, but my head is full of my own."

"I know. You don't scream, though." He smiled.

"Oh, I've been known to," she admitted. "I just don't sleep

very much these days."

He nodded. "Well, don't lose out on your rest on my account. I can take it."

She'd been standing in the middle of the room, her arms around her body as though she was holding herself together. Now she moved to the table by the window and sat down. "Are you really sure about this? Grainger didn't try to sugar-coat it, did he?"

"He gave it to me straight. You fucked up, big time, and it nearly got you killed."

"It did kill the others. If it hadn't been for me…"

"From what he told me, they weren't innocent bystanders. They were in as deep as you."

She nodded. "I suppose." She rubbed her eyes. "But I'm the only one who walked away. I have to live with that. They didn't get the chance. It was all so stupid. I was in it for kicks. Anything to wind up my bloody parents. I wanted them to notice me, even if it was just to read me the riot act. How pathetic is that, eh?"

"What were the others in it for?" he asked.

She sighed. "Equally pathetic reasons. James lived his life in the expectation that he'd inherit a fortune from his aunt, but she changed her mind at the last minute. It's his own fault. He never made any effort to go and see the old girl, so she left it to someone who did – her god-daughter. The trouble is, James had spent money he didn't have in anticipation of his inheritance, and he owed a lot to the wrong sort of people."

"He was your boyfriend?"

She shrugged. "On and off. We were more off than on. What you might call a tempestuous relationship. He was an old school friend of my brother. My parents thought he'd be a good catch when he got his inheritance. Not that I wanted to marry him. He was an arse most of the time."

Jeff didn't want to analyse what he was feeling as she talked about this man. He was dead. It was in the past. "What about your brother?"

"Percy?" she said. "What can I say? He was older than me. I was just a pest to him most of the time. But it amused him to push James and me together. He was clever, ambitious and manipulative. He was our parents' golden boy. In their eyes he could do no wrong." She rubbed her eyes again, as though trying to banish the memories of her brother.

"What happened to him?"

"Hit-and-run, right outside his office. He was a solicitor – a lawyer – and was building a reputation for getting even the dodgiest of people off on technicalities. He thought it was a great game, playing the system and helping these people to walk free when they should have been locked up." She laughed. "I thought he was so cool." Her laughter died as quickly as it had arrived. "Then he did a deal with the casino owners to give James a chance to repay his debts by doing a job for them, and I was sent along with him to make sure he behaved."

"The trip to France?"

"Yes. Where bloody James tricked me and ran off with the goods."

Jeff nodded. Once Faye had told Grainger to give him the truth, he hadn't held back. "Did you know you were carrying drugs?"

She shrugged. "Not really. I never asked and I never looked. But anyone with an ounce of sense should have realised what it was. I just didn't want to know. It was the chance of a free holiday – an adventure. Stupid, eh?"

"So James took the drugs, and left you and your brother to face the consequences?"

She nodded. "I suspect he must've thought the package contained cash. He was never into drugs. Whatever he thought, it left Percy and me in a lot of trouble."

Jeff moved to the table and sat opposite her. It looked as though she was lost in her memories. He waited. Part of him wanted to push her, to force her to tell him everything. But another part of him didn't have the stomach for it. She'd been a fool, a poor little rich girl desperate for attention. But the attention she'd got had nearly killed her, left two men dead and changed her life forever.

"I had no idea what James had done. I thought I'd left him

behind because he acted like he had a stomach bug and said he couldn't travel. So I rolled up in the car in which the goods were supposed to be hidden, expecting them to thank me, only to find he'd stolen the package. God, it was awful. I thought they were going to kill me there and then. But instead they told me to find James and get them their merchandise, or be prepared to pay them fifty thousand pounds in compensation." She dropped her head to her chest for a moment before raising it again to look him in the eye. "Even I couldn't put my hand on that kind of money, so I knew I was in trouble. And just to make sure I knew it, they waited outside Percy's office and mowed him down on the street. He never recovered consciousness."

Jeff nodded. Grainger had told him Percy had been in a coma for a few weeks before he died. "So what did you do?"

"I couldn't find James. So I tried to get the money from Charlotte, the woman who'd had his inheritance. Turns out she's Grainger's god-daughter, too. I nearly backed out – I was ready to make a run for it to the continent. After all, if James could disappear, why couldn't I?" She sighed and ran a hand through her hair. "But they were expecting that. They ran my car off the road into a wall."

"Jesus!"

She gave him a crooked smile. "Grainger wasn't going to help me. Not when I'd done a deal with the devil. The accident wasn't enough to do me serious harm; it was just a warning – get the money or else. So I went back to Charlotte, but Grainger and his sidekick were there waiting for me. I ended up in Holloway Prison." She raised her chin. "Did Grainger tell you that I'm a criminal?"

"He said charges were dropped in return for your co-operation."

"It doesn't take it away though. I committed crimes, and I caused death and destruction." Her voice dropped to a whisper. "I don't deserve to live."

He stared at her. She really believed it. "Tell me what you did next," he insisted.

"You know what I did. I told the police everything – all the times and dates, places and faces that my damned photographic memory had stored away. James had been arrested by then and returned to London. He did the same thing. Between us we were responsible for getting dozens of criminals convicted."

"And that's why you were attacked?" He reached out and ran a gentle finger down her left cheek.

She sat back, out of his reach. "Yes. They got James, too, in prison. Only he didn't survive."

Jeff wondered about that. Maybe Grainger had faked this James's death as well. He doubted they'd ever know. The important thing was that Faye had survived.

"So, there you have it," she said. "My whole sordid past. Are you still sure I should go back to Montana with you?"

"Yeah."

"Why?"

"Because you're family."

She scoffed. "You said yourself, a five-minute ceremony and some papers don't make a marriage."

"No, but my dad made a commitment to you, and I'm sticking with it."

For a moment, he thought she might start crying again. But then she took a deep breath and nodded.

"Okay, so the wicked step-mother stays for the time being. Although I'd appreciate it you didn't tell Sally what you've learned today. I've had enough disapproval to last me a lifetime."

Chapter Forty-Three

Faye was exhausted. She hadn't expected the emotions that had been evoked by meeting her mother again after so many years. Nor had she ever wanted to bare her soul and expose her darkest secrets again. Add to that, the sheer terror she'd felt as she'd faced Tabitha Fairbrother, and the despair that had swamped her when she thought she'd have to leave again, alone, for pastures unknown, and it was no wonder she had no reserves left. The whisky she'd drunk in the hope of forgetting just left her feeling sick and disorientated.

Neither of them felt like eating dinner. Instead they lay side by side on the bed, the TV droning on in the background, each lost in their own thoughts. Later, Faye watched the shadows lengthen as she listened to Jeff's slow, deep breaths as he fell asleep. She didn't know how long she lay there, but eventually sleep claimed her too.

She awoke to bright sunlight. Jeff's body was spooned against her back, his arm was draped across her body, his warm breath fluttered over her neck. At some point one of them had pulled a blanket over them, but they were both fully dressed.

She couldn't remember the last time she'd woken up in the arms of a man. Her last relationship – with James – had never been affectionate. She'd hardly ever bothered staying in his bed after they'd had sex. She could never see the point. Neither of them were the type of people to enjoy cuddles. They'd used each other for their own gratification, nothing more. It was all she'd ever known. Her parents were distant, and her brother never showed her anything but contempt or amusement.

Lying in a bed with a sleeping Jeff Mackay draped around

her was a novel experience, one that left her wishing for more while at the same time filling her with tension and the urge to flee. She closed her eyes and tried to relax, but he must have sensed her anxiety because his breathing changed and she realised he was waking up.

When she opened her eyes and glanced over her shoulder, he was staring at her.

"Mornin'," he said, his voice husky with sleep.

She nodded, not trusting herself to say anything. When she went to move away, his grip tightened.

"No nightmares last night," he said. It wasn't a question, merely a statement. Both of them had been so exhausted they'd slept deeply, safe from their demons. "Maybe we should always sleep in the same bed."

She did move away then, wriggling out of his arms to sit on the edge of the mattress. "Easy, tiger." She laughed. "You'll be wanting to have sex next, and that would be a very bad idea."

He lay on his back, watching her. She'd been aware of what she believed the Americans called his 'morning wood' pressing against her bottom. But that didn't mean he fancied her, or even thought of her in any sexual way. He was just a man; he would be in the same physical state even if he'd been alone.

Of course, if she'd found herself in bed with him a few years ago, she wouldn't have thought twice about jumping on him and enjoying his body. He was a good-looking man, after all. But now... now, she was ashamed of the woman she'd been, and couldn't imagine that someone like Jeff would be interested in her for sex – or anything else. She was just a liability he'd inherited from his father. A scarred, bitter liability.

She stood up. "I'm going to freshen up. What's the plan? I had a bus ticket for yesterday, so I need to make new arrangements."

"We'll fly to Billings. I left my car there. I called the airline and got you a ticket."

"Direct? A bit presumptuous, don't you think?"

"Sure. But it's the best way."

She shook her head. "It's not a good idea. Why don't you go that way and I'll take a more roundabout route?"

"No. We travel together. And the sooner we get back to the ranch, the better."

She sighed. "All right. But…"

"Don't fight me on this, Faye. I said I'd protect you. I can do that better at home."

"Even if we lead them there by failing to cover our tracks?"

"No one is going to follow us. Your mom doesn't know where you live, and the couple we saw think you're heading for Alabama. You have no reason to worry."

She pulled a face at him but didn't argue. Instead, she went into the bathroom and locked the door behind her. She hoped he was right. But she had a bad feeling about this.

As she took her time in the bathroom, she heard him talking on the phone. She was pretty sure he made more than one call, but she was in no rush to go back out there. When she was clean, she wasted more time applying body lotion and cleaning her teeth. She only left the bathroom when he banged on the door and told her he needed to use the toilet.

She emerged wearing the same clothes she'd slept in. She thought about changing into her dress while he was in the bathroom, but decided she'd rather be comfortable than presentable. She wasn't out to impress anyone any more.

The seven-hour flight delivered them to Billings Airport in the early evening. They retrieved Jeff's car and headed into the Crazy Mountains. Faye couldn't help but smile as she remembered the first time she'd been told about the name of the mountain range that protected the Mackay lands. It seemed appropriate. She said as much to Jeff as they drove away from the airport.

"Did anyone tell you why they're called the Crazy Mountains?" he asked.

"No."

"They were originally the lands of the Crow tribe, who called them *Awaxaawapìa Pìa,* which means Ominous Mountains. They would go into the mountains on vision quests, and regarded them as sacred. The story is that white men started settling the area and there were attacks by the Crow. One woman lost her entire family and ran into the mountains. She lived there alone and went insane. They were called the Crazy Mountains after that."

Faye shivered. "How appropriate. Do you think I might be that woman reincarnated? No. On second thoughts, don't answer that."

"You don't need to live there alone, Faye. In fact, I think it's time you became part of the community. You'll be safer if everyone is looking out for you."

She shook her head, her lips a thin line. "The more people know I'm there, the more chance they'll betray me."

He didn't say anything more for a while. Faye relaxed as they left Billings behind and the roads became quieter. When he did speak, it took her by surprise.

"You know, most people aren't as bad as you think they are. It's already common knowledge that you're living at my cabin."

"How do they know? I avoid the town. I don't speak to anyone."

"What about the CB radio, Lavender Lady?" he smiled.

"Huh, hardly worth mentioning." She scoffed. "Your father thought I should have some way of contacting the outside world when I refused to have a phone at the cabin. There was already the radio equipment in the truck. He set up my handle and showed me how to use it, but I've never bothered since he made me join in a couple of conversations in the early days to satisfy him I knew how to use it."

"Yet just about every time I'm in town, someone asks me if that English woman is still at the ranch. And even if you don't stop in town, people have seen you driving through in the truck, walking in the hills with Bear or riding Ebony. You're not a secret, Faye."

She frowned. "It's better that I keep my distance. Let's face it, if they knew what you know about me, they'd probably want to run me off the land pretty sharpish."

"I disagree. Anyway, since you saved Amy's life, you've

gained the reputation of being a heroine. They want to get to know you, Faye. I think maybe it's time."

"How the hell do they know about that?"

"The ranch hands talked about it in the bar. Pete told his teacher. Word gets around."

"Well it's no more than anyone else would do," she huffed. "They need to mind their own business."

"If you hadn't been there, my niece would have died. Hell, I was no good to her."

She was silent for a while; the only sound was the hiss of the tyres on the tarmac. She couldn't imagine wandering through the little town, saying good morning to anyone she met, meeting friends for a coffee in the diner.

"You're crazy if you think I'll fit in. I have nothing in common with those people."

"No?" he asked, glancing at her. He was grinning. "You're good with dogs and horses. You can handle a gun like a cowboy. You've got the best kitchen garden in the county and you can cook up a storm. Sounds like a lot of women round here. How about you concentrate on those things, instead of thinking you're different and trying to find reasons to keep yourself locked up like you do?"

"I'm not locked up," she said.

"Yeah, you are. You're punishing yourself and denying yourself the chance of a good life—"

"I do have a good life," she argued.

"Okay, but it could be so much better, with people around who will look out for you and keep you company." He paused. "And maybe fill some of the gaps left by the people you've lost or had to give up," he concluded softly.

"I don't need any of that."

"Yeah, you do. Or else you'd have lit out of here the minute I showed up. You need people, Faye. The Mackays are your people now, and the whole community would be if you just gave them a chance."

"Oh, like they'll welcome me with open arms as little Amy's saviour, and ignore all the shit from my past? And they'll find out – just like you, they'll keep on asking and poking their noses into my business until they know everything. Then they'll wish I'd carried on hiding and I'll get the cold shoulder every time I walk down Main Street."

"You risked your own life to put a whole mess of criminals behind bars," he said through clenched teeth. "You avenged the death of your brother. In the eyes of folks round here, that makes you a good person."

She turned away, looking out of the passenger window. They were deep in the country now, not far from home. "I grassed them up to save my own skin. I was facing charges of smuggling and extortion. Are you going to excuse that by comparing me to the old geezers who made moonshine during Prohibition? For God's sake, Jeff, don't try to make me out to be justified in what I did. There was no justification. I was a horrible person, and I'm still the same woman who did all those things." She turned to face him. "And in case you hadn't noticed, I'm a bitch. I'm cold. People don't take to me."

"Then you'll have to learn to mind your manners," he said with a smile as he took a turn.

"Where are you going? This isn't the way."

"I'm hungry. Gonna make a pitstop."

"There's a pantry full of food at home. Can't you wait half an hour?"

"Nope." They were on the outskirts of town. He pulled into the parking lot of a large building. It was crowded, but he found a space and parked. "I got me a craving for some of the best pizza in the state. Ever been to Pizza Joe's?"

"Of course I haven't."

"Well, you've been missing out." He took the key out of the ignition and opened the door. "Come on."

"I'm not going in there," she said, crossing her arms over her body and looking straight ahead.

Chapter Forty-Four

Jeff made his way around the car and opened the passenger door. She wouldn't look at him.
He smiled and leaned in and spoke softly, his warm breath moving a stray tendril of her hair across her cheek.

"Folk are already looking to see who I've got with me. If you don't want to come in, I'll have to invite them over here to meet you."

"Bugger off," she said, swiping at her cheek and pushing her hair away.

"Now I don't think that's very nice, Princess. All I want us to do is say hi to a few of our neighbours."

"Don't start with the princess rubbish again," she snarled. "You told Grainger you'd keep me safe."

"And that's what I'm doing. The sooner folk get used to you being here, the sooner you'll be recognised as one of our own. You won't be any safer than that, I promise you."

She turned her head to look at him. "You're so bloody naïve."

He grinned. "So, are you coming in?"

She glared at him. "Under protest, yes. But don't expect me to be nice to anyone."

He laughed and held out his hand. She swivelled her legs out of the car, took his hand and stood up like a true princess. When she would have taken her hand away, he held on to it. "Atta girl. Come and sulk. But I promise you, once you've tasted the pizza in this place you'll be thanking me for making you get out of the car."

He hadn't been wrong about folk wanting to see who he was with. Within moments they were greeted by half the town, all enjoying a family meal at the pizza joint. He introduced Faye to old school friends, neighbours, friends of his father and sister. The place was the gathering place for families on the weekend. He was only surprised Sal wasn't there with her husband and kids.

It took a while to get to a table for the two of them. Along the way they were invited to join several groups who were happy to squish up and make room for them. But Jeff didn't want to push his luck – it was a damned miracle he'd persuaded her to get out of the car at all.

As Faye slid into the booth by the back wall, she visibly relaxed. Her shoulders dropped and she let out a deep breath. Instead of sitting opposite her, he slid in beside her, figuring she'd prefer to have people's view of her blocked by his big frame. She acknowledged this with a brief nod.

"Don't think I'm going to forgive you for this anytime soon," she said softly, keeping a serene smile on her face. He recognised the same smile her mother had worn in the middle of the shit-fest at the Waldorf.

"You can thank me later." He grinned as the waitress approached to take their orders.

While they waited for their pizzas and drinks, there was a steady stream of people heading over to their table.

"Hey, Jeff, my man. Good to see ya!"

He looked up to see Gunther, a classmate from high school. They'd been on the football team together, double-dated and generally caused mayhem as teenagers.

"Gunther, I didn't know you were back in town."

"Well, hell, if you came into town more often, you'd have known. I got back a year ago and took over running the feed store when my dad retired. But now I can see why you've been hiding out in your cabin. Who's this pretty thing?"

As happy as he was to see his old friend, Jeff knew the guy was a player and he didn't want him getting any ideas about Faye. Even though he knew she could hold her own and would probably cut Gunther down to size in a New York minute, he made a split-second decision.

"Honey, meet Gunther, an old friend of mine. Gunther, meet Faye Evens Mackay."

He felt her stiffen next to him. He laid a hand on her thigh, hoping she'd play along with him.

"Wait. What? You got married?" Gunther's voice carried across the busy restaurant and there was an instant pause as everyone turned to look at them.

Jeff just grinned and turned to nuzzle Faye's cheek. "Stay with me on this, Princess. I know what I'm doing."

"No you don't," she hissed. "You've gone stark raving mad."

He laughed and accepted Gunther's hand as his friend congratulated him.

"Why didn't we hear about this? Did you have a party without me, man?"

Jeff shrugged. "No party. My dad…"

"Oh, sure. I'm sorry, man. I forgot. I'm sorry about Jeff Senior. He was a great guy. Maybe we can celebrate on your first anniversary, huh?"

The waitress brought their orders and Gunther went back to his friends after getting Jeff to promise to meet up for a beer sometime soon. Faye kept her head down and ate and drank as though she didn't have a care in the world. But he could feel the rage coming off her in waves.

"It makes sense," he said when everyone had turned back to their own meals and weren't paying any mind to them. "You're already a Mackay. Better people think you're married to me than my dad."

"Better people knew nothing," she said. "You're a bloody idiot."

"I disagree. If ever we need to protect you, you're already known as one of us."

"Until they get to know me and start to wonder about your sanity, tying yourself to a bitch like me."

"Then I guess you're going to have to make nice, sweetheart. You know, keep that regal smile on your face, just like your mama did when Tabitha and Chip ambushed her."

"I'm out of practice and I'm bloody tired," she snapped. "Have you finished?" She pointed to his empty plate. He'd been thinking of getting dessert, but maybe he'd pushed her enough for one day.

"You gonna eat that?" he asked. There were a couple of slices left on her plate.

She shook her head. "I'm full."

He signalled the waitress and got her to put Faye's leftovers in a carry-out box. "No point in wasting good pizza. I'll eat it when we get home."

"Fine. Can we go now? Or have you got any more plans to humiliate me this evening?"

He pulled some notes out of his wallet and handed them to the waitress when she came back with the box. He told her to keep the change, as he didn't expect Faye would be prepared to wait around any longer. He stood and took her hand as she slid out of the booth. She tried to pull away, but he held on.

"Play nice," he said softly. "Smile. People are watching."

With a sigh she looked at him, her eyes promising retribution. To onlookers, the smile on her face was sweet, although Jeff could see that her teeth were clenched tight, making it more like a grimace this close up. He held her close and smiled and chatted to people as they made their way to the exit. All the time, Faye kept silent, letting Jeff do all the talking.

"Well, Jeff Mackay, you've certainly taken us by surprise tonight, son," said an older woman who was dining with her children and grandchildren. "We wondered who the woman was who'd moved into your cabin. Your family never said she was your wife."

Jeff shrugged. "Well, we wanted to wait until I got home and we could tell everyone together. We'd have been out in town earlier, but my leg hasn't been too good until now. I can't wait to take my girl dancing." He grinned and kissed Faye's temple. He felt her tremble, but her smile didn't falter.

Before anyone else could ask any questions, he steered her out of the restaurant. She immediately pulled away from him and marched to the car, her whole body rigid with outrage.

He unlocked the car and she got in before he could help her. With a sigh he got in behind the wheel and started the engine.

"What were you thinking? Are you mad? That was the

stupidest, most ridiculous thing I've ever witnessed."

"It makes sense."

"No, it doesn't. You realise you've messed up your chances of courting any woman in this town now, don't you?"

He laughed. "Who says I want to? I reckon I dated any that were worth the trouble before I enlisted. I don't have any hankering to repeat the experience."

"What about newcomers? Your soulmate could have been in that restaurant, and now you've missed your chance of a happy ever after."

He sent her a sideways glance as they drove out of town. "You been reading my mama's old romance books? I didn't figure you for someone who was holding out for her soulmate and happy ever after."

"Of course not," she snapped. But she looked away. "But every woman in that place thinks you're something of a catch, and no doubt the sisterhood has been working out who to pair you off with. Now they'll hate me for taking you off the market, and then they'll hate me even more when I leave."

"Let's just take it a day at a time, eh? I never was in the market for a wife, so you've saved me a lot of explaining."

She did look at him then. "Why? Are you homosexual?"

"No," he said quietly, suddenly serious. "I just don't see me taking a wife when chances are I could attack her in my sleep."

She sat back and closed her eyes. "That's a really silly reason to pretend to be married to me," she said, the anger in her tone being replaced by weariness.

He turned off the main road without answering. She opened her eyes again.

"Now where are we going?"

"Somewhere quiet. We need to talk. There's a swimming hole along here where we can park out of sight."

"Just take me home," she said. "We can talk there."

"Uhuh." He shook his head. "We have to stop at the ranch house to pick up Bear. We need to decide how much we tell my sister."

She was silent until he parked up on the banks of the small

lake surrounded by trees. "So, let me get this straight, soldier. You have decided to take over my life on the pretext of 'protecting me'." She made quote marks in the air. "And in your infinite wisdom you think we should shout it from the rooftops that I'm living with you at your cabin, and let people think it was you I married and not your father?"

"Yep."

She turned in her seat to look at him. "Who are you really trying to protect? Your father? Because he's gone and took our secret to his grave. Or you? Do you think you're a liability because you've got shell shock and aren't fit to be in the presence of some poor sweet country girl who might not have the wit to kick you in the balls if you attack her?"

He winced. "Don't hold back, sweetheart," he drawled.

"Well?" She crossed her arms and waited.

He looked out into the darkness. "I used to bring dates here to make out," he said. "In fact, I lost my virginity in this very spot."

"Not in my truck, I hope."

He grinned, but didn't confirm or deny. She looked disgusted. No doubt she was used to four-poster beds and feather mattresses.

"My family has lived here for generations. We're well thought of. By letting everyone know you're a Mackay, you gain the protection of the whole town."

"Not when they find out you lied."

"I didn't lie. I never said we were married. I just told them your name. They made up their own minds."

She rolled her eyes. "Lying by implication," she said. "You're as slippery as my brother – he was a master at twisting things and swearing black was white." She frowned. "Don't forget, your lawyer knows the truth."

"Right. I'll call him."

"And so does your sister."

"So we'll have to tell her what's going on."

"No. I told you, I don't want anyone else to—"

"You also said you didn't want to put my family at risk. If you keep them in the dark, that's exactly what you'll be doing.

We have to tell them something."

She blew out a breath. "Well, that'll put paid to your plans for a fake marriage. Sal will have me off your land quicker than you can run at the moment."

He rubbed his thigh. "I think you underestimate her. She's Jefferson's daughter. She'll want to help as much as I do."

She shook her head. "She's a mother who will do anything to protect her children. I'm a bloody liability. I should go."

"No. You should stay. You like it here. Hell, I think you might even like me if you took that spur out of your ass and let yourself relax a little."

She laughed, even though she looked like she didn't want to. "There is nothing up my arse, cowboy. I'm simply being realistic."

"All right. How's this for realistic? We tell Sal that you're on a witness protection program organised by Grainger – no lies so far, and that will be enough to persuade her you're on the side of the good guys. We explain there's a slim chance that the bad guys are still looking for you, but it's unlikely because they think you're dead. But Grainger is monitoring the situation in England, and in the meantime you need to stay here where you're safe. As we both want to occupy the cabin, the simplest way to explain your presence is to let everyone think you're my wife."

"Oh God, she'll have the kiddies calling me Auntie next," she said. But she didn't argue with him.

They sat there in the darkness for a while, each lost in their own thoughts. Jeff was surprised that, the more he thought about it, the more he liked the idea of claiming this uptight fierce warrior-woman as his own.

An owl flew silently across the lake, the moonlight illuminating its path. On the bank, it pounced, then took off with a small mammal in its talons.

"If we do this," she said into the still air, "how long do you expect it to last?"

It was a good question. One he had no answer to. He shrugged. "Let's see what happens, yeah?" He turned the key in the ignition and the car's engine growled in the night. "We can keep checking in with Grainger. He'll know the best strategy. I get the impression he does a lot of this kind of thing."

"He certainly is a man of mystery," she said. "My father always swore he was someone else, but he never actually said who or why – something to do with the war, I think."

"Makes sense. Dad met him in Italy in '44. He did some special operations with the British, and carried on doing work for the government after the war. He and Grainger kept in touch all these years. He even visited the family at the ranch a couple of times. That's how me and Sal know him."

They drove back along the unmade road to the highway and then on to the turning for the ranch. Jeff felt a sense of homecoming he'd missed when he'd arrived home after leaving hospital. Back then, he'd been consumed by physical pain from his injury and gnawing grief for his father, and could barely think straight.

Now, though, he had a purpose. He just hoped his dad would have approved of his plan. Though despite what he'd told Faye, he still wasn't sure his sister would.

Chapter Forty-Five

Faye was feeling tired and irritated as they made the short drive to the ranch from the lake. She couldn't help but think this crazy scheme Jeff had set in motion was doomed to failure. *Who on earth is going to think I'm a blushing bride, for God's sake?*

Her mood was improved a little by the ecstatic welcome they got from Bear the moment they got out of the car at the ranch house. He nearly knocked her over as he leapt up to greet her. She just about kept her feet as she laughed and hugged the over-sized beast. A moment later, he was off, eager to give Jeff the same treatment. They were both laughing as Sal came out of the house.

"Hey, guys. You didn't say you went away together."

"We didn't," said Faye. "He followed me."

Sally raised her eyebrows and looked at her brother. "Does this have anything to do with Grainger calling here, trying to reach both of you?"

Faye felt a shiver of ice run down her spine. "When? When did he call?"

"About an hour ago. He said he thought you'd be home by now."

"Did he say anything else?" Jeff asked.

Sally shook her head. "Only to ask you to call him when I saw you."

Jeff looked at Faye.

"I told you it was a bad idea," she said.

"What's a bad idea?" his sister asked. "What's going on?"

Jeff was still holding on to Bear, who was standing on his hind legs, as tall as the man. With a sigh, Jeff told the dog to sit. He looked surprised when Bear did as he was told. If Faye hadn't been so full of dread since the mention of Grainger, she might have smiled at his expression.

"I'd better call him," he said.

"I'm coming with you," said Faye, chasing him up the porch stairs and into the house.

"Will somebody tell me what's happening?" Sal yelled after them.

"As soon as I talk to Grainger," Jeff yelled over his shoulder.

In the study, Jeff opened a drawer, looking for the address book that contained Grainger's phone number. But Faye didn't need it. She picked up the phone and dialled before Jeff had even opened the book.

When Grainger answered, she didn't bother with any pleasantries. "It's Faye," she said. "What's happened?"

"Ah, Faye. Thank you for calling back. Is Jeff with you?"

"Yes." Much as she wanted to speak to Grainger alone, she knew Jeff wouldn't let that happen. She glanced at him and beckoned him with her finger. He moved to her side, like they'd done in the hotel room, so that they could listen together. "We can both hear you," she said.

"Good. Well, I knew you were nervous about your meeting, Faye, so I arranged for a couple of my people to be in the restaurant to keep an eye on things, just in case."

"You had us watched?" she said. She wasn't surprised. In fact, she was a little relieved. But it reminded her that she had been so overwhelmed by meeting up with her mother after so many years and so much distance between them that she'd failed to take note of her surroundings. "If you sent spies, what's to stop the gang doing the same?"

"Quite. That's why I'm calling. It seems that someone else was watching. My people saw someone take a photograph of you with your mother in the lobby of the Waldorf. He followed you when you left and his companion stayed behind to watch your mother."

She must have made a sound, because Jeff's arm came around her shoulders. When she would have pulled away, he held on.

"Breathe," Jeff said, his voice soft. She pulled in a deep breath and blew it out again.

"Everything all right?" asked Grainger.

"Yeah," said Jeff. "Faye's just worried about her mom."

She looked at him. *How did he know?*

"Understandable, of course. But there's no cause for concern. I've already spoken to Elizabeth to put her on her guard. I've assigned one of my team to stay with her, and he'll be joining her on the cruise. She'll be less of a target as one of a couple. In fact, she'll be safer on the liner than anywhere else."

Faye had visions of her mother's corpse, floating face down in the ocean as the cruise ship steamed off into the sunset. She shook her head, trying to dislodge the image.

"Tell him not to let her out of his sight," she said. "Even on the ship."

"He won't, my dear. I promise you," said Grainger. Faye knew he would keep his word. "But that leaves us with your situation," he went on.

"What do you know?" asked Jeff.

"You were followed to your hotel. He went in and told the receptionist he was part of an international police operation and persuaded her to let him see Jeff's registration card."

"Damn!" Jeff swore. "I had to write my address on that thing."

"So he knows where we are." Faye felt the familiar weight of despair and dread settle in her stomach.

"I'm afraid so."

"Has he followed us here?" she asked.

"No. We've had a twenty-four hour watch on him and his companion. They took a flight back to London this afternoon."

"But they'll be coming back, won't they? Probably with more of them."

Grainger sighed. "I expect so. We'll pick up their tail in London and find out who they're working with. As soon as there's any movement from them or any of their associates, I'll let you know. In the meantime, I think you should prepare yourselves."

"I can't stay here," she said. "I can't risk anyone else."

"Bullshit," said Jeff. "They already know about us. I say you stay and we fight."

"This isn't the Wild West," she snapped. "These people are professional killers."

"So am I," he said. He raised his voice. "You think twelve years in the army and fighting on my own territory is enough experience to deal with these guys, Grainger?"

"It will certainly help," he replied. "And we'll be able to give you plenty of warning when they mobilize. Jeff's right, Faye. I think your best chance of dealing with this threat once and for all is to hold your ground. I'll alert the authorities on both sides of the pond. Jeff, if you can call on help from your local Sheriff, and anyone else, that would give you an added advantage. These people are used to operating in Britain and Europe. They don't have the same support networks in America."

Faye's instincts were screaming that they were wrong, that she needed to run. *But where would I go? How long before they find me again and I have to keep on running? What if they hurt Jeff and his family, even if I moved on?*

"Who needs a support network when you can walk into a shop and buy enough guns to equip a small army?" she said, her voice sharp.

"We'll be watching them, every step of the way, Faye. Trust me. We'll get you through this."

"Yeah, we will," agreed Jeff. "Keep us informed."

"Right-o. In the meantime, Faye, try not to worry. We'll keep your mother safe. And maybe, when this is all over, you can enjoy a proper visit with her."

"Just concentrate on keeping her alive, Grainger," Faye snapped.

She handed the phone to Jeff and walked over to the window while he finished the call. She wrapped her arms around her waist, trying to keep her swirling emotions in check. Just as he put the phone down, she turned and ran from the room to the nearest bathroom, where she threw up, heaving and weeping.

When there was nothing left in her stomach, she washed her face and rinsed her mouth before going back out into the hall. Jeff was waiting for her. She looked at him, wondering what was going through his head.

"You all right?" he asked.

"Of course not," she sneered. "You should have cut me loose in New York. Now you're all in danger."

He sighed and ran a hand through his hair. "It is what it is," he said. "We need to be prepared. I'm not about to let some hoodlum threaten my family."

"You're just a man," she said. "You can't fight a whole gang."

He grinned. "Why not? You did."

She closed her eyes and shook her head. "And look where that got me."

Sally came out of the kitchen, Bear at her heels. "Are you two ready to tell me what the heck is going on now?" she asked.

"Sure," said Jeff. "Where are the kids?"

"Having a sleepover at my mother-in-law's. Nick and me were planning on going to the movies, but when Grainger called, we figured we'd better hang around till you got here."

"Sorry," said Faye. "I'll make it up to you. I can babysit for you."

Sally shrugged. "It's okay. It was some damned action movie that I didn't want to see anyway," she said. "But don't tell Nick that."

"Where is he?"

"Just checking the horses." They heard the back door slam. "Ah, here he is." She turned and went into the kitchen to greet him.

"Come on." Jeff put an arm round Faye's shoulders again, and again, she didn't fight him off. She was just so tired. "We need to tell them what's going on. Then we can make a plan."

Chapter Forty-Six

Jeff did most of the talking, telling his sister and brother-in-law the bare bones of the story, as he'd promised Faye. As he expected, they were surprised but not unhappy about Faye's reason for being on the ranch, and agreed that it was a good thing. Faye thanked them, but said little else. She was pale and quiet. It could have been fatigue or it could have been guilt. Either way, there wasn't anything he could do about it here in the company of his family.

But now he also had to tell them that they'd met with Faye's mother in New York, and her cover had been blown.

"Oh my God," gasped Sally. "You've gone all this time not seeing your mama, and they followed her from England?"

Jeff smiled. It was typical of Sal to focus in on the family first. "The point is, sis, that these guys know Faye is alive and where she is now."

"I'll leave," Faye said. "I'll pack a bag and be gone by the morning."

"No!" Jeff and Sally spoke at the same time.

Nick rubbed his knuckles over his chin and looked at Faye with a wry smile. "What's the point in running? If these guys are coming here, we're likely in for a fight anyway. You're a good shot. We know you can hold your nerve, seeing as how you dropped a full-grown cougar leaping at ya. We're gonna need you."

Faye's jaw dropped at his words. Jeff wanted to punch the air. Nick didn't say much, but when he did, he got to the heart of it. He knew, the moment his brother-in-law said that they needed her, that she would stay.

"He's right," said Sally. "We need you."

Faye looked at Jeff, confusion filling her eyes. He smiled and gave her a slight nod. She took a shaky breath and nodded back.

"All right. I'll stay. I just… I just wanted to keep everyone safe."

Sally reached across the table and took her hands in her own. "That's all any of us want. But you can't do it alone. You need us and we need you. Together we're stronger."

"That's what family's all about," said Nick. He stood up. "Who wants a beer?"

"Erm, actually," said Faye, looking at Jeff. "There's one more thing you need to know."

Nick sat down again and they waited. Faye glared at Jeff, but he just nodded and indicated she should go ahead. He knew she wanted him to explain the whole married thing he'd let happen back in town.

"You tell 'em, honey," he said.

"I'm not your honey," she snapped. She turned to his sister. "For some stupid reason known only unto him, your brother has let people believe that we're…" She looked at him again, but he kept his mouth firmly shut and tried to keep the smile off his face.

God knows why I'm finding this so entertaining, he thought. *But I do.* He could almost imagine his dad standing in the doorway, watching them and laughing his head off. He knew the old man would be right behind them, urging them on.

"He let them think we're married," she said, rushing the words, biting them out like they tasted nasty.

Nick laughed and looked at him. "How'd you do that?"

"I just introduced Gunther to Faye Evens Mackay. In his usual style, he added one and one and got seventy-five."

Sally put a hand to her forehead and shook her head. "And with the mouth on that guy, I'll bet the whole town heard."

"Yup. We were in Pizza Joe's."

"Oh God," Sally looked from Jeff to Faye and back again, then threw back her head and laughed. "Why the heck did you do that?"

"She's family. I figured it was the best way to tell people. Better they think she's married to me than to Dad."

Faye looked around the table at their amused faces. "I don't see what's so funny about this. It's a ridiculous idea."

Sally shook her head. "No, Faye. It's a brilliant idea. Jeff's right. Folk have been asking about you. They've always known you were here. And since you killed the cougar, well, they want to meet you. You saved our daughter's life. That makes you one of us." She looked at her brother. "And I'm guessing Jeff figures now you're an official member of the Mackay family instead of a dirty little secret, we can count on everyone to watch out for you."

"That's what he said," she huffed, rolling her eyes. "I can't see it myself."

Jeff sat back, watching the women, relieved his sister knew him well enough to understand his motives.

"It also makes it easier to explain why you took up residence at the cabin and haven't moved out now that my brother's home. As Jeff's wife, where else would you be?"

Faye looked at him, maybe wanting him to back her up. But why would he? Sal could see how right it was. So he grinned and said, "Told ya, honey. It's a match made in Heaven."

Her look told him to go to Hell, but those English manners of hers kept her quiet.

"You've better get her a ring," said Sal. "People – well, the women – will notice if she's not wearing one."

Jeff frowned. "I didn't think of that. I guess we'd better go into the city to get one."

Faye stilled and blinked. "Wait. The package my mother gave me." She stood up. "It's in my bag."

She ran out of the room before anyone could stop her. Nick got up and finally got some beers from the refrigerator. He was just putting them on the table when she returned. In her hand was the neatly-wrapped package her mother had handed her as they'd left. It was unopened.

"If this is what I think it is…" she said, peeling the tape away and opening the wrappings. "Ah, yes." Inside was a small silver box. She took it out, a soft smile on her face. It made her look younger, more beautiful.

Jeff blinked. *What the hell? I've just tricked this woman into pretending to be my wife and I'm getting the hots for her? Damn. This is not good.*

"What is it?" asked Sally, leaning closer.

"My grandmother's trinket box. She always said I would have it when she died. But my parents told me it was part of the estate, and I never saw it again. Until now."

She opened it and her smile widened. She started taking out things – brooches, hair ornaments, earrings. She laid them on the table and Sally cooed over each piece as Faye told her its history. "I would play with these for hours and hours," she said. "Grandmother loved to tell me the stories of who had given them to her and when she'd worn them." She laughed. "She was quite a girl in her day."

Then she reached into the box one last time and brought out two rings. "Her wedding and engagement rings," she said. "If they fit, I think I'd like to wear them." She looked at Jeff. "Do you think that's all right? It will save the expense of buying a ring."

The wedding band was plain yellow gold. The engagement ring was a square emerald, flanked by two square diamonds. Simple but classy. The stones were a good size, but not flashy.

"Try them on," he said, his throat suddenly dry.

Her fingers shook a little as she slid the two rings onto the third finger of her left hand. They fitted perfectly. Jeff wanted to reach over and take her hand, to kiss it. But Sally was already reaching for Faye's hand and admiring the rings.

"They're beautiful," she said. She looked up at Faye. "You must miss her."

Faye nodded, blinking rapidly. "Yes, I do. But she's been gone a long time now. Just as well, really. She didn't get to see the mess I made of everything."

"I'm guessing she'd be mighty proud of you," said Sally.

Jeff could see Faye swallow down her emotions as she put on what he'd come to realise was her public smile – the one she hid behind.

"Thank you," she said, taking her hand back and turning to the other pieces on the table. She picked up a pair of pearl and diamond earrings and another with sapphires. "You should have these."

Sally gasped. "I can't take your grandmother's jewels," she

said. "You should wear them."

Faye shook her head. "I'll wear the other pieces, but I want you to have the earrings. I can't wear them. See?" Without warning, she pulled her hair away from the left side of her face, revealing her scars and her mutilated ear. Jeff leaned forward and put his hand on her thigh, letting her know he was there for her. She glanced at him, their gazes met and held. She nodded, and looked away. "The reason they thought I was dead is because I was attacked in the courtroom after I'd testified. So, will you wear my grandmother's earrings for me?"

Sally nodded, tears in her eyes. "I always wondered why you wore your hair like that, but I never imagined…"

"It's all right. I'm not likely to change my hairstyle any time soon, and I'd rather you didn't tell anyone about this." She pointed to her scars. "But, well, if we're telling everyone that we're related…" She faltered for a moment before going on. "… then I'd like you to share my family heirlooms."

"I'd love to," said Sally.

"Well, hell," said Nick. "I guess now I'll have to take you someplace fancy so you can show them off."

He looked so pissed at the thought that the rest of them laughed.

"All right," said Jeff. "So, now we have a ring for the bride, we'd better work out a plan to protect us all from the bad guys when they get here."

Chapter Forty-Seven

Faye couldn't get to sleep that night, despite being exhausted. Every time she closed her eyes memories would flood in, leaving her shaken and afraid. In the end, she got up and crept down the ladder and across the living room to the kitchen.

A moment later Jeff emerged from his bedroom, with Bear following close behind.

"Can't sleep?" he asked.

She shook her head. "You too?"

He ran a hand down his face. He looked as bad as she felt. "Damned dog snores," he said.

"You can always make him sleep out here," she said, pointing at the oversized dog bed in the corner of the kitchen. Bear liked to use it for naps during the day, but he'd always slept with her until Jeff had come home. She didn't suggest she took him with her into the attic; there wasn't much space up there with her art supplies all over the place. Bear's wagging tail could cause mayhem, even if she could get him up the ladder.

"I guess," he said. "Bear, in your bed." He pointed to the corner. The dog looked at him for a moment before giving the equivalent of a doggy shrug and settling in his bed. He rested his huge head on his paws and looked up at them.

Faye laughed. "You're getting the hang of it," she told Jeff.

"Good dog," he said, bending to scratch behind his ears. Bear closed his eyes in bliss.

Faye set about making cocoa. She was tempted to hit the whisky, but decided it was better to stay sober now she knew they were definitely under threat. She couldn't afford to be caught with anything less than razor-sharp reactions.

"No whisky?" he asked, sitting at the kitchen table and watching her as she warmed up milk.

"I don't think that's a good idea, given that we could be

expected to fight at any moment, do you?"

"It'll take a while for them to get here," he said. "And we'll be ready for them."

Faye sighed, focussing on her task. "Part of me wishes they'd just turn up and get it over with. But then I think about everyone who will be put in danger because of me, and I pray they'll never get here."

"The waiting is always the worst," he agreed. "Never knowing when the battle will start or where the enemy will come from."

She looked over her shoulder at him. "You're supposed to make me feel better."

"Sorry." He yawned.

She put a steaming mug of cocoa in front of him and sat opposite, cradling her own drink. "Neither of us will be any good if we can't get any sleep. Why don't you go back to bed?"

"What about you? You've been tossing and turning up there for hours."

"You could hear me moving?"

"Yeah. I couldn't settle either."

Faye took a sip of her drink, enjoying its warmth and bittersweet taste. "Do you want some extra sugar in there?" She pointed to his mug. "I make it quite strong. Some people find it a bit bitter."

He tasted it. "Nah, it's good. So, how do we both get some sleep?"

She shrugged. "I don't expect to be able to relax until this is all over. What's the saying? 'I'll sleep when I'm dead.'"

Jeff's hand shot out and grabbed her arm. "You are not going to die," he said, his gaze stern as she looked at him. "We are going to beat this. Understand?"

"You don't—"

"Yeah, I do. This is my territory. Those guys might be big shots in London. But out here they're in an alien land. They'll soon find out no one messes with my family and gets away with it."

She wanted to argue that she wasn't really family, but realised that was irrelevant – just by being here, she had put the

Mackay family at risk. Jeff would do everything in his power to protect them — or he'd die trying. She shivered at the thought. She didn't want any more blood spilt because of her. She nodded.

"All right, soldier. Understood. But that's even more reason why you need to sleep. Go back to bed."

"Come with me," he said.

His hand was still on her arm. She wondered whether he could feel the goosebumps appearing on her skin. "What?"

"The only time I haven't had nightmares was when I was tranquilised in the hospital and when we slept together at the hotel," he said softly. "I'm guessing it was the same for you."

She looked away. He was right. But sleeping together…?

"I won't have sex with you," she said.

"I didn't ask you to. I just need to hold you. Keep my nightmares away, Faye, and let me help you too."

"I'm not much of a cuddler," she said, knowing this was a bad idea, but surprising herself by actually wanting to say yes.

"Let's try it. You never know, you might like it," he said, his voice low and husky.

She fought against the shiver that ran up her spine, unwilling to let him know that she was affected by him and his persuasive words. "You might attack me again."

"I didn't last night," he pointed out. "But if I do, you can always kick me in the balls again."

"Oh, I will, soldier. You can depend on it."

"Is that a yes?"

She looked at him. He was grey with fatigue. She felt her resolve to keep her distance slipping away. She had slept so well in his arms. It was probably a fluke and the whisky they'd drunk, but what if it wasn't? What if the only time she could find peace was when she was held by Jeff Mackay?

She sighed. "All right. I'll give it a try. But no funny stuff."

He smiled. "No funny stuff." He finished his cocoa and stood. She did the same. He held out his hand and she took it. They walked into the bedroom and closed the door to stop Bear joining them.

They both slept, long and deep, their nightmares absent.

Chapter Forty-Eight

Word that Jeff was 'married' spread like wildfire and brought a steady stream of visitors from town to the cabin to check out his bride and wish them well. No one questioned the suddenness, or the fact that Faye had arrived months ago and had kept herself to herself. As he had predicted, she was now one of their own as Mrs Jeff Mackay, and everyone wanted to meet her: neighbours, people he and Sally had gone through school with, and his parents' old friends all arrived within the first few days. It seemed like as soon as one visitor left, another turned into the drive. He and Faye were kept busy making fresh coffee to go with the cakes and cookies people brought along.

Every night they slept together dreamlessly in his bed, with none of the 'funny business' she'd warned him against. But, rested as he was, he was finding it harder and harder to wake up with her in his arms and not kiss her to see where it would lead. He told himself they didn't need the distraction of sex. There was too much to do to make sure they were safe.

Jeff soon realised these visits were the perfect opportunity to explain the bare facts of what Faye was facing and to make sure everyone was on the alert for strangers in the area. He'd also visited the Sheriff's office and filled them in. Before long everyone within a five-mile radius was on the lookout, and he was confident no-one would sneak up on the Mackay lands without being spotted.

"We can't expect everyone to put themselves at risk," Faye had argued.

"We don't," he assured her. "No one will approach them. But any stranger around here will be reported and watched, and we'll have the advantage if they make a move."

"I suppose so," she sighed. "But it doesn't feel right. I've been used to keeping all this to myself. I'm not sure how I feel about everyone knowing my business."

He smiled. "At least you didn't have them reporting back to your mom the minute you looked at a girl."

"Really? Tell me more."

"Let's just say it's a miracle any kid in a small town gets to lose their virginity. There are eyes everywhere and they all know your mom's phone number."

Faye giggled. "Hence the trysts at the lake?"

"Yeah. Although I doubt my generation was the first to find it."

"Mmm. We all think we're the first to do something wicked, but it's been going on for centuries." She looked down at her grandma's wedding rings. "My grandmother told me stories about when she was a girl that made my antics seem tame… until I went too far, of course." She looked up, raising her chin and taking a deep breath. "She was far too smart to cross that line. I thought I was like her, but I realise now that I have quite a way to go before I can claim to be worthy of her."

She looked so damned brittle, like she could shatter at any moment. Yet she still held her chin up, ready to face anything that came her way. She had greeted their visitors with a regal smile and been the perfect hostess, even though he'd known she would have preferred to have hidden away until they left. Jeff put a hand on her shoulder.

"She'd be proud of you," he said.

"Maybe not yet. But I'm working on it," she said. She turned away and headed for the kitchen door. "I take it we aren't expecting any more visitors today? I mean, there can't possibly be anyone left out there that we haven't met, can there?"

"I think we're good," he smiled. "That's phase one of the plan complete."

"So, what's next?"

He took a deep breath. "I need to get back to target practice."

She stopped with one hand on the door handle and turned to look at him. "Want some help?"

He considered it. But the soldier in him balked at the thought of this woman standing by to rescue him if he lost it again.

"Nah. I'm good. It's getting easier." At least, he hoped it would if he just kept going.

She didn't look convinced, but she nodded and went out to tend to the kitchen garden. He watched her through the window for a few minutes. She looked so at home, digging in the soil, picking the produce she'd grown. He couldn't imagine her as the big city party girl who got herself mixed up with organised crime, drugs and murder.

He went out to the barn and let himself into the tack room where the guns were kept in a locked cabinet. He'd persuaded Faye that she didn't need a shotgun under the bed for the time being, although she insisted it must go back there the moment they knew the enemy was on its way. He couldn't blame her for that. But while he hadn't had any nightmares for a few nights, he still worried that one might invade his brain and would send him reaching for the gun before he could come to his senses. He wasn't prepared to put her at that kind of stupid risk.

He selected a pistol and a box of ammo and locked the rest away. For the next hour he practised shooting at various targets he'd set up. The first couple of rounds left him sweating and gasping for breath as the sounds of the shots dragged other sounds and images into his mind. But he kept going, forcing himself to focus on the targets, on his finger on the trigger, on the present threat, and eventually it became easier. When Faye called out to him that she was going to start dinner, he felt stronger.

He returned the weapon and remaining ammunition to the gun cabinet and went into the house to wash up. He didn't fool himself that he was okay, but he was getting there. In the meantime, it wouldn't hurt to put in a couple of calls to his old army buddies. He knew he could rely on them; they were his brothers. After a half-hour on the phone, he had three of them on standby to head to Montana the moment Grainger reported the bad guys were on the move. Until then, he agreed with them that it would be a good idea to put some booby traps and early warning systems in place, like they had when they were in the field in 'Nam. He could set up some simple trip wires and a couple of traps in the woods around the house. That would keep him busy and focussed while they waited.

He wasn't sure how Faye would react to his plan, but he told her about it over dinner. To his surprise, she grinned.

"It's a shame we don't have some of my Scottish grandfather's bear traps," she said. "I'm told his forebears caught a few poachers in them. More than one of them lost a leg."

"Jesus, woman! And there was I, thinking you were so refined. You're pretty bloodthirsty, ain't ya?"

She laughed. "Actually, I hated the bloody things. I didn't like the idea of bears or any other animals being caught in them, let alone some chap trying to catch a rabbit to feed his family. But the men who are coming after me are worse than any poor poacher, believe me. A bear trap would be too good for them."

"Well, no bear traps. But I've got a few tricks that will hold them up and warn us they're out there."

"Good. I'll come with you."

"You don't need—"

"Oh, yes I do. Bear and I enjoy a walk through the woods. I'm not putting him or myself at risk by not knowing where your traps are. I don't relish ending up hanging upside down from a tree, or even worse, trying to get Bear out of something like that."

"You should limit going anywhere alone for the time being," he began.

"Bugger that, soldier. I appreciate your concern, but it could be weeks before this is over. You can't expect me to sit here like a scared rabbit. I won't have it."

"Okay," he sighed. It wasn't worth arguing about. In fact, he thought it was a good idea that she knew where the traps were. "We'll start tomorrow."

She smiled. "Good. We'd better warn everyone at the ranch not to wander through there as well."

"Good point."

They ate in silence, then shared the clear-up duties. There was no need for conversation, they had fallen into an easy companionship once their initial conflict over possession of the cabin was taken out of the equation. It became a habit that Jeff would whistle for Bear once the dishes were done, and Faye would join them for an evening walk. They made sure Ebony was bedded down for the night and the chickens were secure before spending an hour walking the Mackay lands. The summer evenings were light enough to enable them to negotiate the woods as well as the pasture.

"You've lost your limp," she pointed out when they'd been walking for a while.

"I guess the physical therapy and general exercise helps," he said. In truth, he hadn't thought about it. He felt physically stronger every day. It was his head space he was more worried about. Every now and again, he'd wonder whether he could handle the battle to come – or if he might just lose it like he did when Faye shot the cougar. But he pushed those thoughts away. He couldn't afford to be weak. He had to focus and fight or he'd end up dead.

"Good."

They walked on a little whilst Bear snuffled in the undergrowth and marked his territory on several of the trees. Jeff pointed out places on and around the trail through the woods where he intended to plant his booby traps and trip wires. She listened and nodded, making the occasional suggestion. He was impressed that she could understand what he was trying to do and how his tactics would work.

"Can you really trust all those people you've spoken to about this?" she asked eventually.

"Yeah. Why?"

She shrugged. "I just can't believe that everyone is as perfect as you seem to think they are. What if someone is desperate for money and some stranger offers them a reward for information? And how do you know you didn't offend someone years ago and they're bearing a grudge? I'm sorry, Jeff, but I find it really difficult to trust, and right now there seem to be far too many people out there who could easily betray us."

He walked on, considering what she said. "Okay, I can see where you're coming from," he said eventually. "And I guess after the years I've been out of town, I can't give you an iron-clad guarantee that I haven't misjudged any of them. But, well, I grew up with these folk, and I reckon that even if one of them is determined to sell us out, there are enough good people around that would notice what was happening and we'd get a fair warning." He stopped and looked at her. "That's all I can offer you. I'm sorry."

She halted too, staring up at him. He kept forgetting how petite she was – her sassy mouth and fearlessness always somehow made him think of her as being bigger. He could see her considering his words. As he waited, he realised that whenever he was this close to her, he wanted to take her in his arms, to kiss her and more. He remembered holding her at the Waldorf, when she'd leapt on him, her slim legs wrapped around his waist, her lips on his. He took a deep breath and tried to blow his desire for her out of his head. He couldn't be doing with this now. It was hard enough, sharing a bed so they could both get some sleep, pretending to be a loving husband when folk were around. If he came on to her and she rejected him, it would make this whole crazy situation so much more complicated. No, he needed to keep his feelings to himself and focus on the battle to come.

Maybe if they survived it, he could explore his feelings, and figure out if they were borne of his urge to protect or were simple lust because he hadn't had sex for a while – or if it was something bigger than either of those things. Not that he expected this high-class city girl to settle for a washed-up cowboy like him.

"All right. I suppose you're right," she said. For a moment he felt his stomach drop. Had he just told her what he was thinking? *Shit!* But then she went on. "There's nothing we can do to take it back, so I have to trust that someone will warn us if we're betrayed."

Jeff nodded, not trusting himself to speak. *Focus. I need to focus.*

Chapter Forty-Nine

The following days were filled with activity. The woods were booby-trapped. The house was checked and secured – especially the root store. Weapons were cleaned and tested. Bunks were found and set up in the loft of the barn for Jeff's army buddies. Faye thought it was far too primitive for guests, but Jeff assured her they had survived in much worse conditions over the years, and anyway, it wasn't likely to be for long. She hoped he was right.

She cooked up a storm, making pies and casseroles for the freezer.

"I'm preparing to feed our army," she told him when he asked why.

They checked in with Grainger every couple of days. He told them the people who had seen them in New York had met with known associates of Faye's enemies. It was just a matter of time. Faye thought she ought to be terrified. But, somehow, she felt relieved. It would soon be over. They were going to come after her – and, thanks to Jeff, she was ready.

She had given up everything because of those thugs, and she wasn't about to do it again. She'd found her place, and she even allowed herself to think that maybe she might have found her man – but she wasn't allowing herself to dwell on that until these shenanigans were over. She needed to know that her enemies were vanquished before she could examine her feelings for Jeff Mackay.

There was every chance that she was imagining herself falling for him because he was one of the few men she'd ever met who showed her any respect. He didn't put up with her bitchiness. He made her laugh. His presence helped her sleep without being disturbed by nightmares. And he was damned handsome, whether she liked to admit it or not. But was she confusing her feelings of gratitude for a decent night's sleep and his protection – and, she acknowledged, basic lust – for something deeper and more long-lasting? Whatever it was, now was not the time to test it or to make any decisions.

Maybe, if she survived what was to come, they could see what they felt about it all. She only hoped that Jeff and his family and friends stayed safe through all of this. She didn't think she could live with the guilt if anyone else got hurt because of her.

Finally, the day came when Grainger called to say that four men had boarded a flight to Las Vegas.

"I suspect they will meet with associates there who'll supply them with weapons."

"What if these associates decide to join them?" asked Faye, her throat dry. "They could raise a bloody army."

Jeff stood next to her, the phone receiver between them. He squeezed her shoulder and she moved closer to him, taking courage from his warmth.

"We've got eyes on them all the way, my dear. My counterparts in Nevada are already on standby to assist my operatives. We'll let you know the moment they make a move and how many of them are coming."

Jeff nodded. "We'll be ready for them," he said, his expression hard. At that moment, Faye saw the warrior in him. She almost felt sorry for the thugs who were heading their way. *Almost. But not quite.*

When they ended the call, Jeff called his army buddies and they promised to be with them within twenty-four hours. Then they drove over to the ranch house to warn Sal and Nick.

"I'm so sorry about this," said Faye, as they sat around the ranch house kitchen table, discussing their plans. "I never wanted to get anyone else involved."

"It is what it is," said Sally with a shrug, echoing Jeff's words. "Daddy wanted to help, so that's what we're going to do. No one should have to live with this kind of threat hanging over them." She shook her head, her expression angry. "God, I hate the idea that you've lived in fear all this time, and now they think they can barge in here and threaten my family just because you're here with us. The sooner we catch these bastards, the better."

Nick laid a hand over hers. "It'll be okay, honey. We won't let them get anywhere near you and the kids."

Sally blinked back tears of frustration and anger.

"Can't you send the children somewhere safe?" asked Faye.

"They'll go to Nick's mom's the moment these guys cross the state line," said Sally.

"You should go with them," said Faye.

"No," she said, at the same that Nick said, "Yeah, you should."

"I'm not leaving you," Sally told him. "I can fight."

"But you don't need to, honey. We've got plenty of fire power."

"He's right," said Jeff. "Listen to him."

Sally glared at the two men. "Don't you start with the damned helpless woman thing. I can shoot as good as any of you."

Faye leaned forward, resting her hand on Sally's shoulder. "It's nothing to do with that," she said. "But I'd feel happier if you were with Pete and Amy, guarding them. Go armed, by all means. I hope to God these thugs don't decide to threaten the children, but we can't take the chance. You need to protect them."

"But… Nick—"

"… will be more effective, knowing you're with the kids," said Jeff. "Don't make him worry about you when I need him to focus on the plan."

Sally looked like she wanted to argue, but in the end she nodded and sighed. "If they come anywhere near my kids, I'll kill 'em," she said. "And if Nick gets shot, I'll kill you," she told her brother.

"I'd gladly give my life to keep the family safe," said Jeff, kissing his sister's cheek. "You know it. But I'm planning on living, and so is Nick. Ain't that right, brother?"

"Hell, yeah," the quiet cowboy agreed.

Faye breathed a sigh of relief. At least she wouldn't have to worry about Sally and her children. She just hoped that none of the men who had pledged to protect her got hurt. There were a lot of them – Jeff, Nick, the ranch hands, the local Sheriff's department, their neighbours and, of course, Jeff's army buddies were all in on the plan.

"I wish they could just pick them up and arrest them before they got here," she said. "But law enforcement can't act until they've committed a crime." She ran a hand through her hair, unconsciously patting it down over her scars. "If we were in England, they'd get them on just being in possession of a deadly weapon or something. But because anyone in this country can carry a gun, we're scuppered until they actually point it at someone."

"Scuppered?" said Nick. "What the hell is that?"

She looked around the table at their confused faces and rolled her eyes. "Sorry, another example of being divided by a common language. It's from an old naval thing – when you sink your own ship to avoid it being taken, you're scuppering it. I don't suppose you use a phrase like that in a land-locked place like this. We use it to mean we're stuck, our plans are ruined. Does that make sense? If they don't actually shoot at us, we can't get them arrested."

They all nodded.

"Although, I suppose we could get them for trespass, but that wouldn't hold them for long," she added.

"Let's make something clear here," said Jeff. "If these guys set foot on Mackay land, we'll stop 'em. If they get close enough to take a shot, I won't be looking to get them arrested. They'll go down. No one messes with my family. If the authorities want them alive, they need to stop them before we get them in our sights."

"Yeah," said Nick.

Sally and Faye exchanged glances. They had already had quiet conversations about what might happen. Sally was worried for her husband, but she was also concerned about Jeff's state of mind. Faye agreed that the last thing they needed was for him to have another episode in the middle of a gun fight. But she was able to assure his sister that Jeff had been shooting targets, acclimatising himself to the noise. It was also a relief to be able to report he hadn't had any nightmares lately, although she didn't mention it was because she slept beside him every night. For Sally's peace of mind, Faye promised to stick close to him, just to be on the safe side.

As for Jeff's intention to shoot to kill, Faye couldn't blame him. She would do the same if necessary. She'd seen the carnage these criminals had created. The only way to send a clear message to their bosses, and to put an end to this for once and for all, was to meet them with more power than they expected.

"Just make sure you don't end up in jail for killing someone," she said. "This isn't the Wild West any more, and I'm not worth it."

"A man has a right to protect himself and his property," said Jeff. "It's in our constitution."

She noticed he didn't say anything about her own worth. It hurt a little, but she was pragmatic. She really wasn't worth it. But she really wished that she was.

Chapter Fifty

Jeff watched as Faye served up a feast for his buddies. They'd arrived within hours of his call, and he'd spent the afternoon walking the woods and pastures with them, making sure they were familiar with the lie of the land and the locations of his booby traps.

Now they were crowded around the kitchen table, chowing down on steak pie, crisp roast potatoes and green beans from the garden. The guys weren't saying much, they were too busy inhaling Faye's cooking.

Steve Baldwin had arrived first, being closest. He watched Faye with interest, having hit a brick wall when he'd tried to investigate her. When he'd arrived, Jeff had told him about their fake relationship and why. Steve had just grinned and nodded. Jeff was glad he hadn't made some smart joke about it. He didn't want to have to punch his friend.

Chris Hamilton and Pete Iverson had flown in from New York together a few hours later. They'd finished their tours of 'Nam a few weeks after Jeff's evacuation. Hamilton had returned to his family's sporting goods business, and Iverson was working as a part-time firefighter while thinking about his future. They'd both dropped everything to come to help. Jeff just hoped it didn't make like difficult for them.

"Are you sure you won't lose your job, man?" he asked Iverson again.

"Nuh-huh," he replied around a mouth full of food. He swallowed and took a drink of water before going on. "The fire chief is my uncle and an ex-marine. I had a fight on my hands to stop him coming with me."

"It's so useful, having connections, isn't it?" said Faye, her cut-glass accent sounding even more pronounced among the *men's shorthand grunts and army slang.*

"It sure is, ma'am," said Hamilton.

"I've told you, I'm Faye. Every time you say 'ma'am' I think the Queen has walked in and I have the urge to curtsey."

They all laughed. Jeff could see that they were charmed by this strange creature, so different from any other women they'd met.

"I am very grateful you're here, though," she went on. "I just hope none of you get hurt in all this. This isn't your fight, after all."

"Yeah it is," said Iverson. "Mackay is our brother. He'd do the same for us. We're all in until the threat is neutralized."

Jeff watched Faye as she recognised the truth of what he said. She smiled and nodded.

"Well, thank you," she said before turning her focus back to her meal.

He reckoned she was finding it a tad uncomfortable, having all these people looking out for her, determined to keep her safe. From the little she said about her life in England, she wasn't used to that. But, as he'd come to expect, she didn't let on how she was feeling. Instead, she played the perfect hostess, making sure everyone got as many helpings as they could handle and topping up their drinks. They were on water or soda – none of them would touch alcohol until this was over. They needed to keep their minds and reactions sharp.

After dinner, they headed over to the ranch house, where the ranch hands, the Sheriff, Teddy, Gunther and a few other guys and even a couple of women from town had gathered. The rest of the evening was spent going through the plans. They needed to be flexible, ready to respond to whatever the criminals did.

Jeff stuck close to Faye, aware that she wasn't saying much. He knew she felt guilty that she was putting everyone at risk, but no-one had been forced to come here. Each and every one of them had volunteered – although he supposed the Sheriff and his team were just doing their jobs, making sure the citizens stayed safe. No matter their reasons for being here, every one of them was ready to fight.

"Okay, I think that's everything," he concluded. "Any

questions?" There was a general shaking of heads. *"Good. From here on out, everyone at the ranch will be carrying on as normal, but with extra vigilance. Me, Baldwin, Hamilton and Iverson will be patrolling the Mackay property, and the Sheriff and everyone else will be watching for any strangers arriving in town."*

"I'll also send extra patrols out to check some of the empty properties around the area," said Sheriff Harding. *"There are a few cabins and old farms off the beaten track that could harbor these bast– uh, undesirables,"* he said, sending an apologetic look to Sally.

"Thanks, Sheriff," Jeff said. *"Good to know they won't be able to sneak in and surprise us. Okay. We all know the signals. As soon as we're alerted that they've crossed the state line, we'll notify everyone and put the plan into action."* He paused. *"On behalf of all the Mackays,"* he said, putting a hand on Faye's shoulder to let her and everyone there know he included her in this, *"we appreciate your support. These guys need to be stopped. They've done enough harm back in their own country. They got no business spreading their poison round here."*

There were nods and mumbles of "Damned right," from around the room.

"They've got no idea what they're walking into, so let's keep it that way. Keep your eyes and ears open and stay safe, everyone."

Later that night, neither Jeff nor Faye could sleep. They lay next to each other, talking quietly about what might happen.

"I'm worried that Grainger's men might be mistaken for the criminals," she said. *"What if one of us shoots a good guy?"*

"We won't. Grainger's guys have strict instructions to hang back if the targets cross onto Mackay land. They'll only come in on our say-so."

"But what about the federal authorities he's been speaking to?"

"Same deal. They're in contact with the Sheriff, and agreed we've got a solid plan and know the territory. We have the best

chance of catching these guys."

"I didn't think the feds liked leaving it to the locals," she said.

"I don't think they do. But apparently, Grainger has some powerful friends."

"I know," she sighed. "It's hard to believe when you meet him, isn't it?"

Jeff smiled, remembering the pleasant, unassuming English gentleman. "I guess he keeps his power well-hidden until he needs to use it. And that's what we're doing. Those punks won't know what hit them."

They were silent for a little while. "This will be the end of it, won't it? I mean, everyone thought it was over after the trial. But they had friends who were ready and willing to avenge them even then. What if this is just the next battle in a never-ending war?"

Jeff turned on his side to look at her and traced a gentle finger down her scarred cheek and neck. "If it is, we keep on fighting. Sooner or later, we'll win. You don't have to keep running, Faye."

She took a deep breath. "I wish it was over."

"It will be. I'll keep you safe. I promise."

She looked at him, a fierce light in her eyes. "And I'll keep you safe. It's the least I can do."

He smiled. This itty-bitty scrap of a woman was brave, and, even if she wasn't fearless, she would fight with everything she had, pushing right through her fear. He wondered how he had ever imagined she was cold and heartless. She was a warrior. They had that much in common. She was wounded, just like he was. She understood him and had led him out of his nightmares. He was beginning to realise he understood her better than any other woman he had ever met.

He wanted to kiss her, to lose himself in her body. He figured she wanted it too, if the flush on her cheeks and the pulse speeding up under his hand was anything to go by. But now was not the time. They had a battle ahead. When it was over, they would have all the time in the world to explore the attraction that grew between them with every beat of their hearts.

When the battle was won, he intended to win her for himself.

"*Rest,*" *he said, kissing her temple.*

She turned in his arms and rested her head on his shoulder. Within moments, they were both asleep.

Chapter Fifty-One

The next twenty-four hours were tense. Grainger reported that, as expected, the men from London had met with known criminals in Las Vegas, who had supplied them with weapons and extra men. Two car-loads of hired guns were heading for Montana. The make and models and registration numbers were passed to the Sheriff and the network of people standing by to help the Mackays. Everyone was ready for them.

Faye was relieved when Sally and the children left to stay with Nick's parents over in the neighbouring county. She almost asked them to take Bear with them, but Jeff persuaded her to keep the dog close.

"He'll warn you. Just like he did when I arrived," he said.

"But what if they shoot him?"

"Don't think about it."

She noticed he hadn't tried to tell her it wouldn't happen, and she was grateful for that. There were no guarantees. But if she started to worry about everything, she'd be no good to anyone.

"All right," she said.

She kept herself busy. She knew that when it started, things could happen very quickly. The troops, as she had taken to calling Jeff and his army buddies, were on constant alert, keeping watch in strategic spots which overlooked the entrances to the Mackay lands. She saddled up Ebony and rode out, delivering food and flasks of coffee to each of them.

"Can't have you starving when we need you fighting fit," she said.

They seemed to like her cheerful manner, thanking her for the supplies. She didn't hang around, knowing her role was to remain close to the cabin. She doubted the enemy would approach the ranch in broad daylight. It was more likely they would drive by to establish the lie of the land, and then wait until darkness to make their move. Everyone at the ranch had been ordered to carry on as normal, as though they weren't expecting anything to happen. However, to a man – and Faye – they were all armed.

Faye got back to the barn. She groomed and fed Ebony before letting him out into the pasture, then went back into the cabin. She checked that everything was secure – all doors locked and windows shut, then climbed up into the attic. The CB radio from the truck had been moved up there. She switched it on and reported in.

"Lavender Lady here, gentlemen. I've had a lovely ride out and didn't see any cougars in the woods. Has anyone else spotted any wildlife out there?"

She knew she should use the slang the CB *officianados* did, but she thought it sounded ridiculous, especially with her accent. She'd tried over the past few days when Jeff and the others were testing the system out and they all agreed they knew what she was trying to say, even if she couldn't bring herself to use CB slang.

She heard various voices checking in to report all was quiet, including Papa Bear (the Sheriff), Gas Jockey (a fellow who worked in the nearest service station), Jaws, Rhino, Doc, and Pokey amongst the male contingent; as well as Ruby Tuesday, Legs, Lips and Delilah – local women who liked to keep track of their men via the radio waves. She had met all of them over the past few days, and could put a name and face to every voice she heard. It made her nervous.

Jeff remained silent, but she knew that he, Baldwin, Hamilton and Iverson had walkie-talkies with a direct link to Nick at the ranch. They would only break their cover if absolutely necessary. She knew they were trained for this and they had the element of surprise on their side, but it didn't make her heart beat any slower or soothe the nausea in her stomach.

She checked the pistol that was stuffed down the back of her waistband. It was loaded. She had six shots. Her jeans pockets were stuffed with extra bullets, but she couldn't guarantee she'd have enough time to reload. Under the flare of her jeans was a hunting knife, strapped to her calf. Beside her was a shotgun, together with a box of ammunition. She could pull up the ladder, close the hatch and stay up here, which is what Jeff wanted her to do. She could pick off anyone who tried to sneak up to the house from behind. But she couldn't see the front drive, and she didn't like that.

Bear snored softly in his bed down in the living room, seemingly oblivious to the tension. She didn't want to leave him alone down there. At a push she could get him up into the attic, but he could easily give their location away by knocking something over with just a twitch of his tail.

She sighed and lay down on the daybed, knowing that all she could do was wait. She wished Jeff was here, but then again, she was glad he wasn't. If she had to die, she didn't want him to see. He had enough nightmares to deal with.

She smiled, realising how far she'd come since she'd left London. At first, all she'd thought about was herself – her pain, her humiliation, her sense of betrayal. It hadn't occurred to her that she should take responsibility for her own actions, that she always had a choice in what she did, and that many of the paths she'd chosen to follow had been the wrong ones. It hadn't been until Percy and then James had died, and she'd almost lost her own life, that she had finally faced the truth and accepted the blame for everything that had happened.

She was incredibly lucky that Julian Grainger had offered to help her. He didn't have to – after all, Faye had tried to extort money from his god-daughter in order to pay off the criminals who were threatening her. But he had, and for that she would always be grateful. She was also thankful that he'd brought her here and introduced her to Jefferson Mackay Senior. That old man had been more of a father to her than her own had. He actually listened to her, even when she was being a bitch, fighting for survival. And he'd heard what she *hadn't* said but wanted to – that she was sorry, that she was scared, that she didn't want to be Fliss Broughton any more. He had made it clear that she could be anyone she wanted to be – she just needed to take that step. She hoped that he knew how much she had loved him for that.

Much as she missed him, Faye was glad that old Jefferson wasn't around for this fight. He would have fought, and gladly, she knew. But he shouldn't have to. Just as his son and son-in-law and all the others shouldn't have to.

No, it wasn't herself that Faye was worried about this time, but all the others. She didn't deserve their support and protection, but they were giving it to her anyway. If she survived this, she knew she'd spend the rest of her life trying to make it up to them. She only prayed that none of them would get hurt because of her.

"Breaker, breaker," the CB radio burst into life. "Gas Jockey here. Just had a couple of cougar cages filling up with motion lotion. No ears in sight. Heading to the picnic area now."

Faye sat up. So, they had arrived at the local service station and filled up. The pump attendant hadn't spotted any CB radios in either car. That was a relief. They wouldn't know that their every move was being watched.

"Copy that, Gas Jockey." It sounded like the Sheriff. "Anyone got eyes on them now?"

"Yeah, Papa Bear," came a female voice. "Delilah here out on the highway heading east. They're in my rearview. I'm driving like I'm Mrs Clean and dead-peddling to slow the convoy down. We're about two miles from the picnic area."

So, they were on their way to the Mackay ranch.

"Good job, Delilah. Don't rile 'em up, but if you can hold 'em up for a little while, it all helps."

"Ten-four. I'll let you know when we get to the turn-off."

"Roger that."

Faye took a deep breath. After years of fearing this moment, it had arrived. She knew they could well drive on past the ranch this time. They would probably wait until night-time to make their move. But, then again…

"They took the turnoff!" Delilah's shrill cry came over the airwaves. "Repeat, they took the turnoff! Oh, crap. What should I do?"

"Get your butt out of there, girl. Go home. We've got it covered. You did good."

"Roger that. Stay safe everyone. Lavender Lady, we're all rooting for ya, gal."

Faye wanted to say thank you, but she didn't think she could speak through the lump in her throat and the pounding of her heart.

"Okay, everyone. Let's get this show on the road. Gunther, you ready with the tractor units?"

"On our way, Papa Bear."

Faye stood up and looked around, her heart racing. She knew that Gunther had agreed to bring his huge feed container lorries to block all the exits to Mackay lands. The enemy would be trapped. This was it. Either she survived, or she didn't, but they wouldn't be able to escape. The thought had a strangely calming effect. She took a deep breath and stepped towards the hatch. She should pull up the ladder and close it. She could stay up here and they wouldn't find her. But then Bear lifted his head and gave a soft woof. Faye caught his gaze as he looked up at her, and she knew she couldn't leave him on his own.

She turned off the CB radio as she'd been told to. If they got in here and heard it, they would know what was going on and the element of surprise would be lost. But she was also aware that it left her without any means of knowing what was happening. She had to trust in Jeff's plan and stick with it by remaining in the cabin. She grabbed the shotgun and cartridge box and headed down the ladder.

Bear stood as she pulled the hatch closed and manhandled the ladder away from the hatch to rest it against the wall. It meant she couldn't get back up there in a hurry, but if the thugs managed to get into the house it would be too late anyway.

"Good boy, Bear. Now, I'm going to need you to be quiet now. Don't give us away, all right?" She knelt and hugged the dog with her free hand, not letting go of the shotgun. "Stay with me, boy. Come on."

She checked the doors and windows again, as well as the

hatch to the root store in the pantry. She left it unlocked from the inside, just in case she needed to hide down there. No one could get into the root store from the outside now, but she didn't want to go down there unless she absolutely had to. Right now, it felt too much like a tomb for her liking.

The slow rumble of tyres on the dirt driveway reached her ears. She crept towards the window and peeked out through the net curtains she'd insisted on installing. Two dark Buicks were making their way slowly towards the cabin. That meant the plan was working. The entrance to the ranch house drive was blocked by a stack of tree trunks, forcing the cars to follow the track to the cabin. Bear growled.

"Hush now," she whispered, scratching behind his ears. "It's all right. Our troops are out there. It's all going swimmingly."

She giggled a little at that. A group of hired guns were heading her way, intent on killing her, and she was telling her dog that it was *all going swimmingly?* She shook her head and took another calming breath. *This is not the time to get hysterical,* she told herself.

The cars pulled up in the yard in front of the cabin, about twenty yards away. Faye watched through her shotgun sight as the doors opened. She recognised the first two to emerge. They used to work security on the doors of James's favourite casino. There hadn't been enough evidence to charge them when their bosses had been arrested. They were nasty bastards. She'd seen them threaten people, and knew from the fear they generated by their very presence that everyone knew they weren't empty threats.

They looked around, wiping their sweaty faces with handkerchiefs, clearly unused to the sun's heat as it beat down into the wide valley. The mountains stood guard around them, revealing nothing but pasture and woodlands as far as the eye could see. One of them took off his suit jacket and tossed it into the car. He was wearing a gun in a holster over his now limp white shirt and dark waistcoat. His companion did the same.

Faye felt her lip curl as she watched the others exit the cars.

The Englishmen, unused to the heat after travelling in air-conditioned luxury for several hours, stood in a huddle, sweaty and uncomfortable, their weapons on display. She supposed they didn't think it would matter, out here in the back of beyond. Perhaps they thought they were safe, away from the city, confident in their arrogant assurance that they could get away with anything here in the Wild West.

"Well, that works both ways, chaps," she muttered. "I hope you're ready for it."

The Americans who had brought them were more cautious. They stayed close to the cars, their jackets on, although it was clear from their posture and watchful eyes that they were just as threatening as the others.

After a conversation that she couldn't hear, one of the Englishmen headed towards the porch steps. With a quiet command to Bear to follow, Faye crept into the kitchen and the pantry, where no one looking through the windows could see them.

She had already put a chair in there against the back wall. After locking the pantry door from the inside, she sat down and pointed to the floor. Bear lay down at her feet. She rested a hand on his head. "Quiet now, boy," she whispered.

She heard footsteps on the porch and a knocking at the door. She kept her grip on Bear, whispering and soothing him when he would have barked and gone to investigate. When no-one answered the front door, she heard footsteps follow the porch around to the back. There was silence for a while as the thug stopped. Faye imagined he was peering through the windows.

"There ain't no one there, Jim," he called out. "You sure this is the place?"

More footsteps joined the first set. "I bloody hope so. The quicker we do this job and get out of 'ere the better. All these fucking open spaces ain't natural."

The first voice laughed. "Well I reckon someone's having a laugh. Look at that – bleeding chickens, a veggie patch, fucking rocking chairs on the front porch. That Broughton bitch'd go stark raving mad, stuck in the middle of nowhere. A party girl like her would never live here."

"She's here all right. You saw that photo, Charlie. Just 'cause she's changed her hair, the silly cow, don't mean it ain't her. That Fairbrother tart said she looked just like that when she was at school."

Faye buried her face in Bear's fur, trying to keep her breathing steady and the dog calm. He seemed to sense that she needed him to behave.

A call from the front of the house got the their attention and the footsteps receded. When she was sure they were back in the front yard, Faye told Bear to stay and crept out. From the living room window she saw her truck coming down the drive. The American thugs stood their ground, watching while the English – *bloody idiots* – either grabbed their jackets or dived into the car. *As if no one's going to notice they're carrying guns,* she sneered.

The truck pulled up and Jeff got out.

"Hey fellas," he called, doing a creditable impression of the Clampett boy. "You lost?"

Faye held her breath. He hadn't said anything about riding in there on his own. *Where the hell are the others?* She glanced over her shoulder, wondering whether she had time to get up into the attic and call for back up on the CB. But even as the thought formed in her mind, the American thugs drew their guns and pointed them straight at Jeff.

He took a step back and raised his hands. "Woah, fellas. What the hell?"

The English got out of the cars again and came to stand next to their hired guns.

"Where is she?"

Jeff frowned. "Where's who?"

"Don't muck me about, cowboy. You was with her in New York. Where is she?"

Jeff shook his head, scowling. "You mean Mary-Beth? I ain't seen her since she ditched me for some suit in the city. Bitch got me to pay her bus fare and a hotel room then skipped out of me."

A couple of the men laughed. "Sounds like her, boss," said

one of them. "She could always get some daft bugger to open his wallet for her."

Faye felt a wash of shame run down her spine. He was right. She'd been a greedy, conniving bitch. She hated that Jeff was learning that about her from these evil bastards. She wanted to open fire, but they were eight against one and there were too many guns pointing at Jeff. She couldn't take the chance.

"Yeah," Jeff agreed, his hands still in the air. "So, what she do to you? Seems like a lot of you to come after one itty-bitty gal."

"None of your fucking business, mate."

"Okay," he said. "So, can I put my hands down?"

"Nah. You stay there. I ain't convinced she ain't 'ere."

"Look, man, you think I'd protect her?" he scoffed. "I just want a quiet life. Why don't we just forget I ever saw you, and you go look for Mary-Beth some other place, huh?"

"What you reckon, Charlie?" asked Jim. Even through the net curtains, Faye could see he was sweating like a pig. "Let's get out of here."

One of the American thugs glanced over at them. "Boss said no witnesses."

"Fair enough," said Charlie, turning away.

Chapter Fifty-Two

Facing eight guys and as many guns with his hands in the air didn't leave Jeff with a lot of options.

"Wait!" he yelled as the guy nearest him took aim. "You don't wanna kill me," he tried for a dopey grin, but keeping up the act of a dumbass was getting harder and harder. "I can help ya."

"Oh yeah? Now why would need you, mate? We've got plenty of help."

"So has she," he said. "You can't get to her without me."

His would-be assassins were getting antsy. "No witnesses," repeated one of the Vegas contingent.

"Hang on, hang on. If he can take us to her, it'll save a lot of bother, won't it?" said Jim. "I can't be doing with all this chasing around. If I don't get home soon, me missus'll have a fit. We've already been here a week. It's her sister's wedding in a few days. If I miss that, she'll kill me."

"Shut your mouth," said Charlie. "We got a job to do."

The other two Brits muttered and looked unhappy. "You said it was a quick one," one of them said. "I reckon we should just off this bloke and go home."

"Not until we get the girl," said Charlie.

"But she ain't here, mate. What's the point? She ain't likely to go back to London, is she? She can't do no damage if she's out here."

"I said shut the fuck up," Charlie yelled, turning on the other man. "It don't matter where she is. We're gonna find her and kill her. She put my brother behind bars, and yours n'all. She's gotta pay."

Charlie turned back and pointed his gun at Jeff.

"You really don't want to do that, man," said Jeff, his voice calm, all trace of the dopey cowboy gone.

"Yeah? What you gonna do about it?" Charlie sneered.

Jeff shrugged, his hands now on the top of his head. "Well now. I can't do much. Like you said, eight to one. But I got friends. You won't get off my land alive."

Charlie laughed as the others looked around, smirking. "Who'd you think you are, mate? John fucking Wayne? Got the cavalry waiting over the hill, have ya?"

"No. They're right here."

They didn't even notice his signal. A shot rang out. Jeff dropped to the dirt at the same time as one of the suits fell, a neat hole in his forehead.

Chapter Fifty-Three

Faye watched as all hell broke loose. For a moment she was stood in petrified silence, unable to move or act until she saw Jeff roll under the truck, away from the bullets flying around him.

He's all right!

The thugs were shooting in all directions, trying to work out where the shots that had already taken out two of them were coming from. A couple made a dive for the nearest car and they screeched out of the yard, heading for the road. One of the suits tried to run after them, but he was taken down by a shot in the leg. Charlie and Jim headed towards the protection of the cabin. Faye stepped back from the window, her gun trained on it, knowing they couldn't get through the solid front door. She could hear them shouting and cursing.

The second car took off, leaving just those two behind. She grinned. *Now the odds are better.* She knew the occupants of the two cars would be picked up before they got to the highway. The only two men standing were Charlie and Jim. She should have realised about their brothers. *But they should have realised about my brother.*

A soft whine at her side let her know that Bear was with her. She dropped to her knees, wrapping an arm around him. "Shhh, boy. It's nearly over. In your bed, Bear. Go."

The dog whined again before obeying, the sound seeming even louder now that the gunshots had ceased. She could hear footsteps running around the porch towards the back door. Faye raised her shotgun, ready to shoot. The dog watched her. "Stay," she said softly.

She wanted to run and check on Jeff. She knew he was alive because he'd moved. She thought he'd grabbed the gun of the man who'd been shot, so he had at least one weapon to hand. *Surely he had something on him. Only a madman would have gone into that situation unarmed.* She wanted to get out there, to be by his side. But she knew she needed to stay focussed on the threat of the two thugs now lurking outside on the back porch.

A couple of shots, fired in rapid succession, blasted through the lock on the kitchen door and a moment later it was kicked open. Faye stood, holding her aim, waiting for the first of them to run through the entrance. She could hear Jeff shouting orders and footsteps running across the yard towards the house, but she didn't have time to wait for them. It was only a matter of seconds between the shots and the door being breached before the two men charged in.

She pulled the trigger, catching Jim in the chest. He fell, Charlie tripped over him, screaming at her with hatred in his eyes as he pulled the trigger. There was an explosion of noise and pain as she fell backwards.

I'm all right, she thought. *I'm still alive.* She could feel pain in her arm, hear the thud of her shotgun as it landed on the floor beside her. She could smell blood and see Charlie gain his feet again and point his gun at her head. She wanted to reach for the pistol at her back, but she couldn't move her right arm and she knew she wouldn't be able to shoot him quick enough with her left.

"Didn't you learn nuffink when we offed your brother?" he snarled. "Did you really think we'd let you get away with it? You should have died the day you put my brother away. But you're gonna die now, bitch."

She looked up at the barrel of his gun, her vision going woozy as her blood dripped onto the floor. "I'd do it again," she said, using her best ice-cold princess voice. She was aware of a movement just behind her assailant. She smiled at the beautiful furry animal crouching, reading to pounce.

"I'm gonna off you, then I'm gonna get that fucking boyfriend of yours." Charlie laughed. "Think some cowboy's gonna get the better of me? He don't know nuffink."

She smiled, blinking against the darkness that was

threatening to engulf her. "Oh, I think you'll find he knows a great deal more than you," she said. "For example, he knows to stay away from bears. Do you?"

Charlie looked angry and confused. He was shaking with rage. "What the fuck are you talking about?" He waved his gun in the air. "Why ain't you begging me? You're gonna die – d'you hear me?"

"Everyone dies," she said. "But at least I won't get eaten by a **bear**."

"What? Shut up, you fucking bitch." He took a swing at her with his gun hand but it didn't make contact. A scream rang out as Bear leapt, his teeth sinking into the flesh of Charlie's arm, making him drop the gun, just as his fingers squeezed the trigger.

The scream and the explosion of sound were the last things she was aware of before the darkness closed around her.

Chapter Fifty-Four

Jeff managed to grab the gun off the goon who fell next to him before rolling under the truck and out the other side. Shots were flying from all directions. He knew his guys would have everything under control.

One of the cars gunned its engine and slid past him, one of the doors still open as a couple of the thugs tried to get away. Jeff took a shot at their tires and grinned as there was a satisfying pop and the rear end of the car slewed sideways before straightening out and speeding away. He didn't go after it. The Sheriff and a whole crowd of law enforcement officers were waiting for them, and the tractors blocking the road would prevent any escape.

He turned back towards the cabin and took stock of the situation. Two goons down, that left four. One had reached the other car and was screaming at his *compadres*.

"Get in the fucking car!"

A shot shattered the rear window of the Buick, sending the driver screeching up the drive, leaving his friends to their fate. Jeff shook his head. A true soldier never leaves anyone behind. These bastards had no honour.

One of the goons was running after the escaping car. A shot from the woods got him in the leg and he went down.

"Two left," he breathed. *The English guys. The ones with the most reason to hate Faye.*

He heard a shot, then another and the crack of the kitchen door hitting the wall. Another shot. Jeff took off running. He could see the others emerging from the woods and the barn, but he didn't stop. He took the porch steps in one leap.

"Why ain't you begging me?" The voice from inside the cabin froze his blood. "You're gonna die – d'you hear me?"

"Everyone dies," she said. Jeff moved; she was still alive. He had to get to her. He barely registered her next words. "But at least I won't get eaten by a *bear*."

As her assassin's yell turned to a scream, Jeff saw Bear launch himself at Faye's attacker. The explosion rang out, and debris rained down on them as he launched himself over the body in the doorway, desperate to get to Faye. He covered her body, frantically checking her for signs of life. She groaned as he touched her arm and his fingers came away covered in blood.

She's alive, but shot.

More screams came from across the room as Bear shook the arm in his jaws. Jeff smiled as he heard the bones crunch. He moved, gently cradling Faye in his arms as he carried her out of the room, kicking their guns away as he went. Iverson arrived on the porch as he emerged.

"Let me take her," he said. "I've got a first aid kit in the barn."

Jeff didn't want to let her go, but the screams from the kitchen were getting higher.

"We'd better go and stop that, man." Baldwin grinned as he joined them. "You don't want Bear to get in trouble for eating the evidence. Do ya?"

Jeff transferred Faye to Iverson's arms. She groaned but didn't open her eyes. "You take good care of her," he ordered.

Back in the kitchen the big guy was screaming and crying like a baby, cradling his chewed arm while Bear had his lower leg gripped tightly in his jaws.

"Get him off! Get him off me!" he screamed.

Jeff and Baldwin stood over him, arms crossed. "What d'you think," Jeff asked his friend. "Do we let Bear eat him, or hand him over to the cops?"

"Don't let him eat me! Oh God, he's eating me!"

Baldwin rubbed his chin. "I think he wants the cops," he said. "Shame."

Jeff signalled to Bear to still, but the dog didn't let go. He waited, eyes on his master, his tail wagging.

"I think maybe you deserve to be eaten, you lousy scumbag.

You just shot my woman. That animal loves her, y' know. He don't take kindly to you turning up here, shooting up my place and hurting my woman."

"For fuck's sake, call him off!"

"Not yet."

Charlie screamed again, even though Bear had ceased chewing on his flesh.

"If I call him off – are you listening to me?" Jeff leaned towards him and yelled over the man's cries.

Charlie flinched and began to whimper. Jeff continued to stare at him.

"I'm listening," he said eventually.

Jeff straightened up and nodded. "Good. Now listen up. Your life depends on it. You're going to spend a lot of time in jail, I guarantee it. Because you're scum. You should have learned your lesson when my woman took your organisation down. But you didn't. Now, you've run out of choices. This is the end. If you ever even think of coming near her again, I will end you and Bear here *will* eat you. No one will ever know what happened to you." He kicked at Charlie's bloody arm. Just a nudge, but enough to have the guy screaming in pain again. "Understand?"

Through his screams, Charlie swore that he understood. Jeff nodded and turned to Baldwin. Hamilton was standing in the doorway.

"You guys okay to watch him until the Sheriff arrives?"

"Sure thing, Sarge."

"Good. I gotta check on Faye."

"She's okay," said Hamilton. "She just woke up."

Jeff nodded, relief flooding him. "Thanks." He turned towards the door. "Come on Bear, good dog."

The beast dropped the man's leg and stood over him, snarling at the snivelling wreck. With a final bark, he leapt over his prone body and followed Jeff out towards the barn.

Chapter Fifty-Five

Faye became of aware of light and pain as she slowly regained consciousness. She groaned.

"Don't move, Faye." It was Iverson. "I know it hurts like a bitch, but it's just a flesh wound. Those dumb asses couldn't shoot fish in a barrel."

"Lucky me," she said, her voice cracked and dry. "There's nothing worse than inept assassins."

Iverson laughed. "You're one tough lady, Faye. No wonder Mackay's so taken with ya."

She gave him a smile that turned to a grimace as he applied pressure to her wound. She turned her head just in time to see him pour some liquid into the bullet hole in her arm. With a yelp, her good hand shot out and she punched him on the chin, forcing his head back. He dropped the bottle and put his hand to his face.

"That bloody stings," she said.

He tested his jaw, moving it from side to side. "Yeah, sorry. Maybe I should've warned you."

"Yes, you should," she huffed. "But I'm sorry I hit you."

"What's going on?" Jeff stood in the barn doorway, looking from Faye to Iverson. "Who's hitting who?"

"She punched me," he said. "My fault. I didn't warn her I was pouring iodine into her wound."

"And it bloody hurt," she complained.

Jeff smiled as he approached. "I guess you're not dying if you're feisty enough to punch this big guy."

"I've already apologised," she said. "Is everyone else all right? Where's Bear?"

At the sound of his name, the dog rushed into the barn and would have leapt all over her if Jeff hadn't grabbed him in both arms.

"Woah, boy. Get down!"

The dog lay down, but then began crawling along the floor towards Faye, whining and tail wagging the whole way. Faye laughed and held out her good hand for the dog to nuzzle and lick.

"Good boy," she crooned. "You saved me."

Jeff raised an eyebrow. She laughed. "You too. You all saved me. I can't believe it's over."

"I reckon so." He took a walkie-talkie from his back pocket. "I'd better check in with the Sheriff." He knelt by her side, his hand on her thigh as he asked for a 'sit rep'. Faye assume it meant situation report.

"Got the two guys in the cars," came the response.

"Wait, there were three in the cars – two in the first, one in the second."

"Damn! We only got one in each car. I reckon one must have bailed. He must have headed into the woods. I'll get…"

"No, Sheriff. The woods are booby-trapped. Can you get your guys to cover the perimeter so he doesn't get away?"

"Sure thing. We're moving the tractor to let in an ambulance for Faye. What about the others at your end? Any other casualties?"

"A couple of the bad guys, the rest dead. Faye's the only casualty on our side."

"I'm all right," she called. "Iverson says it's just a flesh wound."

"Okay. Ten-four that. Good to know. The feds are ready to move in. That all right with you, boy?"

"Sure thing. Just tell 'em to stay out of the woods for now."

Faye tried to sit up, but Iverson gently but firmly pushed her back down. She glared at him but he smiled. "Stay where you are."

"There's one of them still out there," she glared at him.

"And I'm going to get him," said Jeff, checking his gun was loaded.

"Not on your own," she said.

He smiled, leaned down and kissed her on the lips. "Don't

worry. I'm a smart man. I'm taking Bear with me." The dog woofed as if in agreement. "That's right, boy. We're going to hunt down a bad guy. Maybe I'll let you chew on this one like you did with the other guy, eh?"

Faye laughed, but then groaned as the movement of her shoulder caused pain to shoot down her arm. In the distance, she heard the sirens of the ambulances. She beckoned Bear to her and he licked her cheek.

"Good dog, Bear. You guard Jeff for me, all right? I want him in one piece." She looked at Jeff over the dog's furry head. "And you take care of my dog," she told him. "I don't want to hear he's been caught in a trap. If that happens, I'll shoot you myself."

He nodded as Iverson snorted. Faye closed her eyes and laid her head back. Her arm was throbbing, but she could feel her fingers, so she knew it wasn't serious. But she knew she was weak from blood loss, otherwise she'd have insisted on going with Jeff herself.

"In fact," she raised her head again. "I don't think you and Bear should go in alone. Iverson, leave me with a gun and go with them." When Jeff would have refused, she shook her head. "I know you know what you're doing, but the man out there is desperate. He's in a strange place, and his friends are dead or have buggered off and left him. I don't want him to get the chance to hurt you or Bear. Take Iverson, Jeff. Please."

She saw the moment she won the argument. It was the moment she said *please.* She hid her smile, not wanting him to think she was gloating, even if she was.

"Okay, but only because the medics are here." He gestured over his shoulder as more vehicles pulled up in the yard. Iverson went out to meet them, no doubt to report on her injury as well.

"Be careful," she said to Jeff.

"We will." He straightened up, checking his weapon again.

"Take my knife," she said, pointing to her leg.

He grinned. "Now, the thought of handling your sexy little ankle is mighty tempting, Princess, but I've got my own." A switchblade appeared in his hand as if by magic.

"Darn it," she said in her best Mary-Beth voice. He laughed. "Another time."

The medics came in, rolling a stretcher. Jeff touched her cheek, then he was gone. She felt fear return as he walked out of sight, but she pushed it back and tried to concentrate on answering the questions the ambulance crew were asking as they transferred her to the stretcher and checked her over before they took her to the ambulance.

There were police officers and people milling around. Three bodies were laid out on the grass, their faces covered with blankets. She realised that one of them was the man called Jim, whom she'd shot. Did that make her a murderer, in addition to all of her other sins?

There was a commotion as another crew carried another stretcher down the porch steps from the cabin. When a bleeding and moaning Charlie spotted her, he began shouting.

"Keep that fucking bitch away from me! She set a bloody beast on me! Tried to eat me, it did. I want her arrested. She killed Jim and she tried to feed me to that fucking bear."

One of the officers called over to Faye. "Does he mean Bear?"

Faye nodded and the policemen all started laughing and hooting. She grinned. Everyone knew that Bear was the softest, daftest dog in the state.

"Man, you must have really pissed him off if Bear bit ya," called another man.

"Hey, Joe. You'd better tell the doc to give this guy an anti-rabies shot."

"Yeah, that's what I need," cried Charlie. "She set her bloody rabid beast on me."

The guys guiding Charlie's stretcher into their ambulance joined in the fun. "You sure you want the shot, man? It's a six-inch needle and they jab it straight into your belly. And it ain't just one shot. You have to have a whole course. Every day for a week or two, depending on the size of the animal that bit ya."

"Oh fuck," Charlie gasped.

"Take the shots, Charlie," she called, her mirth easing her

own pain. "The full course. I can't guarantee Bear's healthy. He does love to wander round the woods, picking up carrion. He ate a skunk the other day. It was very nasty."

Everyone was openly laughing now, except Charlie who was swearing as they closed the doors on the ambulance.

"I don't suppose we can be taken to different hospitals?" she asked as she was loaded into the other vehicle.

"Don't worry. He's going to Billings. They've got a secure hospital wing at the jail there. We're going to the local emergency department."

"Good. But… Is there any chance we can wait for a while? My… Jeff's in the woods, rounding up the last fugitive. I just want to—"

"Sorry, ma'am. Our orders are to get you out of here," he said. "Don't worry. Jeff knows what he's doing."

She wanted to argue, but her head was beginning to ache and she was starting to shake. She knew enough to know that she'd lost a lot of blood from her wound and might be suffering from shock.

"All right," she said. "Let's go."

Chapter Fifty-Six

Jeff and Iverson made their way slowly into the woods with Bear at their heels. The sun was beginning to disappear behind the mountains, bringing a chill to the air as the light faded.

"If he bailed from a car on the drive out, he'll have come in from the east," said Jeff, his voice soft. He checked his watch. "He's been in here about thirty, forty minutes tops."

Iverson nodded. They stayed off the tracks kept open by wildlife and horses, checking the trip wires they'd set along the way. Ten minutes in, they found a wire that had been dislodged. There was blood and a tiny scrap of grey cloth stuck to it.

"Bingo," Jeff gave a grim smile. "Bear, come here, boy." He held the cloth to dog's nose, along with a drop of the blood. "Where'd he go, Bear?"

The dog snuffled around for a moment before picking up the scent. As expected, the fugitive had left the path and was heading west. Jeff kept his hand in Bear's fur, making sure the dog didn't encounter any of their other booby traps. Iverson followed, both men moving swiftly and silently as they'd been trained.

Every few yards they saw signs of their quarry. He clearly wasn't a woodsman. There were broken twigs and footprints in the dirt, as well as occasional spots of blood.

After a few minutes, Bear's head came up and the men stopped and listened. A crackle of dried leaves was the only warning they had before a man emerged from behind a tree and took aim at them. Jeff pushed Bear away and dropped to the ground, firing his pistol as he went. He was aware of Iverson taking cover behind another tree and Bear slinking away in the other direction.

The suit yelped and ran, his shots going wild as he crashed through the undergrowth. Jeff didn't think he'd hit him. But that was okay. He wouldn't get far.

He stood and signalled to Iverson and they moved off after their target. He could see Bear creeping through the undergrowth parallel to them. *Damn, that dog is a born soldier,* he thought. *We gotta get him some big-ass bones as a reward when this is over.*

Their quarry was getting tired, and making too much noise. They took their time. He wasn't going anywhere. There was a cordon of cops and cowboys around the perimeter of the woods. Jeff wondered if maybe he should yell and tell the guy to give it up. But then he remembered the fear he and the other thugs had put Faye through – *Goddamit, she got shot back there!* – and he knew he wanted to hunt this bastard down and make him pay. He patted his arm where his switchblade was concealed. *Let him sweat, then I'll help him bleed.*

He realised where they were, close to the main trail through the woods. If they could corral him a little further on... He signalled to Iverson and gave a low whistle to Bear, calling him to his side again. The two soldiers moved in unison, making sure that their quarry could hear them. The guy was probably out of ammo, but they proceeded with caution, just in case they were wrong. They could hear him stumbling along ahead of them, and caught glimpses of him through the trees. He was going right where they wanted him to.

A sudden yell had Jeff grinning. "Got him," he said.

They cleared the trees moments later to find the suit dangling by his ankles from a Ponderosa Pine, his gun on the ground below him. Bear let out a bark and ran at him, leaping and snapping at his arms as he swung and twisted.

"Call it off!" he yelled.

His voice set Bear off again, and Jeff stood back as the dog leapt at the hanging man, pushing him like a papa with his kid on a swing.

The soldiers watched for a few moments, enjoying the show. Then Jeff called to Bear and the dog sat, his tongue hanging out, his tail wagging, his dark eyes never leaving his prey. Jeff stepped forward, scratching between Bear's ears. "Good dog," he said.

"Let me down," demanded the suit. "You hillbillies got no idea what you're dealing with."

Jeff looked at Iverson. "Did he just call you a hillbilly, soldier?"

"I think he did, Sarge."

Jeff shook his head and moved closer to the man. "Lower the rope by a couple of feet," he told his friend. "Mind you don't drop him on his head."

"Yes, sir." Iverson did as he was asked. The suit squealed as he dropped a couple of feet – not enough for him to touch the ground, but fast enough to worry him. Jeff stepped closer, bending down to stare in his captive's face.

"Now, we're gonna have us a little parlay. 'Cause I'm thinking you got the wrong impression of folks round here, man."

"Just let me down and we'll forget about it, okay?"

"Or what?" asked Iverson. "It don't look like you got much to bargain with."

The man wriggled on the end of the rope. Bear woofed, scaring the guy enough that he stopped moving, his eyes on the dog.

"Look, I just came along for the ride, all right? Those limey bastards wanted to off the woman. Said she was a stool pigeon. They didn't tell us she had the damned army guarding her."

"So, why did they want you along?" asked Jeff. When there was no reply, he went on. "I'm guessing you and your associates work for the operations around Las Vegas. Maybe you owed them a favour. Or did they pay you? Thought it was easy money?"

Again, his questions were met with silence. Jeff tutted and shook his head. "I don't think he wants to parlay. So I guess we'd better cut to the chase." He reached over and unzipped the suit's fly, shoving his hand inside and pulling out the guy's soft cock.

"What the fuck?" The suit wriggled and twisted, trying to

get his John Thomas away from Jeff's hand.

"It's the law round here, man. Didn't you know?" Jeff asked him. "You talk, or you get your dick cut off and fed to Bear here." He grinned as the switchblade appeared in his other hand and he opened it with a quick flick of his wrist.

"You're kidding, right?" the suit snarled. "Just get your hand off my cock and let me down."

Jeff twisted his hand, making the guy gasp. "You're not in any position to tell anyone what to do, punk. Your pals are either dead or in handcuffs. You're on my territory now. We play by my rules." He held up his other hand and moved his knife towards the hanging man. "We could leave your body up in the hills and no one would ever find you."

"I got other friends. They'll come after you."

"Yeah? I guess you must be some big shot," said Iverson. "So why the hell are you here in the woods and not in some fancy casino with a couple of chicks and bottle of Jack?"

"It was a job. Nothing personal. For fuck's sake, will you tell him to quit holding my cock, man? Just let me go and we'll forget all about this."

"No can do," said Iverson. He came up behind the guy and grabbed his arms. In seconds his wrists were tied together behind his back. "You broke the rules, *man.* Time to pay."

Jeff brought the knife a little closer.

"No! No, please!" The guy screamed in panic, trying bend his body upwards to protect his crown jewels.

"But you messed with his woman, man," said Iverson. "Don't you know better than that?"

"I didn't know who she was. She was just a bitch who – *ooofff!"*

He swung away as Jeff's hand left his cock and his fist connected with the suit's gut.

"Never, *ever* call my woman a bitch. You hear me?"

The suit swung and coughed, trying to catch his breath. Jeff pulled back his fist for another blow.

"Okay, man. I hear ya."

Jeff nodded and opened his fist, his fingers playing with the blade in his other hand. "Now, tell me why I shouldn't feed my dog your cock and balls. And don't lie to me, boy. I hate liars."

All sign of his bravado gone, the guy begged for mercy.

"You're not telling me what I need to know, man," Jeff went on. "Who told you it was okay to come to Montana and trespass on my land? Why'd you end up out here with those slimey limeys, eh? Ain't the action in Vegas enough for ya?"

"How'd you know we're from Vegas?" he asked.

Jeff grinned. "We got friends."

"Fuck. Who you working with? The Canadian families? The natives in Wyoming?"

Jeff shook his head. "None of the scum that you deal with, boy. Our friends are international. You mess with us, you mess with something bigger than you'll ever believe." He let that sink in for a moment. "Now, if you want to get out of this... *intact*... you need to give up your limey friends and whoever sent you to work with them."

"Jesus Christ, man. I'll be signing my own death warrant."

"You think?" said Iverson. "Looks like you got a choice, man. Slow and painful, watching Bear feast on your balls while you bleed out." The man whimpered. "Or turn state's evidence and maybe get a chance of protection if you give up enough to make it worth our while."

"You're crazy, man. I can't— What the fuck are you doing? No!" He screamed as Jeff grabbed his limp cock and ran his blade along it – not hard, but just enough to draw a couple of beads of blood.

"Here, Bear. Ready for dinner, boy?" Jeff crooned. Right on cue, the dog barked.

"No! Please God, no! All right! I'll talk. I'll tell you everything you wanna know. But don't feed me to him, please!" He twisted and turned, desperate to escape.

Jeff and Iverson both petted the dog, pretending to hold the beast back from the snack hanging in front of him. Iverson kept his back to their captive as he tried not to bust a gut laughing. After a few minutes, Jeff stepped away, pulled out his walkie-talkie and called for the cops to come and get their captive.

"You remember now, boy. You talk, or we'll come and find

you," said Iverson.

"Yeah," said Jeff. "And we'll bring Bear. You hear me?"

"I hear ya," said the suit as swayed in the breeze.

Jeff stepped forward and tucked the guy's junk back in his pants before zipping him back up. "And don't, whatever you do, ever come back to Montana, y'hear?"

"No, sir. I'm done with Montana."

"Atta boy," said Jeff, patting his face before turning and walking away with Iverson.

"Wait, where are you going? Don't leave me here with that…"

Jeff turned and whistled to Bear. "Come on, boy. I got you a nice big bone back at the cabin."

The dog bounded after the men as they walked back to the cabin, leaving the suit swinging in the breeze, waiting for the cops to cut him down.

Chapter Fifty-Seven

Faye hated hospitals and she hated fuss, but she had to put up with both as her wound was dressed and she was surrounded by law enforcement officers asking questions. So it was with relief that she greeted Julian Grainger when he appeared in the doorway to her hospital room. It took just a nod from him to her chief inquisitor to have the room cleared of all but the medic finishing her observations. Moments later, they were alone.

"How are you, my dear?" he asked as he sat beside her. "You're pale, but seem to be in remarkably good condition, considering you've just been shot."

She scoffed. "Another inept assassin. The idiot couldn't shoot a fish in a barrel, as Jeff would say."

Grainger smiled. "Thank the lord for that."

"Any news of him?" she asked. "I assume from your presence here that you've been in charge of operations."

"I believe the last of the fugitives has been apprehended. Jeff and his associates are speaking to the authorities."

"They'd better not be arrested," she said. "All they were doing was protecting me."

"I don't think there's any danger of that, my dear."

She nodded, satisfied that he was telling her the truth. That thought led her to others. "Tell me," she said, her eyes narrowed. "Did you set us up?"

"I'm sorry," he said, his expression bland. "I'm not sure what you mean."

She shook her head, which was still aching, and waved a finger at him. "Don't give me that, Mr Grainger. If it wasn't a set-up, why would you be here? You wanted to finish what we started, didn't you? Were you intending to help the American authorities mop up some of the Las Vegas criminal fraternity at the same time, or was that just pure, dumb luck?"

He smiled, looking a little bashful. "I keep forgetting what a sharp brain you have, Faye. Have you ever thought about a career in the security business? We could use someone like you."

"No, thank you. I have no desire to make myself any more of a target than I already am." She sighed. "I suppose we'll have American gangsters after us now. I'm not sure I can forgive you for that. The Mackays are good people. They don't deserve this kind of trouble."

"Nor do you, my dear. However, I believe that your fears are unfounded. The men we arrested were merely hired guns with little loyalty to any particular group. They are mercenaries, if you like, who sell their services for the right price. They are likely to prove very useful. It appears they're willing to exchange their extensive knowledge of the criminal fraternity in Las Vegas in return for the opportunity to start a new life in another part of the country. The Americans have a very efficient witness protection programme. I've studied their methods, and it has helped me keep you and others safe over the years."

She rested her head against the pillow and absorbed this. She should be angry, and she was – on behalf of the Mackays, Jeff's army buddies, the ranch hands and all the local people who had stepped in to protect her. She certainly felt used. But her overwhelming feeling was one of relief.

"So, can you assure me it's all over? That there won't be any more thugs coming after me and the people I—" She had been about to say *I love*, but stopped herself. "The people around me," she said, not looking him in the eye.

Faye couldn't remember the last time – if ever – that she had considered that she might love someone. Her family didn't love. They didn't know how. She'd been brought up to believe that love was a weakness, something the lower classes subscribed to in order to make their miserable existences more palatable. Declarations of love from various lovers had made her angry. How could they possibly be in love with her when she treated them like dirt? She'd known they only wanted her for her connections and her family fortune. The only reason she and James had lasted more than a few months had been his honesty. He was as selfish and entitled as she was.

"I think I can confidently say you're in the clear now. Felicity Broughton will have to stay dead, but you could reinstate direct contact with your mother, so long as you're both discreet. But if you still don't feel safe, I can arrange for you to move on, make another fresh start."

"Again?" She shook her head. "No thank you." The thought of leaving the ranch and the Mackays now made her feel sick. *I want to stay. I want to belong,* she thought. "I'll probably call my mother occasionally. But I'll stay here. Unless, of course, they want me to leave. I wouldn't blame them, would you?"

"I'm sure they won't. As you quite rightly surmised, my dear. None of this was your fault, and Jeff is aware of that now."

"I suppose that's the nearest I'm going to get to an admission that you set us up," she said.

He smiled that polite, bland smile he used so often. The one that said that he wasn't going to tell her, no matter how often she asked, or how much she demanded answers.

He stood up, patting her hand. "I'll leave you to rest. Don't worry about the authorities. I'll deal with them."

"I'm not likely to see you again, am I?"

"Probably not. You're safe now. My people will keep a watching brief, just to make sure, and you can always contact us if you feel the need. But I don't expect you'll encounter any more trouble from your old life. Enjoy your new life without fear, my dear."

"Thank you."

"You're very welcome. Be happy, Faye. You deserve it."

As the door closed behind him, Faye gave in to tears. She wanted to believe that it was all over, that she didn't have to spend her life looking over her shoulder in fear. But as that threat receded, another fear was growing within her. *What if Jeff wants me to leave? He's fulfilled his duty to his father, so there's no reason for him to want me around any more, is there? He'll probably be glad to see the back of me.*

She wallowed in this, letting her tears fall freely for the first time in a long, long time. Her mind knew that she needed to let it all out, that she would feel better and stronger when she'd cried it all out. Then she'd be ready to be told she wasn't wanted back at the Mackay ranch. Then she'd be able to make plans for her future alone. She didn't need Grainger or Jeff or anyone for that. She had money, and she was strong and healthy. She could cope.

But her heart was breaking. In Montana, she had found a place where she felt she belonged, and people who accepted her for who she was, not for her pedigree or how much money she had. No one had ever talked to her like Jeff did. He cut through her snootiness, her coldness, and made her laugh. She giggled and hiccoughed through her tears as she remembered some of their acerbic exchanges. She'd met her match in Jeff Mackay. He didn't let her get away with anything. He was good for her.

But am I good for him? Probably not. I've brought gangsters to his home. I've never shown him how much I appreciate him. Am I too late?

She tried her best to shut down her silly, silly heart, and eventually she slept.

Chapter Fifty-Eight

Jeff had been questioned for what seemed like hours. He wasn't worried about being arrested – he knew the operation had been sanctioned by both the local cops and the feds, thanks to Julian Grainger and his connections. So he answered everything honestly, only failing to mention the small incident with his knife and the hanging man's cock. No one needed to know about that, and Iverson wasn't likely to blab about it.

When he was finally done, it was the middle of the night. He was assured that Faye was fine and staying in the hospital overnight for observation due to the amount of blood she'd lost. The cops advised him to wait until morning to go and see her. He wanted to argue, but then Grainger said he'd seen her and she was better left to sleep and recover.

Back at the cabin, he noticed a light still on in the barn. He went in to find Iverson, Baldwin and Hamilton drinking beer and playing cards. Bear was with them, curled up on a blanket on the concrete floor. Ebony whinnied a greeting from his stall.

"Hey, Sarge. About time you got here," said Baldwin.

Hamilton nudged up on the hay bale he was sitting on, and Jeff sank down beside him. Bear got up and nuzzled him.

"Hey, boy. You did good today. These bozos fed you, huh?"

"Yeah," said Iverson. "We grilled some steaks for dinner. Bear got the biggest one we could find."

Jeff smiled. "Thanks. And thanks for being here, guys."

"Where else would we be when one of our brothers needs help?" said Baldwin. "You'd be there for us."

"I sure would. Any time."

Someone handed him a beer, and Jeff clinked bottles with them in a silent toast before drinking.

"So, what now?" asked Hamilton. "Did Grainger offer you a job? He offered to hire all of us."

Jeff grimaced. "Yeah, he did. Right before I tried to punch him. Turns out he set us up. Said it was the only way to make sure Faye stayed safe in the future."

"Did you say you *tried* to punch him?"

"Yeah. Slippery bastard knows martial arts. He had me in a headlock before I made contact."

His buddies hooted and howled with laughter. Eventually, he joined in. The idea that he had been bested by a man three decades older than him was damned humiliating, but he had a grudging respect for the guy. He imagined his dad would be looking down on him, laughing his ass off, just like these clowns.

"So, did he withdraw the job offer?" Baldwin asked when he stopped laughing.

"No. But I turned him down," he said, his mood sobering. "I'm needed here."

"Faye's safe now," said Hamilton, his tone gentle. "Do you think she'll stay?"

Jeff shrugged. His head was telling him she would probably take off for a city somewhere, or even England, and never look back. But his heart was hoping she'd stay. She seemed at home here, no matter where she came from. They'd been slowly getting to know each other, finding more things they had in common than not. The thought of her leaving made him feel sick to his stomach.

"I guess it's up to her now," he said. "But whatever she decides, I'll stay. Sal and Nick could do with some help. It's not fair to leave all the work of running the ranch to them."

"Fair enough," said Iverson. "It's a mighty fine spread you've got here."

"Yeah." But he wondered how he would feel about it if Faye left. It wouldn't be the same.

"I might take him up on the offer," said Baldwin. "It would fit in with my PI work, and the money's a damned sight better.

"Not me," said Hamilton. "I'll stick with sports training. I don't need no more nightmares."

Jeff looked at him. "You have nightmares?"

Hamilton looked down at the almost empty beer bottle in his hand and nodded. "I've been seeing this chick – a real sweetheart, you know? Might be the real deal. She got freaked out when I started screaming in the middle of the night. I reckoned she'd kick me out of bed and out of her life for sure. But her dad's a psychologist. She made me see him. He calls it Post Traumatic Stress Disorder. He's getting more and more vets on his books these days."

Jeff took a swig of his beer. "Does it help?" he asked.

"Not at first. It got worse. But then it did. I haven't had a nightmare or a flashback for a couple of months now."

"Flashback?" said Baldwin, sitting up straighter. "Like when you feel like you're back in 'Nam?"

Hamilton nodded. Jeff ran a hand down his face.

"Fuck, man. I thought it was just me," he said.

"You too? Man, how'd you cope with all the shooting going on around here today?"

He frowned. "I spent some time on target practice, getting used to gunshots. When it came down to it, I didn't think about it. I just did what needed to be done." He shook his head. That sounded too simple. "And Faye helped." The only time he'd slept without being plagued by his terrors had been when she was in the bed with him. "She understands. She has her own nightmares."

Iverson nodded. "I saw her scars," he said. "I guess those limeys and their associates had something to do with that?"

"Yeah." He didn't share the details. That was Faye's story to tell, if she ever wanted to. "What if all this brings them back for her?" He didn't want to think about whether his own nightmares would now feature her, covered in blood.

"She's tough. She'll be okay. But I'll give you my guy's number just in case. Hell, he's likely to be my father-in-law soon if my gal will have me. Should be able to get you a family discount, man."

Jeff nodded. "Appreciate it."

Iverson stood up. "Well, I reckon I'll hit the hay." He looked up at the hayloft where their bunks were, amongst the stacked bales. "Literally," he grinned. "Man, I'm looking forward to getting back to my own bed."

Jeff stood and hugged him, slapping him on the back. "Thanks, man. I owe ya."

"Any time, brother. You know it."

The others joined them, all of them ready to get some sleep. It wouldn't be long before the sun rose over the mountains, and they'd all been up and on full alert since early the previous morning.

Jeff walked over to the cabin with Bear. Someone had already fixed the lock on the kitchen door. The guys had given him a couple of new keys for it. He unlocked the door and walked in. There was still a pool of blood drying on the floor, some plaster was missing from the kitchen ceiling and there was a broken chair, but otherwise the place was untouched. He would clean up later. Right now, the adrenaline that had kept him going had drained out of him and he was exhausted.

"Come on, boy," he said. Man and dog went into the bedroom and collapsed on the bed. Jeff thought he'd be asleep as soon as his head hit the pillow, but his mind kept going over everything that had happened in the last twenty-four hours, and a particular piece of information Grainger had let slip just before he'd left. Then he got to thinking about Faye and what would happen with her now. He was trying to work out what he wanted when sleep finally overtook him and he fell into a deep, dreamless sleep.

Chapter Fifty-Nine

Faye was ready to go when Jeff walked into her hospital room at eleven the next morning.

"You took your time, soldier," she said. "Have they been interrogating you all this time? You look like hell."

He rubbed at his jaw. He hadn't bothered to shave when he'd finally dragged himself out of bed after not nearly enough sleep to let Bear answer the call of nature. "Don't hold back, sweetheart," he grinned.

"Just get me out of here," she said. "I've had enough of being prodded and poked."

She was wearing her jeans, with a t-shirt that said *Montana Rocks* with an image of the mountains on it. When she saw him looking, she glanced down at her chest. "They cut off my shirt. Someone brought me this from the hospital gift shop."

"It looks good. Ready to go home?" he asked.

Faye gave him a sharp look. Did he mean back to the cabin, or was he suggesting she go back to England? His expression gave nothing away. She decided to worry about it later. For now, the cabin was home. And that was where she wanted to go.

She nodded. "Let's go," she said, getting up from the chair where she'd been looking out of the window, waiting for him.

She must have stood up too quickly because the movement made her feel dizzy. Before she could fall, Jeff was there, a steadying hand at her waist.

"Thanks," she said, her voice a little breathless. "I moved too fast."

"Take it steady. Lean on me," he said.

She did as he suggested, resting her head on his broad chest as her senses settled. She could have sworn she felt his lips on the top of her head, but it was probably wishful thinking. She stayed there as long as she dared before stepping back.

"I'm all right now. Let's go home."

He studied her face for a moment, then nodded. He crooked his elbow and she took his arm, leaning on him as they made their way out of the hospital. As they passed the reception desk, Jeff paused. She pulled on his arm.

"It's all right. Grainger took care of the bill."

"That's the damned least he could've done," he growled.

"You worked it out then – that he set us up?"

"Yeah. Bastard."

She laughed. "I hope you didn't try to hit him. Someone once told me he knows fifty ways to kill a man."

He looked sheepish. "I know that now," he said.

She laughed again, feeling better with every step.

Bear was waiting for them, his furry body taking up the whole of the back seat of the car. He greeted her with happy woofs and tried to lick her face.

"No tongues, Bear," she said sharply.

The dog huffed and settled his head on her shoulder over the back of the car seat, his warm presence making her feel safe. She smiled as Jeff got into the car and shook his head at the sight.

"I guess we both missed her last night, eh, Bear?" he said, his gaze searching her face.

He must have been satisfied with her smile, because he nodded and started the car. The drive back took no time at all and soon they were pulling up outside the cabin. She took her time getting out of the car, cradling her injured arm, but she didn't wait for Jeff to help her as she walked up the steps to the porch. He came up behind her, reaching round and opening the door then stepping back for her to enter. Bear followed close behind.

"I don't think he's gonna let you out of his sight any time soon," Jeff observed.

She scratched between the dog's ears. "I don't mind. I missed him too." She wanted to say more, but suddenly felt shy. It was a strange feeling she'd never experienced before. She didn't like it, even as she understood it.

She looked around the living room as she stood in the doorway. "I wasn't sure how it would feel, coming back," she said as he came up behind her.

"If it freaks you out, you can always stay at the big house. Sally won't mind."

She shook her head. "No. This is home," she said. "At least…"

"At least what?"

She took a deep breath and turned to face him. "I know it's your property and I understand if you want me to leave – especially after everything that's happened. But—" A quick glance at his expression silenced her. He gave nothing away. Was she making a complete fool of herself? She'd never begged, not once in her entire life. But right now, she wanted to get on her knees and beg him to give her a chance. The thought made her angry. Broughtons never begged.

"You were saying, Princess?" he said.

Her temper flashed at his goading. Then she caught a twinkle of humour in his eyes and her anger disappeared as fast as it had arrived.

"Nothing," she said, losing her nerve. "I'm going to have a cup of tea." She turned towards the kitchen.

His hand shot out and he stopped her. "Not yet. Let's get this out in the open first."

"What?"

"The fact that you want to stay and I want you to stay."

"Oh!" She couldn't stop her smile. "Well, that's good, isn't it?"

"It could be," he agreed. "It depends on how mad you're going to get when I tell you what else Grainger told me."

She was immediately on her guard. *What else could he possibly have revealed?* She didn't think there was anything that Jeff didn't already know about her. "What did he say?"

He hesitated, then walked into the bedroom. She heard him open and close a drawer. A moment later he was back, an envelope in his hands. She frowned as he indicated she should sit down. She sank down on one end of the couch, her eyes never leaving his face as he sat at the other end and opened the envelope. He took out a folded sheet of paper and opened it out. He checked something, nodded, then held it up for her to see.

"It's my marriage certificate," she said.

"Yeah," he said. "But did you know that marriage by proxy is legal in Montana?"

She frowned. "What?"

"It's legal in this state for someone to stand as proxy at a wedding for someone who is on active service."

"But… I married your father," she said. "Didn't I?"

He shook his head. "Look – Dad was Jefferson Andrew Mackay, born 1913. I'm Jefferson Andrew Mackay, born 1943."

She took the paper and examined it. She hadn't bothered before because it had been a marriage of convenience; it hadn't meant anything to her other than a means to get an American passport. She'd simply signed where she was told. When old Jefferson had died, she'd had no further interest in it. Now, she studied the document and saw that the groom was stated to be Jefferson Andrew Mackay, born 1943, and it was signed by Jefferson Andrew Mackay as proxy for his son, a serving member of the US Army.

She looked up. He was watching her closely.

"I knew nothing of this," she said. "Bloody hell. How did I miss it? They didn't say a word."

"Me and Sal didn't notice either when we first saw it. We were both so mad and shocked we barely glanced at it. Grainger said you didn't know. They decided it was better that way."

"The crafty old buggers. They couldn't resist playing God, could they? But why on earth would your father do this to you?"

"Well, according to Grainger, you needed to marry to get an American passport. They figured that if Dad really had married you, the authorities might look into it to check it wasn't a marriage of convenience, seeing as how he was old enough to be your father. So they used the proxy to marry you to me, because we're of a similar age and it would look more likely to be a genuine match."

"I'm so sorry, Jeff. We'll get an annulment. They had no right…" She felt so confused. She didn't know what to think. It was a horrible thing to do to your own son, and she felt responsible. If she hadn't…

"I had no idea he did it until now. But it's okay."

"What? This is acceptable to you?" She didn't know what to think. Her emotions were all over the place. She didn't understand why he wasn't spitting mad about it.

He sat back, relaxing into the sofa, resting his arms along the back of it. "Well, I guess if I'd taken the time to notice the details when I first saw that, I'd have been as mad as hell. But now? Well…" He shrugged. "We've been telling folks we're married anyway."

"Yes, but that was… Stop it, Jeff. You can't want me to stay! Why aren't you angry?"

"Maybe I've gotten used to having you around."

"Like the dog?" she asked, not impressed.

He laughed. "No, honey. Bear snores. You don't."

She went to cross her arms as she glared at him, but the jolt to her wound had her hissing with pain. "Bugger. I wish you'd stop taking the piss. This is serious."

"I know," he said, his tone mild. "And I think we should take this seriously. Don't you?"

"Of course. I just said so, didn't I?" She was getting even more confused. "What do you mean?"

He sat forward, resting his elbows on his thighs. "I don't pretend to know what my dad was thinking about all this," he said. "But I reckon he was the best judge of people I ever met. He probably expected to be here when I got home so he could explain it to me. He must've figured you and me could make a go of it. Why don't we see if he was right?"

She blinked once, twice. Her body and mind felt frozen. *Did he mean it?*

"Please don't tease me," she said.

"You got your princess voice back," he observed. "Does that mean the idea of being married to me is a total disaster?"

"I don't know. Is it?"

He sighed. "Look I know you probably want to hightail it out of here now the bad guys are off your tail. But I'd really like you to stay."

"All right," she said softly.

"Think about it, it makes se— What did you say?"

"I said all right. If you mean it, I'd like to stay."

"And be married to me? I mean really married. Not some fake arrangement."

She nodded, hoping this wasn't all one big prank. She braced herself, waiting for him to tell her it was all a joke, especially when his smile grew wider.

He stood up and held out a hand to her. She put her hand in his and he pulled her up and into his arms. She winced at the twinge of pain as her injured arm made contact with his body, but she didn't pull away when he enveloped her in his arms. She felt herself stiffen automatically, before she consciously relaxed and let him hold her.

"I'm not used to this," she said. "I've never been much of a cuddler."

"Well you'd better get used to it, Mrs Mackay. This family is pretty hands-on, and frankly, after seeing you passed out and bleeding yesterday, I'm inclined to keep you right here for a long time." This time she was sure of it when he kissed the top of her head. "You got a problem with that?"

"Not at the moment," she said. "But don't expect miracles, soldier. I'm still the same bitch you tried to kick out of here."

He laughed. "We can work on that."

She stood in his embrace, wondering whether she was dreaming. Never in a million years did she think any man – let alone this grumpy, handsome, straight-talking, honourable, honest, damaged one – would want her after the horrendous mess she'd made of her life. But, it seems, he did.

"Yes," she agreed, and her face broke into a slow smile. "We can."

THE END

Fantastic Books
Great Authors

darkstroke is
an imprint of
Crooked Cat Books

- Gripping Thrillers
- Cosy Mysteries
- Romantic Chick-Lit
- Fascinating Historicals
- Exciting Fantasy
- Young Adult
- Non-Fiction

Discover us online
www.darkstroke.com

Find us on instagram:
www.instagram.com/darkstrokebooks

Printed in Great Britain
by Amazon